"THANK YOU FOR COMING. I HAVE BEEN EXPECTING YOU," SAID A WARM AND GENEROUS VOICE.

Then the floor opened up, and Remo and Chiun were plunged into icy water. Even as Remo realized that the water was rising, he felt his ankle enclosed by a beartrap-like device.

Chiun, his skirts billowing like a floating jellyfish, had also been caught. Remo reached for the anchoring cord, and was yanked off balance before he could touch it.

Remo thrashed in the water. He had nothing to pull or push against. No leverage for his muscles at all. And the air in his lungs was running out.

It was something Remo had never encountered before. The perfect trap for someone with his abilities. And why not? It had been designed by the one enemy that knew his every strength and weakness. . . .

The Destroyer

#75

RAIN OF TERROR

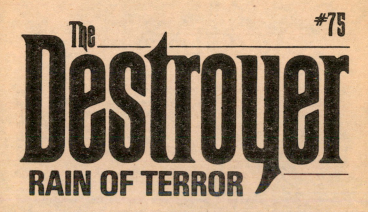

Created By

WARREN MURPHY & RICHARD SAPIR

A SIGNET BOOK

NEW AMERICAN LIBRARY

PUBLISHER'S NOTE

This book is a work of fiction. Names, characters, places, and incidents either are the product of the author's imagination or are used fictitiously, and any resemblance to actual persons, living or dead, events, or locales is entirely coincidental.

Copyright © 1988 by The Estate of Richard Sapir and Warren Murphy

SIGNET TRADEMARK REG. U.S. PAT. OFF. AND FOREIGN COUNTRIES
REGISTERED TRADEMARK—MARCA REGISTRADA
HECHO EN CHICAGO, U.S.A.

SIGNET, SIGNET CLASSIC, MENTOR, ONYX, PLUME, MERIDIAN and NAL BOOKS are published by NAL PENGUIN INC., 1633 Broadway, New York, New York 10019

First Printing, January, 1989

1 2 3 4 5 6 7 8 9

PRINTED IN THE UNITED STATES OF AMERICA

For Robert Sampson, a gentleman beside whom the likes of Richard Wentworth and Lamont Cranston pale into shabby insignificance.

And for technical adviser John Dinan.

Introduction

"For an attic on Garfield Avenue and bologna sand-
wiches on cheap white bread and Pathmark gin and
rolling inner tubes across backyard pools . . . when
all the world made sense and even dreams had right
sizes."

That was Dick Sapir being nostalgic in a Destroyer dedica-
tion a couple or three dozen books back. And why not a
little nostalgia? We had written a book that nobody would
buy for eight years and then we were "overnight" successes. Nostalg away, Dick. You earned it.
And now Destroyer Number 75.

Seventy-five books in seventeen years. Almost five mil-
lion published words. And still at it, still trying to get it
right.
Five million words. Maybe you'll understand better
how many that is if you remember that Arthur Conan
Doyle wrote about five per cent that many about Sherlock
Holmes before he got tired of him and tried to kill him off.
Five million words. As many memories. As many laughs.
This wasn't one of them: "Before tackling a novel you
ought to try writing short stories." That was the first agent
we sent the Destroyer manuscript to.
And the second agent. This genius, after cashing our
check for reading fees, suggested we end the book by
killing off the hero, Remo Williams. "You wrote this like a
series book," he told us, "and *nobody* publishes series
books."
Nothing's more stupid than the conventional wisdom, so
we sat on the sidelines and waited and eight years later, in
1971, got published—thanks to Dick's father, the dentist,

and a publishing secretary with papier-mâché teeth—and after our series had sold its first million copies, Sapir sent both agents a telegram—ten years later now—and said, "Go to hell." He never forgot; he never forgave.

Five million words. About one argument every million words.

One screamer. In Destroyer 5, *Dr. Quake*, Sapir kills Chiun, the old Oriental assassin around whom the series revolves.

"Can't do this," Murphy says. "Can't kill Chiun."

"It's a great scene," Sapir says. "Why can't I kill him?"

"Because everybody will stop reading the books and we'll have to go back to work at the car wash."

"Well, if you're going to nitpick everything I try to do . . ." Sapir says.

Chiun survived. So did the books. In America. Then in Europe. Eventually all over the world. Twelve languages. Twenty-five million copies.

Five million words.

A telegram arrives. It reads: "Murphy, you're done. Partnership is over. Contact my lawyer. Richard Sapir."

An hour later, another telegram. "Dear Warren. Ignore previous telegram. Some dastard has stolen my Western Union credit card and is offending all the people I hold most dear. Your friend, Dick."

It was never brought up again. Never knew what it was about.

Five million words.

Sometimes it's good not to think too much about what you're doing and just go ahead and do it.

If we knew that what we were writing was a satire on the whole men's adventure genre, maybe we would have started taking ourselves seriously.

And then maybe we would have missed out on seizing that radio station the day Dick bought the bad gin and we got away with doing fifteen minutes of Radio Free Hoboken until they got the door open and threw us out.

Maybe if we had known we were promulgating one of the most enduring myths in all pop fiction—the brash young Westerner trained in the secret arts by a wily aged Oriental—maybe it would not have been so much fun.

Maybe we couldn't have kept boa constrictors in that ratty hotel room in Jersey City or thrown pizza dough at the opera singer.

Five million words and maybe if we had thought they were important, maybe we wouldn't have overturned the boat and had to swim for it. Maybe Dick would remember where and when he totalled Murphy's new car before delivering it back with two flat tires, a ripped-off door and a red presentation ribbon on the hood.

Maybe we never would have had that football game in the hotel hallway in Atlantic City.

Maybe we wouldn't have liked each other.

But it was a long time ago and we didn't know any better and dreams still had right sizes.

Five million words. Seventy-five books. Not as good as we wanted, because nothing ever is, but a lot better than those early covers would lead you to believe.

Sapir went off on a separate career and wrote a handful of wonderful, enduring books, like *The Far Arena*, *The Body*, *Quest*, masterworks of myth that belatedly started to get him the critical attention something called The Destroyer series never could.

But he never gave up The Destroyer, and in many of these books are a lot of people he met and liked and a lot more he met and hated and things he appreciated and things that annoyed him, including, often, his partner.

Five million words and now book number 75. And not so much fun anymore.

Richard Ben Sapir died in January 1987, in the sunny afternoon of his life, in full control of his wonderful talent; in the warm surrounds of his loving family and friends. A lot of words have been written about him since then, some look-Ma-I'm-writing encomiums from people whose warm words would have been appreciated more while he was living.

But he never needed anybody else's words and he still doesn't, even in a valedictory. In a big piece of almost five million words he wrote his own.

Asked once how he could equate his career as a serious novelist with his other career doing The Destroyer, Dick Sapir said: "The Destroyer is what it is. It is good. And that's enough. There are not many good things in this world and Warren and I are part of one."

Amen, brother. We keep trying.

—Warren Murphy

1

Captain Claiborne Grimm was not at his command post when the Sonalert started beeping.

Although he was missile warning and control officer at the PAVE PAWS radar tower at the far end of Georgia's Robbins Air Force Base, national security did not preclude a trip to the john. And there was nothing in Air Force regs about bringing along a book to pass the time.

There was a lot of time to pass in the ten-story PAVE PAWS complex. Especially at three o'clock in the morning with an unheeding moon silvering the wedge-shaped blue building. The entire structure was run by computer. From the Modcomp system steering the phased array of 2,677 radiating elements that were shielded behind the building's eastern face to the twin CDC Cyber 174 data processors, there was little need for human beings at the console screens.

One of four identical sites scattered throughout the United States, the PAVE PAWS radar system's primary task was to detect the launching of submarine-based ballistic missiles. It was the last line of detection in the event of global war. Conventional wisdom had it that World War III would begin with massive land-based launches targeted at opposing land-based launch sites. NORAD's Spacetrack satellite system was responsible for detecting those first-strike launchings. If anyone survived to give orders for a second strike, America's submarine fleet would presumably still be intact to discharge that mission. By that time, Captain Grimm reasoned, the PAVE PAWS network designed to detect enemy submarine launchings would be so many floating particles—and never mind the Pentagon's crap about survivable mission-critical circuits.

So when the alarm beeped, warning of a possible submarine launch, Captain Grimm turned the page of his book. He was at a really good part. The blond with the big knockers was about to go down on the hero. Besides, the system had probably just picked up another satellite decaying out of orbit. But because he was a trained Air Force officer, Grimm kept an ear cocked for the status officer to hit the reset button, indicating a nonthreat situation.

When the beeper finally cut out, Grimm relaxed.

Then from the tactical operations room came a fearful cry.

"An event, sir!"

Captain Grimm stumbled out of the john, his feet tripping over his lowered trousers. He did not pull them up even after he found his post among the bank of six consoles. If this was real, there would be less than fifteen minutes from launch to impact.

Grimm shot a hard glance at the Global Display screen. Outlined in luminous green was the continental United States, centered between Europe and Asia.

Over the black space that represented the Atlantic Ocean floated a green tracking symbol that he'd seen only in training exercises. A glowing letter U. The U stood for "Unknown."

"Satellite?" he demanded of the status officer.

"The software says no."

"Then it's gotta be an air-breather."

"Negative, sir. Software confirms that it's not a conventional aircraft."

"Can't you—I mean it—identify it?" Captain Grimm shouted.

"Mission software refuses to sort it, sir!" the status officer, a lieutenant, said sharply.

Still in his shorts, Captain Grimm got behind a second console. According to his Global Display, the unknown object was approaching the apogee of its trajectory. He touched the glowing U with his lightpen and hit a console key. The U was magnified by a factor of two. Tiny jagged-edged boxes suddenly became visible as they flew off from the U symbol.

"It's shedding fragments," Captain Grimm said in a relieved voice. "It may be breaking up." But then he saw the speed of the thing. It was very fast. Faster than any known missile.

"It should be dropping its final stage at this point," the lieutenant said worriedly.

"No," Captain Grimm said. "No stages. Nothing."

"It has to. Maybe you're reading a tank box for a fragment."

Hitting a key, Captain Grimm deleted the fragments from the display. Only the U symbol remained.

"Damn," said the lieutenant, fervently cursing the automated system that made the operator as redundant as the backup console. "What have we got here?"

"A drill. It's gotta be a drill," said Grimm, reaching for a phone. "Maintainance, we in a test mode?" he barked into the receiver.

The reply was surreally flat.

"No, sir."

"Training mode, then?"

"No. Everything's up. Everything's running."

Captain Grimm lowered the phone with a trembling hand.

"It's gotta be a glitch in the software," he said.

"Sir, the software confirms that the unknown is ballistic."

"Oh, my God! Launch point?"

"The system can't pinpoint, sir. It's a ground launch. Point of origin beyond our operating parameters."

"Ground! Then why are we dealing with it? Where's Spacetrack? This is their responsibility. They should already have this thing in inventory and be feeding it to us."

"I don't know, sir," said the lieutenant, looking at the Object Table display. "But it's heading for the east coast."

"We gotta call it. High, medium, or low?"

"We can't go low. There's definitely something up there."

"Threat or nonthreat?"

"It's not a known missile, but it's ballistic. I'd go high."

"High it is," said Captain Grimm, hitting the high-confidence button that alerted the entire complex that they had a real situation. He tapped a key, touched the screen with his lightpen, and an expanded outline of the U.S. filled his screen. On the lower east coast a glowing green circle encompassed an area from North Carolina to New York City. As the inexorably moving U on the other screen inched across the Atlantic, and the software steadily computed the probable impact point, the circle shrank.

"Could be Washington," the lieutenant said in a shaky voice.

"There's only one object. It has to be Washington," Grimm rasped. "They must be crazy to launch only one object." He reached for the direct line to NORAD.

Deep in the North American Air Defense Command's Cheyenne Mountain complex, the Air Force general designated as CINCNORAD put down his red telephone. He looked out the Plexiglas of his command booth at status officers hunched over computer consoles like space-age scriveners. On the huge status panel overlooking the room, a blinking green object showed above a simulated horizon. It was larger than a warhead but smaller than a missile. And it was coming down fast. There was no time to think, never mind identify the unknown. Trembling, he picked up the White House hot line and asked for the President.

The President of the United States snored happily. It had been one of the great days in his life. He could hardly wait to get up the next morning to tackle the challenge of the Oval Office. But even an eager new President had to sleep, and so he slept.

He did not sleep long.

Two Secret Service agents burst into the room.

The President's wife bolted up from her pillows the instant the light clicked on. She reached for a dressing gown. Her fingertips grazed the pink chiffon briefly, and then one of the grim-faced Secret Service agents literally pulled her out of bed and hustled her out the door to a waiting elevator.

The First Lady screamed.

That woke the President. Seeing a hulking man looming over him, he asked a natural question.

"What is it? What's happening?"

"No time," the agent snapped. "It's for your own good, sir. Now, come with me, please."

The President reached for the nightstand drawer, where a red telephone lay. The Secret Service agent plucked the receiver from his hand and picked him up bodily. The chief executive was carried out of his bedroom, his eyes on the red telephone as if it were water and he was lost in the Gobi Desert.

The President was not set down until he was in the elevator. He stood in candy-cane pajamas, blinking rapidly. The Secret Service agents had faces that resembled cut stone. But they looked healthy compared to the face of the man carrying the aluminum suitcase. Sleepily the President tried to remember who the third man was. He could not. But he did remember the briefing when they had told him that the aluminum suitcase was called the "football" and it contained the special codes needed to launch America's nuclear arsenal.

Then it dawned on the President that the elevator had passed the White House basement and kept on going—deep, deep into the sub-sub-subbasement nearly a mile under impenetrable bedrock and lead radiation shielding.

And he knew.

"It's not fair," the President of the United States moaned. "This was going to be my first day in office!"

At the PAVE PAWS station at Robbins Air Force Base, Captain Grimm watched at the green circle shrank remorselessly, like a closing noose. It became the size of a half-dollar. Then a quarter. Then a nickel. Before it irised down to the size of a dime, a letter I appeared directly over Washington, D.C.—and then there could be no question about the point of impact.

The green circle squeezed into a dot and froze like a dead man's pupil.

"That's it," Grimm said huskily. "Washington is gone." He felt drained. Then he remembered to pull up his pants.

The precise point of impact was Lafayette Park, directly in front of the White House. The naked trees were rimed with late-January ice. It was exactly 3:13 A.M., so the park was deserted.

Washington, D.C. woke up to a sonic boom mixed with a noise like a tape of a car-crashing machine being played back at high speed. The ground jumped. The tremors were felt as far away as Alexandria, Virginia.

White steam hung over the hole in Lafayette Park. It was not a large hole, perhaps fifteen feet in diameter. But the superheated air escaping from the pit instantly melted the ice off the trees and turned the hard-frozen ground into the consistency of oatmeal and created billows of steam.

First on the scene was a police cruiser. It pulled up and two patrolmen spilled out. They approached the hole, which glowed cherry red, but the heat beat them back. After some discussion, they called it in as a brush fire. That brought the fire department.

Firemen lugged hoses as close as they could and poured water down the hole. That was a mistake. The water turned to steam. Those closest to the pit were scalded and had to be rushed to the hospital. The hoses were dragged back and, from a safer distance, the firemen tried again.

The next jets of water brought more steam. From deep within the hole there came loud snapping and hissing like water on a skillet magnified a thousand times. For several hours the Washington fire department sprayed water into the hole. Every hour, there was less steam. Gradually the cherry glow turned dull orange, then yellow. Finally it faded altogether.

The fire chief put on an oxygen mask and, carrying a heavy flashlight, approached the edge of the pit. He lay on his stomach and peered down. The rising air hit his exposed brow with tropical humidity. He turned on the flashlight.

The hole was much deeper than he'd expected. Whatever had hit, it had impacted with incredible force. The bottom of the pit was very black and buried under a foot of water. There was no way to discern what lay under the water, although the fire chief spent the better part of twenty minutes trying. He gave up when he leaned over too far and the flashlight jerked from his hand. It disappeared in the water.

It was nearly dawn by the time an Air Force investigation team arrived. They wore white anti-contamination suits and raced around the now-quiescent hole with clicking Geiger counters. The counters picked up only normal background radiation. The suits came off and heavy equipment was brought up as the firemen were ordered to vacate the site by a two-star general.

General Martin S. Leiber kept his suit on. He was a senior procurement officer with the Pentagon. No way was he going to get a face full of radiation. In fact, he wouldn't be here at all, but he happened to be senior officer at the Pentagon when word came from the White House. The President wanted to know if Washington was still standing. General Martin S. Leiber promised the President of the United States that he would look into the situation and get back to him within a few days. The fact that Washington looked perfectly normal from his office window was of little consequence. General Leiber was only five years from retirement. No way was he going to get his ass in a sling this close to the jackpot. Especially with a new President.

General Leiber had returned to his poker game, looked at his hand, and decided to play it out. A major beat his two pairs with a royal flush. General Leiber called the game and ordered the major to get the poop on the Washington survivability question. That would teach the bastard.

When the major returned with word of the possible missile strike on Lafayette Park, General Leiber saw stars. Specifically, one more on each shoulder. Although it was against his best bureaucratic instincts, he personally led the Air Force team to Lafayette Park. But just to make sure, he put Major Royal Flush in operational command.

Now, with the sun climbing toward noon, the general walked up to the major, a serious expression on his gruff face.

"What do you think this sucker is?" he demanded.

"We have unusually high levels of magnetism," the major said. "But no radiation or other lethal agents. I think we should fish for a piece of whatever's down there."

It sounded noncontroversial, so General Leiber said, "Do it!"

A derrick was driven onto the dead grass. Its treads sank into the mushy ground at the edge of the hole. It looked as if it would tip into the pit, but eventually it stabilized.

The steel jaws descended into the hole. And got stuck.

They finally came up with a jagged swatch of metal that dripped water. The metal was black and pitted. The derrick deposited it on a white tarp that had been laid on the ground.

The Air Force team swiftly surrounded it. The major tapped it with a retractable ball-point pen. The pen stuck too.

"I don't understand," he said softly.

"What's that?" General Leiber asked.

"Iron. This appears to be solid iron."

"I never heard of a nuclear missile with iron parts."

"We don't know that this is any such thing," the major pointed out. "Could be a meteor. They contain a lot of iron."

"Bull," said General Leiber. "NORAD picked it up at apogee. It was ballistic. What else could it be, if not a missile?"

"Let's find out," the major suggested. "Bring up another piece."

The next piece was iron too. Cast iron. So was the third. General Leiber began to feel very strange.

Then the derrick brought up a crushed and charred object that was somehow attached to a pitted iron stanchion. Everyone took turns examining the object.

"I'd say this crushed part is not iron," the major said, scraping at the charred surface with a thumbnail. He exposed a line of shiny brownish-yellow metal. "Looks like it was hollow and the impact compressed it. See this lip here? Some kind of opening or mouth."

"What's that thing sticking out, then?" General Leiber asked. "A tongue?"

The major looked. Out of the flattened mouth protruded a tiny ball of metal on the end of a rod. His brow wrinkled doubtfully.

"This thing looks familiar. I can't place it. Anyone?"

The object was passed from hand to hand.

Finally someone offered a suggestion.

"I don't know if this is possible, but I think this was a bell."

"A what?" asked General Leiber.

"A bell. A brass bell. You know, like you would hang in a church steeple."

Then everyone looked at everyone else with the expression of children who had wandered into a very wrong place.

"Let's get it out of the hole," General Leiber said swiftly. "All of it. Every piece. I'll requisition an empty hangar at Andrews. You boys can reconstruct it there."

"It may not be that simple," the major said reasonably. "It's badly compressed and fused. We don't know what it might be. Where would we start?"

"Here," General Leiber, said, slapping the crushed blob of brass into his open hands. "Start with this. If that thing in the hole is some new kind of enemy weapon, the future of your country may depend on learning what it is and what it was supposed to do."

"What if we end up with a church steeple?" the major joked.

"Then you better get down on your knees, son. Because if the Russkies have turned God Almighty to their side, America doesn't have a prayer."

The major started to laugh. He swallowed his mirth. The general was not smiling. In fact, he looked serious. Dead serious. The major hurried off to carry out the general's orders.

2

His name was Remo and he couldn't remember ever being in this much trouble before.

As he ran down the wooded road, his deep-set eyes searching the trees on either side, Remo Williams did not look like a man in trouble. He looked like a jogger. Except that he wore shoes of excellent Italian leather, gray chinos and, even though the temperature was hovering just under the freezing mark, a fresh white T-shirt.

He clutched a coil of rope in one fist. The skin was drawn tight over his high cheekbones. His dark eyes looked stricken.

A sporty red Corvette zipped past him and Remo broke into a floating run. Showing no apparent effort, he caught up with the Corvette and, checking the two-lane road to see that no cars were coming at him from the opposite direction, he drew alongside the driver's side of the car.

The car was doing a decorous forty-five miles an hour. Remo knocked on the driver's window.

The window hummed down and a blue-eyed woman with mahogany hair looked him up and down with a dreamy expression.

"I'll bet you could go all night, too," she said. She didn't seem surprised to see a man keeping pace with a speeding automobile. Remo looked so ordinary that some people refused to accept the evidence of their eyes when they saw him perform the impossible.

"Have you seen an elephant walking along this road?" Remo asked. There was no pleasure in his eyes.

The woman raised an ironic eyebrow. Her smile broadened.

"Maybe you could describe him," she suggested.

"He's an elephant. Gray. Wrinkled skin. Small for an elephant. No tusks."

"A lot of elephants fit that description," the woman said breathily. "Could you be more specific?"

"Lady, I guarantee you he's the only elephant in the neighborhood. Now, have you seen him?"

"I'm trying to think," she said slowly. "It's possible. Maybe if you drew me a picture. I have some crayons back at my apartment."

"No time," Remo said, and pulled away.

The woman frowned, and deciding that the conversation had ended prematurely, hit the accelerator. The needle jumped to seventy and clawed at seventy-five. But try as she might, the Corvette kept losing ground at each whipsaw turn in the road.

The turns didn't seem to stop the man in the white T-shirt. She lost sight of him after he topped a rise in the road and never caught up. She decided to drive down this road every day at this time until she encountered him again. It was crazy, of course. But there was something about the guy. She just couldn't put her finger on it. . . .

Remo was close to panic. There was no way he was returning without the elephant. Chiun would kill him. Not literally, of course. Although Chiun was the head of an ancient line of assassins and could snuff out a man's life with a casual gesture, he wouldn't kill Remo. That would be too merciful. Instead, the Master of Sinanju would make Remo's life miserable. He knew many ways of doing that, most of them verbal.

Seeing no sign of an elephant on the long stretch of open road before him, Remo plunged into the woods. For the thousandth time he wished he hadn't left the gate open.

It had been Remo's turn to water Chiun's pet elephant. Remo had led the pachyderm out of the shed where he was kept, and had gone to find the hose. The gardener of Folcroft Sanitarium—where Remo and Chiun currently resided—had walked off with it. By the time Remo had talked the man out of the hose, the elephant, whose name was Rambo, had strolled out the opened gate of Folcroft.

Remo had unlocked the gate earlier. After he had hosed Rambo down, he intended to take him for a walk. Open-

ing the gate first was meant to make Remo's job easier. It
was Remo's turn to walk the elephant, too.

Remo had run out immediately, but the elephant had
already melted out of sight. Remo hesitated near the gate,
and decided two searchers would be infinitely better than
one. He hurried to find Chiun, who would certainly understand when Remo explained the accident.

Remo found Chiun doing his morning exercises. He sat
in a lotus position on the Folcroft gymnasium floor, tapping a bar of chilled steel suspended between two up-
rights with his long fingernails. He was a happy little
mummy of a Korean gentleman, with pleasantly wrinkled features and the merest wisp of hair on his chin. He
wore a canary-yellow kimono. He looked frail enough to
snap in a stiff wind.

But when Remo blurted out, "I'm sorry, Little Father,
but Rambo ran away," Chiun paused in mid-stroke. Then
one fingernail continued down to sever the half-inch bar. It
clattered to the pinewood floor in two neat sections.

Chiun got to his feet, his venerable face turning to
granite.

"I'm sorry, I'm sorry. I was only gone a minute," Remo
repeated.

"Find him." Chiun's normally squeaky voice was like
chopsticks breaking.

"I thought two heads would be better than one," Remo
said meekly.

"You thought wrong," said Chiun. "Why should I ex-
pend precious moments of my declining years cleaning up
after your mistakes?"

"It's your elephant."

"Entrusted to you. And misplaced by you."

"He walked off. It was his own idea."

"And if he is now lying in some filthy ditch after being
struck by a careless motor-carriage driver, I suppose that
would be his fault too?"

Remo started to get angry. He checked himself.

"C'mon, Little Father. You can at least help out."

"I will."

"Good."

"I will give you an additional impetus to search faster."

"Huh?"

"I will hold my breath until my precious baby is restored to me."

And Chiun inhaled mightily. His cheeks puffed out like a blowfish. He stopped breathing.

"Awww, no, you don't have to do that."

When Chiun's cheeks puffed out further, Remo threw up placating hands.

"Okay, okay. I'll find him. Stay right here."

Remo ran out of Folcroft and down the road, knowing that Chiun was not bluffing. He would stubbornly hold his breath until Remo returned with the Master of Sinanju's "baby," no matter how long it took.

Already it had been half an hour and Remo had found no trace of Rambo. He had no idea how long Chiun could hold his breath without exhaling. Chiun was a Master of Sinanju, the sun source of the martial arts. Masters of Sinanju were capable of incredible discipline. Remo was a Master too, and had once tried to test his own ability at holding his breath. He went exactly thirty-seven minutes before he got bored. Chiun, having trained Remo in Sinanju, was probably good for an hour. At least.

So Chiun was in no immediate danger. But he would make Remo pay for every breath not taken.

Remo found no tracks in the forest. He stopped in the middle of a stand of poplars, their dead, frozen leaves making no sound under his careful feet. He went up a tree to get a better view.

Back the way he had come, Remo spotted a police car pulled over to the side of the road, its light bar painting the surroundings a washed-out blue. Two cops stepped gingerly from each door with guns drawn.

They advanced carefully on a small elephant who looked like a corrugated gray medicine ball balanced on stubby feet.

"Oh, hell!" Remo said, sliding down the tree. He flashed through the woods like an arrow.

Remo skidded to a stop beside the police cruiser.

"Hey, fellas, hold up," Remo called.

The cops turned in unison. Behind them, the elephant regarded the scene with tiny dull eyes. His trunk seemed to wave to Remo.

"Don't shoot him!" Remo pleaded.

One cop jerked his thumb at Rambo.

"Yours?" he asked.

"Not exactly."

Uncertain how to handle an elephant, the cops turned their attention to Remo, their weapons dropping into their holsters. They were in their mid-forties, with hulking shoulders and meaty faces. They wore nearly identical expressions, like clones. Remo decided they were typical robot cops who had seen too much and liked so little of it that they had shut down emotionally long ago. Remo knew how it was. A long time ago, he had been a cop too. Back before he had been framed for a crime he didn't do and executed in an electric chair that didn't work.

"Whose is it, then?" asked the first cop. Remo thought of him as the first cop because his nose hadn't yet been discolored by burst capillaries.

"A friend of mine. And he's very anxious to get him back."

"This friend. He have a permit to keep an elephant?" This from the second cop. The one with the Santa Claus-red nose.

"I don't think he's gotten around to it yet. The elephant's only been in this country a month. But I'll be sure to bring it up."

"Is that a leash?"

"This?" Remo asked, hefting the coil of rope. "Yeah."

"Can you control this animal?"

"He'll come with me if I approach him right."

"In that case, we're going to ask you to leash the elephant and follow us to the station."

"Why?"

"You've allowed him to roam a major road, where he could be injured by a car. That's reckless endangerment of an animal."

"He ran away on his own."

"We'll look into that too. And you may have to prove ownership."

Remo's shoulders sagged. He could neutralize these two faster than they could blink, but they were cops. And they were only doing their jobs.

Then Remo suddenly had a vision of Chiun's face. It was red, on its way to turning purple.

"I'll put the leash on him," Remo said, and started to approach the elephant.

Rambo saw the rope in Remo's hand and reared up. His trunk waved like a wrinkled python. He trumpeted in warning. The two cops pulled their service revolvers just as two blunt forefeet came down on the hood of the cruiser.

"Oh, no!" Remo groaned as Rambo smacked the light bar with his trunk. The light bar abruptly shut down. Then the elephant stepped off the hood. The hood bore a shallow dent.

The first cop turned to Remo and said, "That's destruction of police property, buddy, and you're under arrest."

The red-nosed cop took aim on the elephant's head and Remo knew that choice no longer entered into the picture.

He disarmed the first cop in the simplest manner. He grabbed at the buckle of his gunbelt and tugged sharply. The gunbelt ended up in Remo's hand. He threw it into the woods. Then Remo tapped the cop in the exact center of his forehead. The man's bloodshot eyes rolled up in his head and he fell like a slab of beef.

The other cop was about to shoot. Remo chopped at the side of his neck and the man fell into his waiting arms.

Remo made a quick noose of the rope and snared the elephant's trunk. But Rambo threw off the noose and reared up on his hind legs.

"Don't make this any harder than it has to be," Remo muttered.

Rambo started to drop back to all fours. The way his trunk flayed the air told Remo he was upset. He would run the moment his feet touched ground. Remo moved in first.

When the front feet came down, Remo was there to catch them. He pushed at the elephant's padded feet with both hands. Rambo trumpeted angrily. He pushed harder, his entire wrinkled weight leaning against Remo.

Remo kept the stumpy forefeet above the ground. Seeming to exert no effort, he kept Rambo off balance. When the elephant tried to step back, Remo stepped forward, still pushing.

Anyone who had driven down the road would have

been treated to the sight of a rail-thin man doing the minuet with an Asian elephant. And the man was leading.

Remo kept the elephant off balance until the pachyderm began to tire. When he sensed that moment had come, he stepped back. Rambo's forefeet struck the ground. Remo lassoed the knobby head with a quick, easy motion. He tugged Rambo over to the side of the road and tethered him to a tree.

"Stay," Remo said firmly.

Then Remo hurried back to the prowl car. He dug into the glove compartment and found, as he expected, a flask. He uncapped it and poured a mouthful down the throat of each recumbent cop, kneading their larynxes so that they swallowed safely. Then he placed one behind the wheel and the other in the seat beside him.

Before untying Rambo, Remo popped the hood and, balancing on the front fender, flattened out the dent with the palms of his hands. He looked like a cook kneading pizza dough.

When he closed the hood, the car looked as good as new. And when the two cops woke up and realized that they had been drinking—even if they couldn't remember tasting a drop—they would dismiss what they'd seen as a hallucination.

The Master of Sinanju wasn't purple when Remo found him. His face was blue. Light blue. Kind of a robin's-egg blue. But he was definitely blue.

Remo figured he had been gone not quite two hours.

"I found him," Remo said hastily. "He's outside."

The Master of Sinanju folded his arms stubbornly. His cheeks still puffed out defiantly.

"Look for yourself if you don't believe me," Remo said.

Chiun shook his head, which was bald but for tufts of hair over each ear.

"You want something else?" Remo asked frantically.

Chiun nodded.

"What?"

Chiun did not say. His hazel eyes regarded Remo pointedly.

"I already apologized," Remo said.

Chiun nodded.

"It won't happen again."

Chiun nodded as if in agreement.

"You want more?"

Chiun raised a long-nailed finger in assent.

"Look, if you want to stick me with some punishment, okay, but do you have to make me work for it too?"

Chiun's eyes brightened. Remo was starting to get the idea.

"I'll walk him every day. No more taking turns."

Chiun's upraised finger indicated acceptance of Remo's offer. But he still did not draw breath.

"And hose him down daily."

A second finger joined the upraised one.

"Twice daily. Okay! Twice daily. Now, come on. You're turning bright blue."

Chiun made sweeping motions with both hands.

"No, not that. I'm not cleaning up after him. No way."

Chiun folded his arms, and deep inside him, he coughed. But he refused to let the cough escape his lips. He seemed to shrink. The bluish cast to his face darkened and he suddenly clutched at his thin breast.

"Okay, okay! You win. I'll clean up after him too. Anything else?"

Chiun released his breath in a long, gusty exhalation.

"How should I know?" he squeaked. "You are doing all the negotiating."

And then he floated out of the room like a happy elf.

Remo stood in the middle of Folcroft Sanitarium, his teeth clenched and his face slowly turning red.

Dr. Harold W. Smith picked that moment to enter the room, peering owlishly at Remo through rimless glasses.

"Could I see you one moment?" Smith said in a serious tone. "It's about your elephant."

3

"It's not my elephant," Remo said in a defensive voice.

He had followed Dr. Harold W. Smith up to Smith's Spartan office. Smith closed the door after them and retreated to the security of his shabby desk.

"You brought it back from Vietnam," Smith said flatly.

"Chiun made me. It was his idea. I wanted no part of this. If you want to get rid of the elephant, you have my total, unconditional moral support. Just don't quote me."

"We can't have an unlicensed animal like that on the grounds. This is supposed to be a private hospital. On that basis alone, I'm risking health-code violations and problems with AMA recertification." Just the thought of those bureaucratic hassles brought that old, haggard look to Smith's gaunt, lemony face. Smith reached into a desk drawer and Remo made a mental bet with himself that out would come the aspirin. Smith's haggard look suggested aspirin. His sour look usually signaled a liquid antacid binge. On occasion, it would be Alka-Seltzer. Smith was not wearing his Alka-Seltzer face today, so Remo was dead certain it would be aspirin.

"Talk to Chiun," Remo said exasperatedly. "You have good security reasons. Just give him the chapter and verse."

"The health-code matter of course is not uppermost," Smith told him. "Folcroft is a secret government installation. Security must be our primary concern at all times. An elephant is bound to attract attention."

"Save it for Chiun, Smitty. It's out of my hands."

Out of the desk drawer came a paper cup, and a worried notch appeared between Remo's eyes. A paper cup usually meant aspirin, but Smith always took his aspirin with water from the office dispenser. Why would Smith have a

paper cup in the desk when they were racked next to the
bottled mineral water?

"I hold you responsible for this elephant situation,"
Smith said, digging around in the drawer.

"Why me? I told you it was Chiun's idea."

"Which he wouldn't have gotten had he not been forced
to follow you to Vietnam. Need I remind you that you
were in that country despite my strict orders?"

"I don't want to rehash that mission."

"It was not a mission," said Smith. "It was a renegade
action on your part."

"Rub it in, why don't you?" Remo slouched onto the
office couch. Why was everyone on his case today?

"I am not even mentioning the expense to the taxpayers
of having the elephant shipped to Folcroft. I'm sure there
are naval officers who are still trying to learn how an Asian
elephant came to be on a United States submarine. By the
way, how *did* you get the animal into the sub in the first
place?"

"Through the weapons-shipping hatch," Remo said sourly.
"I told Chiun he wouldn't go down the conning tower, but
it didn't discourage him. The sub captain tried to bluff
Chiun too, but Chiun's been on too many subs in the past.
He knew about the big hatch. He made them open it and
Chiun prodded Rambo inside."

"Hmmm," said Smith absently. He pulled out an aerosol can, on which the words "FREE SAMPLE" were
marked in red. Remo had never heard of aerosol aspirin,
and he wondered if Smith was going to fool him and shave
instead. But Smith's jaw looked as if it had seen a straight
razor in the last hour.

Remo watched with growing puzzlement. Smith's odd
New England habits fascinated Remo in a peculiar way.
For many years Remo had resented the cold Smith. It was
Smith who had set Remo up, so that his faked execution
wiped away all traces of Remo's existence. It wasn't done
out of malice, but because Smith had been charged with
running a supersecret government agency called CURE.
It was set up to deal with national-security problems in an
off-the-books manner. Officially, it didn't exist. So its single agent, the former Remo Williams, could not exist

either. Twenty years and countless operations later, the
bitter edge of their working relationship had softened.

And so Remo watched with faint amusement as Smith
upended the tiny aerosol can and squirted a white, foamy
substance into the paper cup. It was not shaving cream. It
lacked the pungent medicinal smell—although there was a
faint lime scent.

"Free sample, huh?" Remo said to fill the lull in the
conversation.

Smith nodded and brought the cup to his lips. His
skinny Adam's apple didn't bob as it usually did when
Smith drank something. He tilted his white-haired head
back further. Smith looked very uncomfortable. Maybe it
was whipped cream, Remo thought.

"Can I get you a cupcake or something?" Remo offered.

Smith's head came back down and the cup dropped
from his face. His expression was especially sour, and
annoyed. There was a dab of the white stuff on the tip of
his nose.

"I must be doing something wrong," Smith muttered.
He turned the can around in his hand as if looking for
directions.

"Try squirting it directly into your mouth," Remo suggested in a pleasant voice.

Smith considered Remo's suggestion with a serious expression. Remo hadn't been serious. He leaned forward,
anticipating Smith's next move.

But instead of squirting the stuff into his mouth, Smith
dipped a finger into the cup and brought the foam-laden
digit to his lips. He licked the finger clean, and went
back for more.

"This is very inconvenient," Smith said to himself.

"Use your tongue," Remo prompted.

Much to Remo's surprise, Smith did. He scoured the
bottom of the cup, getting more foam on his nose. Some of
it collected at the corners of his mouth too. Remo decided
not to bring it to his attention.

Finishing up, Smith capped the can and returned it to
his desk. He looked at the cup as if considering its reuse.
Reluctantly he threw it into a green wastebasket that
Remo happened to know was purchased used from a gram-
mar school that had been forced to close down. Smith had

sat through a three-hour auction to get it, thereby saving forty-seven cents.

Smith looked up, his face businesslike except for the dabs of white substance.

"When did you become a whipped-cream fiend?" Remo asked with a straight face.

"Never," Smith said humorlessly. "That was an antacid product."

"Aerosol?"

"It's new. Supposed to be easier to take, but I didn't think so."

"I'll bet you go back for more anyway."

"Can we get back to the matter at hand?"

"Talk to Chiun. It's his elephant."

"I will need your assistance, Remo. I sometimes think the Master of Sinanju does not understand my concerns. He seems to listen, and gives positive answers, but then he forgets our conversations ten minutes later."

"Chiun understands more than you think. If he doesn't understand something, it's because he doesn't want to. He loves that elephant. I know. He's got me trained to see to its every need. You tell him he has to get rid of it and I guarantee you he will not understand a word you say."

"I have to try. Every day that elephant remains at Folcroft places us at risk."

"So talk to Chiun. I'm not stopping you."

"I would like you to back me up. Help me get through to him."

Remo sighed. "Normally, I'd say no way. But I'm facing a lifetime of stable cleaning if Rambo doesn't go. I guess it can't hurt to try. Chiun can't get any madder at me than he already is."

"Good," said Smith, buzzing his secretary.

"But I'm telling you right now, it won't work."

The Master of Sinanju arrived moments later. He ignored Remo and bowed politely before Smith.

"A thousand greetings of the morning, O Emperor Smith," he said roundly. "Your servant informed me that my presence was required, and my sandaled feet flew with wide-eyed anticipation to your sanctum sanctorum."

"Er, thank you, Master Chiun," Smith said uncomfortably.

Chiun beamed at his emperor.

Smith cleared his throat. He cleared it a second time.

Chiun cocked his head to one side inquisitively.

"I . . . I crave a . . . a boon," Smith said at last. He fidgeted with a pencil.

"A boon?" asked Chiun, who had never before heard Smith use such kingly words. It was good at last to see Smith embrace his true state in life. Although Chiun knew that Smith did not exactly rule America, he understood that Smith wielded power second only to the President. And for centuries Chiun's ancestors had worked for royalty of all nations. Therefore Smith was royalty of a sort.

"What boon?" Chiun asked in a delighted voice. "Merely state it and I will consider it my duty."

Smith hesitated. He looked at Remo helplessly.

On the couch, Remo tensed. "Here it comes," he said, bracing himself for the explosion.

"I wish . . . that is, I request . . . I mean, for security reasons your pet elephant presents serious problems."

Chiun clapped his hands suddenly. The sound was so loud Smith jumped in his cracked leather chair. Even Remo was taken by surprise. He wisely started to inch toward the door.

"Say no more," proclaimed the Master of Sinanju in a loud voice. Loud, but not angry. Remo hesitated with his hand on the doorknob.

"But I—" Smith began.

Chiun lifted a quelling hand imperiously.

"I had not planned for this so soon," said Chiun, "but so be it. Be so good, Emperor, as to gaze out yon window."

Uncertainly Smith swiveled his seat around. He stared out the big picture window overlooking Long Island Sound. There, by the docks, Rambo grazed contentedly.

"Your elephant?" Smith said hesitantly.

"No, O Emperor," Chiun corrected. "Not my elephant."

"It's not mine," Remo said quickly.

"Of course not," Chiun said. "It is the Emperor Smith's elephant. His *royal* elephant, to do with as he pleases."

"As I please?" Smith asked unsteadily.

"Yes, did you think I have had Remo training him all these weeks for my own pleasure? No. As a Master of Sinanju, I must be ready at a moment's notice to travel to any corner of the globe to do your bidding. As much as I love pets, I cannot be so encumbered. I knew this when I rescued the poor beast from the cruel Vietnamese. I knew that you were a lover of pets, and would therefore delight in owning him. Consider it a token of my esteem for long years of fruitful employment."

"Smith?" Remo said incredulously. "A lover of pets?"

Behind his own back, Chiun made quieting gestures at Remo.

"I . . . I had a pet turtle once," Smith muttered. "That was a long time ago. It died."

"The loss still marks your kingly visage," Chiun announced. "But now you have many years of joyous pleasure to catch up on and I will not take up any more of our valuable time."

Without another word, the Master of Sinanju floated out the door. As he brushed past Remo, there was a mischievous gleam in Chiun's bright eyes that Remo had seen before. He grabbed for the doorknob as Chiun closed the door behind him. But it would not budge. Remo strained. The doorknob came off in his hands and it was then that Remo knew he had fallen into a trap. Chiun was holding the door closed from the other side. Chiun, who knew Smith's next words before Remo heard them. Probably even before Smith himself formulated them in his mind.

"Remo," Smith said, "I must ask you to find a home for that creature. Keeping him is of course out of the question."

Remo said nothing. His groan was eloquent enough.

After Remo had left, Smith touched a concealed stud that brought his CURE operations-desk terminal rising out of its desktop recess. From this terminal, which was connected to a bank of mainframe computers concealed in Folcroft's basement, Smith had instant access to virtually all nationwide data links. The CURE computers were the heart of his day-to-day operation. Through them, his ability to correlate endless, seemingly unrelated trivia alerted Smith to domestic problems before they exploded into full-blown crises. Through his computers, Smith anonymously tipped off normal law-enforcement agencies to these problems. Only when a crisis did occur, would Smith unleash Remo and Chiun.

As he scanned news digests of the evening, Smith found only the usual situations. One oddity was a sketchy report of a fire in Lafayette park in the District of Columbia. The CURE software had flagged it only because of its proximity to the White House. But it appeared to be a routine matter.

But when Smith switched over to monitor message traffic between the various branches of the government and the military, he suddenly sat up in his chair. Milnet and Arpanet traffic were virtually nonexistent. The systems were up. But no one was passing data. It was as if there was a blackout or a paralysis of communications.

It was very puzzling, but it seemed to be centered in the Washington, D.C., area. That might have been because Washington was the home of most government agencies. But even on a dull day, CIA message traffic was not this light. And the intermilitary lines were unusually quiet too.

Nothing was happening. The few messages Smith did intercept were so routine as to border on trivia. It was as if even though these computer links were considered secure, the government had clamped down on their use so that even in the upper levels of the U.S. government, there were no leaks.

Fascinated, Smith switched over to other information-gathering sources. Everyone was acting as if nothing was happening. That alone was suspicious. In the government, something was always happening. And Smith was determined to discover just what it was.

He hunched over his terminal, his gray eyes coming to life. Interfacing with his system, Dr. Harold W. Smith was in his element. Something close to a smile of satisfaction hovered at the edges of his dry lips. Absently he licked the remnants of the aerosol antacid from their corners. He was so deep in thought, the chalky taste did not even register.

4

General Martin S. Leiber finished shoving his desk over so that it blocked the door to his Pentagon office. He had sent his secretary home. He pulled down the window shades and turned on all the lights even though it was barely noon.

Tough times called for tough measures. He got behind his desk and laid a hand on the telephone. He waited. Every minute increased the risk. If the Joint Chiefs of Staff wanted him, they would have to come for him. The longer they held off, the better his chances improved. He could almost feel the weight of those extra stars on his shoulder epaulets. Never mind the extra perks; they meant a stiff ten thousand dollars a year in retirement benefits.

If he could stall the Joint Chiefs just a little longer.

They were calling for answers. General Leiber had put them off with some military double-talk. He had already fielded one call from the President of the United States this morning. The President was concerned.

"Is it safe to come out?" the President had asked.

"Negative, Mr. President," General Leiber told him. "We have not yet identified the threat."

"But Washington has not been destroyed?"

"It would be premature for me to comment on that, Mr. President."

"Premature!" The President's voice skittered dangerously toward falsetto. "The nation's capital is either standing or it isn't. Which is it?"

"It's not that simple, Mr. President," General Leiber went on, sweat gathering under his iron-gray toupee. "The city has experienced an attack of unknown origin."

"But it failed."

"The first strike may have failed. But it may not. Mr.

President, I will be frank. We do not know the meaning of this attack. That is bad enough. But we are desperately attempting to establish the nature of the weapon itself."

"I was told that it was a missile."

"You have been misinformed, sir. We know no such thing. At present, the threat object is unclassifiable. It's true there was no explosion or release of radiation, but in the absence of knowing what this thing was supposed to do, we can't rule out the possibility that it won't develop into a threat situation."

"I don't understand. The thing was a dud, right?"

"We don't know that. In fact, we know so little that any conclusion or action we might contemplate would be premature—even downright dangerous. I strongly advise you to stay underground until we know that it is safe to come up. Even if this object—which is now being evaluated by the brightest minds in the Air Force—is a nonthreat, we cannot assume that a second strike might not be imminent."

"Maybe I should be talking to the Joint Chiefs. What do they say?"

"I have already spoken with them and we are in complete . . . um"—General Leiber searched for an apt word that was not exactly a lie and, he hoped, not in the President's vocabulary—"equanimity about the situation," he said. In for a penny, in for a pound, he thought.

"Well, if they think that's the best course, I guess I could stay down here another few hours. But dammit, this is my first day in office. I'm anxious to get up there and lead."

"I understand, sir. But your security is top priority. And please, do not call again. We don't know if those phones are tapped. We don't want the enemy to know where you are."

"Yes, I see," said the President vaguely. "I appreciate your patriotism. It was fortunate a man of your caliber was on duty when this thing happened. I hope you will continue to act as my surrogate in this crisis."

"Don't worry, Mr. President, I'm on top of it."

General Leiber hung up. His eyes were bright. If this didn't work exactly right, he could kiss his pension adios and be up for high treason to boot. If only that fool of a major would call. How long could it take them to analyze that thing?

The phone rang and General Leiber reached for it eagerly. He hesitated, scratching absently at his mustache. Might be the Joint Chiefs. Carefully he picked up the phone but said nothing. If it was the Joint Chiefs, he'd crackle some paper against the receiver and try to bluff it out as a bad connection.

Finally a voice asked, "Hello?"

"That you, Major Cheek?"

"Yes, General. You said you wanted to hear the minute we confirmed anything".

"Yes," said General Leiber. "But speak carefully, man. This line may be tapped."

"Yessir, General," Major Cheek said.

"Now, what have you got?"

"Confirmation, sir."

"Outstanding! Outstanding, Major. Confirmation of what?"

"The object we discussed, sir."

"Yes, yes, I know. But what is it? Come on, out with it."

"A bell."

"A what?"

"I can confirm that the mashed brass object is definitely a bell."

General Leiber looked at the receiver clutched in his whitening hand and his eyes got sick. His mouth moved, but nothing came out. Finally he got control of himself.

"A bell?" he asked in a hoarse voice.

"Total confirmation. We even got it to ring. Listen." From the background came a discordant sound like a sick buoy.

"A bell," General Leiber repeated. "You've been at it half the day and all you have is a bell. What about the zillion tons of scrap you pulled out of that hole, mister?"

"Mostly iron, sir. Scorched and pitted. Some of it has fused into slag. We do have several less-damaged sections we are still analyzing, but they're a real mess. This could take days."

"Days," General Leiber said. His voice cracked. Then he pulled himself together. His voice became tight. "We don't have days, mister. The security of the United States of America is at stake here. Do you understand the seriousness of this situation?"

"I think I do, General."

"Think! I know! I know how damn serious it is!"

"We'll need better equipment."

"Anything. I can procure anything you need. What? Name it. Spectroscopic analyzers. Metallurgic equipment. I can probably rustle up an electron telescope if necessary."

"I think you mean microscope, General. There's no such thing as an electron telescope."

"Don't split hairs with me. Just give me a list."

"First we'll need anvils."

"ANVILS, right." General Lieber started a list. "Refresh my memory. That's an acronym for what?"

"Nothing, sir. An anvil is a block blacksmiths use to hammer metal on. We've got a lot of mangled iron here. The only way to deal with it is to heat it up and try to restore the parts to their original forms."

"I understand, but we won't call them anvils. We'll call them Metallurgical Component Restoration Bases."

"With all due respect, General, I think you could get them faster if you simply asked for anvils."

"How much would you guestimate an anvil would cost?"

"Oh, less than a hundred dollars each."

"If we call them Metallurgical Component Restoration Bases, I can add an extra zero to the end of that figure."

The major sighed. "I understand perfectly, sir."

"Now, what else?"

"Hammers."

"High-Impact Reshaping Implements. Hi-Rimps for short."

"Something to heat the metal pieces for reforming. I don't know what they call those things."

"Free-Standing Tripodal Heating Stations," the general said, thinking of a blue-tag special on barbecue grills he had seen at a hardware store. He could buy those himself, jack up the price, and pocket the difference. He wrote it down.

"Tongs."

"Manual Securing Tools," said General Leiber, adding Mansecs to the list. "Anything else?"

"The work would go a lot faster if we had experienced blacksmiths."

"Metallurgical Consultants!" the general shouted, his eyes lighting up. "Now you're talking! Consultants are a big budget item."

"Yes, sir," said the major, who wondered where national security fit into all of this.

"You'll have all this stuff by midday." And the general hung up. He quickly made a series of phone calls. His years of wheeling and dealing as a procurement officer had built up a network of contacts and suppliers. If it could be bought or bartered, General Leiber could get it.

An hour later, he had everything but the blacksmiths and the barbecue grills. The latter items he intended to pick up himself. But the blacksmiths were tough. His regular network of suppliers did not deal in such people. There wasn't even a listing for blacksmiths in the yellow pages. They were hard to track down.

This called for extraordinary assistance, General Leiber told himself. He asked the Pentagon operator to put in an overseas call to Zurich, Switzerland.

A flat, emotionless voice answered in the middle of the first ring.

"Friendship, International," it said.

"Hello, Friend."

"Hello, General Leiber. It is good of you to call."

"I didn't think you'd remember me, Friend," General Leiber said.

"Your voice registered instantly. I never forget a customer."

"I have something more urgent than our last deal."

"I trust the Cuban cigars were satisfactory."

"I'm down to my last box. But we can chew that over later. I need something special and you're the only guy I know who might be able to help."

"How may I help?"

"Blacksmiths. I need maybe twenty of them. But we can't call them blacksmiths. We'll have to put them down as Metallurgical Consultants."

"I can supply. For the right price."

"I can offer seven hundred dollars an hour. Plus meals.

But they have to be on a plane to Washington within an hour."

"Feasible. But your price is too low."

"For crying out loud, they're only blacksmiths."

"Metallurgical Consultants," the other voice corrected.

"Okay, one thousand dollars an hour. And I'll put them up in the best hotels for the duration of the assignment."

"I would prefer to barter. Like the last time."

"I don't know about that. I almost got caught last time."

"I do not require any more shoulder-fired missiles. My shoulder-fired-missile stock is satisfactory. I have another client who requires something special. Something you may be in a position to supply."

"What?"

"A substance called carbon-carbon."

"Never heard of it."

"It is a filament substance used to coat the nose cones of missiles to protect them against reentry burnup. It is very expensive and very difficult to secure. I need thirty miles of it."

"Sounds like NASA stuff," the general said. "I can't make any promises, but I can look into it."

"Look into it. I will have your Metallurgical Consultants assembled by the time you call back."

"Gotcha," said General Leiber, hanging up. He dialed another number, thinking that he should have thought of Friendship, International sooner. That funny-voiced guy had always come through in the past. If only he didn't always ask for the moon. . . .

By three P.M., exactly twelve hours after the unknown object had impacted on United States soil, the carbon-carbon spools were on their way to Zurich and the Metallurgical Consultants were en route to Washington. General Leiber had even found time to get the barbecue grills. He had them delivered to a roped-off aircraft hangar at Andrews Air Force Base while he returned to his coveted window office in the outer ring of the Pentagon.

But when he stepped into his office, he knew that the Joint Chiefs of Staff could no longer be denied. They were there, waiting for him. They were also rummaging through his desk.

General Leiber gave them a snappy salute. The Joint Chiefs, representing the highest officers of the combined United States military, returned his salute. Their faces were stern.

"General Leiber, we demand to know what is going on."

"I have the situation in hand," General Leiber said. He chewed his mustache concernedly.

"The President won't take our calls. We understand he has delegated all crisis-management responsibility to you."

"I happened to be on duty when the threat object impacted. I am the only one with operational knowledge of the situation."

"For God's sake, you're only a two-starrer."

"Not my fault, sir. I was passed over last time."

"That's not what he means and you know it," said an Army general. General Leiber declined to reply. He did not deal with the Army. Even if the Army general did outrank him by two stars.

"Where is this threat object?" an Air Force general asked. General Leiber had to answer him.

"In a secure area being analyzed, General."

"Where?"

"I cannot tell you that."

"Cannot? Why not?" the general roared.

"Because if I reveal its location, you very important officers will rush to inspect it."

"That's our damn job."

"And expose yourselves to unknown risks. As the President's surrogate, I would be derelict in my duty if I allowed you to expose yourselves to possible death."

"Death? Then the object is armed?"

"My team is attempting to confirm that."

"Is Washington still in danger?"

"My people are unable to say at this time. They are trying to identify the nature of the KKV."

"KKV?"

"Kinetic Kill Vehicle," said General Leiber.

An involuntary gasp came from the Joint Chiefs. They sounded like spinsters who had stumbled into a massage parlor.

"That is what I have designated the unknown. Until we

know its mission and capabilities, I am assuming it is hostile."

"Then it's not a dud missile."

"I can safely say that its constitutional elements give a strong indication of belonging to an offensive weapon hitherto unknown to the global stage."

The Joint Chiefs looked edgy. And General Leiber knew he had them right where he wanted them.

"Sirs, I realize I may be overstepping my authority, but it is my professional opinion as an officer that we face two scenarios here."

"Go on."

"Scenario one: we have been attacked by an unknown weapon launched by an unknown power. The double nature of the unknownness clearly indicates that none of our normal tactical responses are necessarily viable."

"What does that mean, exactly?"

"That we would be foolish to assume that just because the KKV has not gone off on impact that it was designed to go off on impact. It may be a delayed-reaction device of some kind."

"Yes. It's possible. Good thinking."

"Scenario two," General Leiber went on, feeling the mood shift in his favor. "It was a misfire. The KKV failed in its primary mission."

"In that case, Washington may be in no immediate danger."

"Wrong. The danger is just as great. Even greater. Whoever launched the KKV knows by now their first strike failed. They are right now evaluating the situation. They must assume that we are analyzing their weapon. Once we succeed, we should be able to identify its origin. And when we do that, we have no choice but to take retaliatory measures."

The Joint Chiefs nodded. The general was absolutely correct. Once they identified the aggressor, they would have to take retaliatory action or risk showing weakness in the face of a brazen attack.

"Therefore," General Leiber said quickly, "it is incumbent upon this enemy to launch a second strike. To take out our command structure before we can identify and retaliate. Every minute that ticks by brings us closer to a second strike."

The Joint Chiefs looked at one another. General Leiber had analyzed the situation with terrifying clarity. Either way it stacked up, they were standing on ground zero.

"Well," said the Air Force general, clearing his throat. "If the President has designated you as surrogate, I don't feel we are in a position to second-guess him. What do you gentlemen think?"

There was a chorus of agreement. A ribbon-bedecked admiral turned to General Leiber.

"General, if this great nation is facing a crisis of such vast proportions as you describe, it is incumbent upon us to advance to a position of command. If Washington goes, someone will have to manage the next phase."

"Yes, sir," said General Leiber.

"If you want us, we'll be down in the Tank. Carry on."

General Leiber saluted snappily. Sweat trickled down the gully of his spine. It was as cold as day-old dishwater. And after the Joint Chiefs had marched out of the room, he sank into his chair trembling.

It was a hell of a gamble, but it had worked. The Joint Chiefs were riding a high-speed elevator down to the nuke-proof command bunker under the Pentagon. They wouldn't dare stir until he gave the all-clear signal.

And General Martin S. Leiber wasn't about to give the all-clear until General Leiber was in the damned clear. He grabbed the telephone and got down to the high-risk business of career advancement.

5

Something was definitely wrong.

Dr. Harold W. Smith's ordinarily pale face was greenish from the backglow of his CURE terminal. If he leaned any closer to the CRT tube, he would bump it with his nose.

Official Washington seemed to be operating under a blanket of secrecy tighter than anything Smith had ever seen before. It was ominous. In the past, no matter how grave the crisis, there was a storm of leaks and rumors. Not this time. This time the routine political games were not being played. It was as if the situation was so grave everyone from the CIA to the Pentagon had decided to work as if they were on the same team, which of course they were.

Smith paged through his on-screen interceptions. There was unusual activity at Andrews Air Force Base. Movements of classified individuals and matériel. The Joint Chiefs of Staff had abruptly left their offices. Among the NORAD and Spacetrack early-warning systems, every unit had been quietly ordered to narrow its field of focus on a certain segment of the sky over the Atlantic Ocean. They were searching for something. Or they expected something. An attack.

As usual, it was the press who first noticed something was amiss. The media did not have a news story, per se. In fact, it was the absence of a story that started the rumor mills buzzing.

Specifically, where was the President of the United States?

The Washington press corps had expected a round of photo opportunities today. After all, it was the first working day for the new President. But the press corps was turned away by a nervous press secretary with the explanation that the President was "indisposed."

Smith frowned when that item greeted his eyes. He punched up the whereabouts of the Vice-President. The Vice-President was not in Washington either. He had returned to his home state very suddenly. The whereabouts of the Acting Secretary of Defense was unknown. And Congress wasn't due to reconvene for another week.

Smith made a series of untraceable phone calls. Pretending to be a wire-service reporter, he tried calling the heads of the CIA, the FBI, and other intelligence services. They were all out of town for the day, he was told.

When Smith hung up the phone, he was trembling slightly. The President had apparently disappeared and everyone else had left town. What the hell was going on? Who was in charge down there?

Smith picked up the dialless red telephone that was direct line to an identical phone tucked away in the nightstand in the President's bedroom. He listened to the ringing at the other end. One ring. Then two. Then three. It was a new President, so there was no telling how long he would take to get to the phone. The last President usually took six rings.

After twenty rings, Smith replaced the receiver, his face gray. The President was not going to answer. Smith was forced to conclude that he could not answer. The President was either not in the White House or no longer among the living.

Smith ordered the CURE computer to scan all official Washington phone lines for high activity. But even the phones were quiet. Small wonder. There was no one down there to man them.

With one exception. A single phone in the Pentagon showed constant use. Smith called up an identification code and instantly the computer relayed the information that the line emanated from the office of General Martin S. Leiber. Smith punched up the file on Leiber. It was brief. The man was a two-star general with an undistinguished field record and a flair for procurement. Some of his methods were unorthodox and there was some question about cost overruns in projects under his control.

Smith's fingers went to work. In a flurry of keystrokes

he instituted a tap on General Leiber's line. Instantly the computer converted the audio feed into an on-screen display.

Someone was complaining to the general. Something about barbecue grills. They weren't hot enough to do the job.

Barbecue grills? Smith wondered. It must be an open code. He asked the computer to identify the source of the incoming call.

The computer told him Andrews Air Force Base. Smith remembered that he had indications of strange activity at Andrews.

General Leiber's response to the complaining call was to ask what the hell did the caller need.

The caller needed brick ovens. And bellows. Lots of bellows.

General Leiber promised the caller immediate delivery on several high-temperature organic kiln-constructs and dynamic exhaust oxygenators, and then hung up.

Smith wondered what had happened to the requested ovens and bellows.

"Code," he mutterd. "This must be a code."

He saved the phone intercept in memory and ordered the computer's decrypting software to attack the text.

After five minutes of listening to the program hum, an error message flashed on the screen.

"EXPLAIN ERROR," Smith keyed.

"OPTIONS FOLLOW," the computer told him.

"OPTION 1: CODE UNDECIPHERABLE.

"OPTION 2: INSUFFICIENT TEXT TO EXECUTE PROGRAM.

"OPTION 3: TEXT IS NOT IN CODE."

"It must be," Smith muttered. "Washington has been virtually abandoned. No one in his right mind would be procuring ovens at such a time."

Smith switched back to the tap on General Leiber's phone. It had saved the last ten minutes of intercepts. As it played back, Smith's jaw fell. The idiot was ordering ovens. And bellows. They were being requisitioned for immediate shipment to Andrews.

"This makes no sense," Smith said in frustration. But because he believed that his computers could crack any problem, he attacked the puzzle again. Somewhere in the miles and miles of data transferring between the nation's computer networks, there was an explanation for all this. All Smith had to do was find it.

He wondered again what had happened to the President.

The President was very much alive. He was doing his best to be presidential. It was very difficult. Especially when one was stuck under nearly a mile of rock in one's pajamas.

"I'm the leader of the free world," the President said in anguish. "I should be up there leading."

"I'm sorry, Mr. President," the senior Secret Service agent said. "We have to wait for the all-clear."

"What if it doesn't come?"

"Then we'd all better try to get along. Because we are stuck here until the fallout radiation drops to survivable levels."

"That could take weeks."

"Months, actually."

"But no one has said anything about radiation. There hasn't even been an explosion."

"Yet," the Secret Service agent pointed out.

"I'm afraid I'm going to have to insist," the President said in a stern voice.

"I'm sorry, Mr. President. I have my orders."

"From whom? I'm the Commander in Chief!"

"I know that, sir," the Secret Service man said politely, "but I do not take my orders from you, but rather from my superior."

"Since when?" the President barked.

"It's our prime directive. Your security is more important than any other factor, including your demands and wishes. In short, the Secret Service will do everything in its power to safeguard your life, whether you want it or not."

The President looked at the Secret Service man in stunned silence.

"I'm sorry, Mr. President," the man told him. "That's how it is. Don't you think you should be watching the tactical displays?"

The President nodded numbly. Being President, he was discovering, wasn't all it was cracked up to be. For one

thing, there wasn't anything near the absolute power he
had envisioned. Everyone else seemed to have his own
agenda.

The President found a set and joined the grim-faced
Secret Service agents as they watched the tactical feeds
from NORAD. Every screen was on Threat Tube Display,
searching for incoming unknowns.

Not for the first time, the President wished the direct
line to CURE had a duplicate down here. Right now, Dr.
Harold W. Smith was the only person he trusted. Perhaps, the President hoped, Smith would set his own people into motion when he learned what was going on.

Dr. Harold W. Smith could no longer delay his decision. It was growing dark. The evening news programs
were leading with the vague but ominous story that on his
first day in the Oval Office, the new President of the
United States had not yet put in an appearance. The
reporters claimed that a cloud of low-level apprehension
had settled over the nation's capital.

By the time the media were through, Smith realized
grimly, the so-called low-level apprehension would be
full-blown panic. Still, Smith had to admit, the press did
have a story. They just didn't have any facts to back it up.

It was time to bring in Remo and Chiun. He buzzed his
secretary to have them summoned to his office.

"I believe they've just left," Smith's secretary replied
crisply.

"Left! Left for where?"

"I'm not certain, but they had me sign a requisition
form for a truck rental."

"Oh, God," Smith said in a husky voice. "That damned
elephant."

6

Remo backed the rental truck up to the shed. He got out and, undoing the restraining chains, let the steel ramp down.

The black maw of the truck faced the shed. Only two feet of clearance stood between the open truck and the shed door. No way was Rambo going to squeeze past the truck. Once he opened the shed, Remo reasoned, it should be a breeze.

Remo took off the padlock with a quick wrench of his hand. He knew Chiun had the key but he would be damned if he was going to ask the Master of Sinanju for any favors. Especially after this latest stunt.

Remo opened the sliding door. Inside the shed, illuminated by a single bare lightbulb, Rambo the elephant sat on a pile of hay. His trunk lifted in greeting.

"Up yours," Remo said back. He stepped in and walked around the elephant. Remo clapped his hands once sharply. The sound brought dust spilling off the rafters.

"C'mon. Up! Let's go," Remo barked.

Rambo fluttered his ears unconcernedly.

"Before, I couldn't get you to stay still," Remo said accusingly.

He tugged on the elephant's ropy tail, not hard, but enough to motivate the beast. Rambo's trunk curled around a swatch of hay and flung it back over his head.

Remo's face wore an annoyed expression as hay fell all over him.

"I'm willing to do this the hard way," Remo said, leaning one shoulder into the elephant's rump. He pushed. The elephant's tail swiped at him without effect. Remo pushed harder. He felt the elephant move.

Great, thought Remo, pushing some more. Slowly, inexorably, he shoved the large gray hulk out of the shed and to the ramp. The hay made it easier. Rambo slid on top of it like a sled.

But when Remo stopped to figure out how to make the elephant mount the ramp, he saw that his problem was far from solved.

Rambo climbed to his feet and walked back into the shed. He got down on his stomach again. His tiny piglike eyes regarded Remo with infinite sadness.

"Ohhhh," a squeaky voice said sorrowfully, "he knows what you intend."

Remo turned. Chiun was standing there. He had changed into a severe gray kimono. His face was unhappy.

"No, he doesn't," Remo snapped back. "If he knew what I was thinking right at this minute, he'd head for the hills."

"You never liked him. He recognized that."

"Tough. I've done enough for him."

"Where do you intend to take him, assuming you succeed in tricking him into this conveyance?"

"I was hoping a zoo would take him."

"Ah," said Chiun. "A zoo. He would be happy in a zoo. There would be others of his kind in a zoo. Yes, I think a zoo would be an excellent place for him."

"I wish someone would tell him that."

"I will try."

"Don't do me any favors," Remo said sourly.

"Do not fear, I will not," said Chiun, marching up to the elephant. With delicate fingers he pulled back one of Rambo's fan-shaped ears and whispered softly. Remo strained to hear what was being said. Chiun's words seemed to be in Korean, but Remo couldn't make them out.

Abruptly Rambo climbed to his feet. His trunk swaying from side to side, he stepped up to the ramp and walked into the truck's container section. He stood patiently, his tail hanging docilely.

"What are you waiting for?" Chiun asked. "Close the door."

Remo rushed to shove the ramp back into place. He slammed the doors shut and threw the locking lever.

"Thanks, Little Father," Remo said grudgingly.

"Thank me by allowing me to accompany you."

"Why do you want to do that?"

"So that I may say a proper good-bye to my faithful steed."

"Then let's go before Rambo changes his mind," Remo said, climbing behind the wheel. Chiun settled into the passenger seat and Remo got the truck in gear and headed for the Folcroft gate.

"Oh, he will not change his mind. I explained everything to him."

"You did, huh?" Remo said skeptically. "I didn't know you spoke elephant."

"I do not. I spoke truth. Even elephants understand the truth."

"Right," said Remo, and piloted the truck down the road. He wondered where the nearest zoo was. He would have to ask at the first gas station.

As the gates of Folcroft Sanitarium receded in the rearview mirror, Remo noticed a frantic figure in gray running after them and waving his arms. Smith. He probably wanted to say good-bye to the elephant too. Remo decided to pretend he didn't see him. He hit the accelerator, knowing that Smith's ancient car would never catch up. No way was he going to stop until he found a zoo.

7

General Martin S. Leiber was beginning to enjoy himself.

He was senior officer at the Pentagon now. When he spoke, other officers jumped. Word had gotten around that the President had left him in charge during the crisis. No one knew what the crisis was and General Leiber wasn't about to tell anyone, except to hint that it was very, very dire.

When he realized how much power he wielded, he sent out for lobster. Might as well grab the perks while he could. He was cracking the last claw when the phone rang.

"General Leiber," he said through a mouthful of lobster meat. Melted butter ran down his chin.

"General, this is CINCNORAD."

"Who?" asked Leiber. He fumbled through a Pentagon directory. He knew what NORAD was, sort of. But what the hell was a CINC?

"I've been in touch with the Joint Chiefs and they tell me you're in charge out there."

"That's right. Who did you say you were again?"

"Commander in chief of NORAD. You mean you don't recognize my designation?"

"It's starting to come back to me," said General Leiber, who usually didn't associate with real military types. He was more at home among lobbyists and defense contractors. Where the true power lay.

"Under orders from the Joint Chiefs, we've completed our tactical search. I thought you should have the results as soon as possible."

"Shoot," said General Leiber, wondering what the heck he was talking about.

"We've been over our logs and satellite reconnaissance

photos a dozen times. We find no evidence of any hotspots or launch blowoffs."

"Is that good or bad?" asked General Leiber, wondering what a blowoff was.

"I'm not sure," said the other man. "It's very strange. We've been assuming a ground launch, but our recon photos show that all Soviet missile silos are on standdown. So are the Chinese launch sites. There have been no ground launches from any known missile sites we monitor."

"Then it's a submarine launch, right?"

"That would be a logical guess, but Spacetrack would have detected it before PAVE PAWS. They didn't. In fact, Spacetrack inventory lists nothing going up. Nothing at all."

"Well, it didn't drop out of deep space."

"I don't think we should discount that possibility," said CINCNORAD.

"Correct me if I'm off base here, but we don't currently have a defense against extraterrestrial hostiles, do we?"

"No, General, we do not."

"What do I tell the President?"

"If I were you, I'd advise him to lie low until we have the straight skinny on this incident."

General Leiber hung up the phone, trying to decide if it would be better to call the President now or after he heard back from Andrews. He decided to polish off the last lobster claw first. If he ended up in the stockcade, it would be a long time before he tasted hot melted butter again. Maybe never.

But the last lobster claw went uncracked. The phone rang again. Leiber picked it up. It was Major Cheek.

"What have you got for me?" he barked.

"Progress, sir," Major Cheek said crisply.

"I don't give a hang about progress. Can you identify the hostile?"

"We can narrow it down to a limited number of possibilities."

"Good. Then it's a known threat."

"Well, yes and no," the major said unhappily.

"What do you mean—yes and no?"

"Well, sir, I think we can determine exactly what the object is, but the threat factor may be up to others to evaluate. We may know more after we go through some reference books. I've sent a man out to buy some."

"Buy? You don't have one lousy copy of *Jane's* at Andrews?"

"*Jane's Aircraft* won't help us here, sir. The object is definitely—repeat—definitely not found in *Jane's.*"

"Goddammit, man, stop talking in circles. Spit it out."

"It's like this, sir. Once we had the brick ovens—"

"High-Temperature Organic Kiln Constructs. Remember that if we're questioned later. No way will the taxpayers pay three hundred and fifty thousand dollars for ordinary brick ovens."

"Yessir. In any case, we isolated the pieces and restored what we could to their original shapes. A lot of it was slag, of course, from reentry heat, but we estimate only the leading third of the object was incinerated. The back two-thirds was intact right up until impact."

"Go on, man."

"Well," the major said hesitantly, "fortunately, several sections of what I guess you'd call the propulsion system survived. I had the smiths—excuse me, the Metallurgical Consultants—I had them try to weld what they could of it together. The propulsion system told us a lot."

"Look, I don't care about how it got here. I want to know about its offensive system. How many kilotons? What's the yield, man, what's the yield?"

"It doesn't have a yield. Exactly."

"Exactly what does it have?" the general asked, touching the remaining lobster claw with his thumb. It felt cool. He couldn't eat it now.

"Um, as I was saying, General, when we put together the propulsion system, we were able to measure one of the rods. By that time we had a fair idea of what we were dealing with. The gauge turned out to be four feet, eight and a half inches. That's very important. It told us right away the object was American-made. Because the rods in the European versions are usually three feet, six inches."

"It's American-made," General Leiber said angrily. "What kind of traitor would sell out his own government?" Then he wondered if he had sold any nuclear missiles lately. He couldn't remember having sold anything that big. "Give me specifics, will you? I'm writing this down."

Major Cheek vented a hot sigh. "We estimate the object to weigh approximately five hundred tons at . . . er . . . launch."

"God, I've never heard of a missile with that kind of throw weight. Thank God it didn't detonate."

"Actually, there was no danger of that, General."

"Why not?"

"It couldn't. I mean, it's not possible."

"It wasn't armed?"

"No, sir. I can safely say that it was not armed."

"If it wasn't armed, then what the hell was it supposed to do?"

"As near as I can tell, sir, it was meant to impact with maximum damage."

"Well, of course, you idiot."

"But it's neither explosive, nor nuclear, nor chemical in nature."

"I'm not following you."

"Sir, perhaps you should come down here yourself. I don't think trying to explain this over the phone can really do the situation justice."

"I'll be right over," said General Martin S. Leiber.

General Leiber was allowed through the Andrews gates only after he shouted down the guards. They tried to tell him the base had been declared off-limits except to cleared personnel.

"I know, you noncommissioned jerk," Leiber shouted, flashing his Pentagon ID. "I'm the man who ordered it."

They waved him through.

General Leiber drove to the hangar. He hadn't been there before. It was simple prudence. No way was he going near that thing. It might go off. But the major had assured him the device was no longer a threat. On the other hand, the major was stupid enough to raise his bid and then lay down a royal flush in the face of a superior officer. A man that foolhardy was capable of any imbecility.

As he was let in through a side door, the general thought the major had just better be correct. If anything happened to him, the President would be stuck underground for a long, long time.

Inside the cavernous hangar, light was furnished by

banks of fluorescent tubes. It was hot. At one end, the orange glow of the kilns flared angrily. They were surrounded by an assortment of heavy anvils. Tools lay on the concrete floor. But there was no sign of the blacksmiths.

Major Cheek came running up. He was in his shirtsleeves and sweating.

"Where are my blacksmiths?" General Leiber snapped. "I hope they're not goofing off. They cost the government plenty."

"I sent them to a secure area, General. Their job is done and I thought it was better that they not be privy to the evaluation process."

"Harumph. Good thinking. Now, let's have the poop on this thing."

"This way, General."

General Leiber followed as he unknotted his tie. "Blasted hot in here," he muttered.

"It takes a lot of heat to make iron malleable," the major said. "That's why your barbecue grills weren't enough. We needed extremely high temperatures."

"Blacksmiths on TV westerns always used stuff that looked like barbecue grills to me. How was I to know the difference?"

At the far end of the hangar there were no lights. Major Cheek started speaking as he began hitting switches, illuminating one section of the floor at a time.

"In a way, you were right, General," he said. "The bell was a good starting point. But even so, we would have had a hard time working from there. It was really superfluous."

As the general watched, piles of twisted metal came into view. Closest to him were simple jumbles of blackened slag. Beyond them were the unfused pieces. They lay about in neat groups. It reminded General Leiber of photos of the destroyed space shuttle *Challenger* after the pieces had been recovered and laid out for inspection. There were a lot of pieces. Leiber saw bent metal bars, strange constructs, and in a corner pile, huge round flat things that reminded him of impossibly large gears.

"As I said," the major went on, "when we assembled one of the propulsion units, it dawned on us what this thing was. But even then, I doubt if I would have recognized what we had if my son hadn't been into HO models."

"HO?" asked General Leiber, clutching at his cigar for support. "My God, are we talking about hydrogen ordnance?"

"Why, no. I've never heard of hydrogen ordnance."

"Never mind," said Leiber. "I thought you said this thing was safe."

"It is. Now. Please come with me."

General Leiber followed the major through the aisles between the debris. Although many of the pieces had been restored from their impact-mangled states, they were not perfect. Exteriors were blackened and pitted and many of the pieces only approximated the original parts. They had been too badly compressed to be completely reconstructed.

"This is the heart of it," Major Cheek said, gesturing to a huge black cylinder set on a wooden frame. It lay open and half-melted at one end.

The general poked his head in. The open end was easily seven feet in diameter and very black both inside and out. It smelled of scorched metal—like an old cast-iron stove. He ran his fingers along the outer skin, which was still warm from being welded.

"From the pieces, we were able to reconstruct this portion."

"The fuel system?"

"You might say that, General."

"Then it *is* a missile."

"Uh, yes and no."

"Don't 'yes-and-no' me again. Out with it! It is or it isn't."

"It's not a conventional missile. But it acted like one in flight. In other words, it was ballistic."

"That makes it a missile," General Leiber said decisively.

"No," said the major. "A missile is a fuel-propelled rocket. This is no such thing."

"No? Then how did it get to Washington? By slingshot?"

"That's the part of this I can't answer, General. We haven't a clue there."

The general stubbed his cigar into his mouth. He tilted his service cap off his lined forehead and his hands went on his hips.

"If you know what it is, you oughta be able to tell me what its motive power was."

"*That* I can tell you," the major said, patting the long drumlike cylinder affectionately. "They usually run on kerosene or coal."

The general blinked.

"Say again."

"Kerosene or coal. That's the fuel. But the propulsion system is a by-product."

"What?"

"Steam."

"Steam." The general's cigar dropped to the floor, shedding sparks. "My God. Do you realize how serious this is? Steam. Every ratass little nation in the world possesses steam technology. If this is true, we could be facing a terrible new era of steam missiles."

"That's the bad news, General. Every nation on earth already possesses these devices."

"They do?"

"General, I don't quite know how to tell you this, but the object we dug out of that pit is a locomotive."

The general looked blank.

"A what?" he asked quietly.

"A steam locomotive. See this wheeled section? It's part of the propulsion system."

The general looked. Beside the big cylinder was a distorted truck sitting low to the ground. It sat on heavy flanged wheels.

"Locomotive. As in choo-choo? As in the little engine that could? Are we talking about that kind of locomotive?"

"I'm afraid we are, sir."

"That's preposterous," the general sputtered.

"I agree."

"A steam locomotive runs on rails. It doesn't have a propulsion system."

"Not for flight, anyway."

"Steam locomotives don't have guidance systems."

"Exactly. And neither did this one."

"They don't have warheads."

"This one is perfectly harmless. Unless it fell on top of you."

"Then what the hell was it doing falling out of the sky if it was so goddamned harmless?"

"Well, had it landed another hundred yards to the north, it would have demolished the White House."

"That's a hell of a small target to take out for the throw weight involved. Only an imbecile would attempt such a thing."

"I can't explain it."

"How the hell did it get airborne? You can at least explain that, can't you?

"I wish I could. I have no idea. The front end is fused from reentery and the rear end, where you'd expect to find a propulsion system, is . . . just the rear end of a locomotive."

"There's got to be something more. Something you've overlooked."

"There is one other phenomenon."

"Yes?"

"The individual pieces. As you can see, we've kept them well-separated. Watch what happens when I push them closer."

The general watched as the major walked over to an isolated fragment. With his shoe, he nudged the piece across the floor until it neared the wheeled truck. Suddenly the smaller fragment jumped across the concrete and hit the truck with a bang.

"Magnetic," the major said. "Every bit of it is magnetically charged."

"We knew that at Lafayette park. It was one of the first things we discovered."

"Highly magnetic. Unusually magnetic. It must have taken an incredible application of electricity to magnetize a five-hundred-ton locomotive."

"That's it?"

Major Check shrugged. "It's all we have."

General Martin S. Leiber looked at the chunks of blackened iron surrounding him. He looked at the major. He felt suddenly very small, as if he were surrounded, not by the pieces of a demolished locomotive, but by dinosaurs which had come to life with ravenous appetites. And he was the only piece of meat in sight.

"How am I going to explain this to the President?" he said in a shaken voice.

The major shrugged again. "I think you should tell him exactly what we've discovered. It's disturbing, but it's not as if we've had a dud nuke dropped on us."

"Dud nuke!" the general roared. "Dud nuke! A dud nuke we can handle. With a dud nuke we could read the serial numbers and identify the aggressor nation. Can you tell me who's responsible for this?"

"Once the reference books on locomotives arrive, we might."

"Can you tell me how it was launched?"

"Not from a book," the major admitted.

"No, of course not."

"I don't see the problem. Even if one of these hits a critical target—and I don't see how, without internal guidance systems—the damage on the ground would be very limited."

"On the ground! You don't win wars on the ground anymore. You win 'em in the back rooms. At cocktail parties. This is the fucking twentieth century. Do you think America and Russia haven't had a major war this century because neither side thinks it can win a ground situation? Hell, no."

"I'm aware of the balance of power, General. But this thing doesn't figure in. It's nonnuclear."

"*This* one was. But what about the *next* one?"

"We don't know that there will be a next one."

"Do you want to tell the President that there won't be a next one? Do you, soldier?"

"No, sir," the major said hastily.

"Let me explain something to you, son. There are two absolutes in national defense. Our ability to detect and intercept an incoming threat. And our ability to retaliate in the event of an attack. We have no defense against this thing. It went up so fast our satellites couldn't read it. Hell, we barely had time to get the President into deep cover before it hit. But more important, we don't know where the bastard came from. We can't admit it hit sovereign territory without admitting weakness. Therefore, we can't warn the world that it had better not happen again. And if it does happen again, chances are we'll just have enough time to kiss our fat, contented assess good-bye."

"I think you may be exaggerating, sir."

"We're sitting ducks. Do you know how many steam locomotives there are in Russia? In China? In the third world? Thousands. Maybe tens of thousands. And every one of them a potential threat. How are we going to defend ourselves? Nuke the rest of the world and hope we get the enemy?"

"There may not be a next one," Major Cheek said stubbornly.

"I want total security on this. Who knows that this is a locomotive?"

"You and I. And three of my men."

"Confine them. They are not to breathe a word of this. No one talks about trains or locomotives or any of it. I'll figure out what to tell the President. In the meanwhile, you get your shiny nose into those reference books. I want to know when this thing was built, who built it, how many more of them are out there, and I want the answers tonight. You got that, soldier?"

"Yes, sir, General."

"I'll be at my office trying to hold this country together. Don't let me down."

And General Martin S. Leiber turned on his heel and stormed out of the overheated hangar. When he got outside, the rush of cold air made him shiver and frosted his mustache. He wiped the sweat off his face with a handkerchief and got into his car.

He was still sweating when he reached the Pentagon.

8

"You don't seem very broken up, Little Father," Remo said as he tooled the lumbering truck through darkened city streets.

"I am not broken at all," sniffed Chiun.

"I didn't mean literally broken," Remo said. "I meant unhappy. As in heartbroken."

"Why should I be unhappy? It is true that I agreed to accompany you on what should have been a short pleasure ride but has turned into an expedition second only to Odysseus' voyage home from the Trojan Wars. But I am not grief-stricken."

"How was I to know that the first three zoos we'd try would refuse to accept Rambo?"

"You could have called ahead."

"I was in a hurry. I want this albatross off my neck."

"Albatross? What albatross?" Chiun asked, looking around.

"Never mind," fumed Remo.

"I wasn't going to mention this, but this is all your fault."

Remo braked the truck in anger. It skidded and he had to wrestle the wheel to the left to avoid hitting a mailbox. He succeeded. He hit a fireplug instead.

"How odd," said Chiun when the truck jounced to a halt. "It is raining, yet there are no clouds."

Remo threw the truck into reverse and backed off the hydrant so the engine would not be flooded. Wordlessly he got out of the truck.

The fireplug was cracked at its base. Water gushed up from the shattered main. Because Remo was upset, he did not approach the problem logically. He kicked the hydrant. The casing flew into a wall. Without the hydrant to cap it, the water geysered upward.

Remo was instantly soaked, which did not improve his mood.

Seeing no other alternative, he plunged into the geyser. Eyes clamped shut to the overpowering column of water, he felt for the sharp, broken water-main mouth. When his fingers found it, he began working the metal. Shrill metallic squeals emanated from the main.

Slowly, as Remo squeezed the water main shut, the torrent turned to a gush and then dropped off to a spastic trickle.

When Remo stood up, only a little water still stubbornly bubbled up. Remo stamped on the source, and the water stopped.

Soaking wet, he climbed back into the cab and tried the ignition. It caught after several tries and he backed the truck off the sidewalk.

A beat cop stood watching the truck depart. He hadn't seen the accident, only the sight of a thin man with unusually thick wrists angrily beating a water main into submission. He decided he hadn't seen enough to warrant questioning the man. If anyone asked, he had no idea what had happened to the hydrant.

"How is it my fault?" Remo asked bitterly after several blocks. He blew water off his lips. It kept rilling down his face. He tried wringing it out of his hair with his fingers.

"We would not now be having this problem had it not been for your rashness," Chiun told him evenly.

"I think we've had this conversation before," Remo said. "Is this the one that starts with: if I hadn't gone back to Vietnam, none of this would have happened?"

"No, this is the one that ends with my humiliation at your hands."

"I think I walked out before we got to that part last time."

"That is why I bring it up now."

"You can get off here if you want."

"Nonsense. You drive. I will talk. Hopefully, you will listen in spite of your stubbornness. It was your stubbornness that created my dilemma."

"What dilemma is that?" Remo asked in spite of himself.

"Smith ordered you not to go to Vietnam."

"So I went anyway. I had an obligation. American

POW's. It's about something you can't seem to understand. Loyalty."

"I understand loyalty. I also understand higher obligations. My obligation to Smith. Your obligation to Smith."

"Sometimes I don't give a rat's ass about Smith."

"Ordinarily I would give even less. But emperors are hard to find in the modern world. Especially emperors with vast stores of gold. I may not value Smith, but I value his gold. It supports my village. Your village, now."

"So what's the beef?"

"The beef is that while I may turn a blind eye to your disobedience toward Smith, you have a deeper obligation to me. I gave Smith my word you would not go to Vietnam, and you did."

"I don't know what came over me," Remo said vaguely. "Must have been those flashbacks I was having."

"A convenient excuse," Chiun sniffed. "But I will continue my tale. I cannot have you disobeying me."

"It was a special case. It won't happen again."

"So you say. Your word was not good enough before. I cannot trust it now."

"Where is this leading? I'd like to take a shortcut."

"Impatient white," Chiun snapped. "We will probably be driving about all night and you do not even wish to converse. Very well. This is where this is leading: you asked me why I did not shed tears for the giving up of my elephant and I will tell you. He is a nice elephant, but truly I have no interest in him. He was merely a tool."

"To do what?"

"To educate."

"I get it," Remo said. "As a Master of Sinanju I'm supposed to learn all there is to learn about elephants because your ancestors had to. Is that right?"

"No, it is not right. You disobeyed me and I had to teach you. Rambo was my choice to teach you a lesson."

"Whaaat!" Remo said, open mouthed.

"I made you wash him, feed him, and walk him so that you would learn the consequences of your actions."

"Wait a minute. You told me he was being abused. Then you tricked me into getting him aboard the sub. When did it occur to you to use him like that?"

"Before then. When I first came upon him."

"I thought he was your transportation through the freaking jungle."

"He was," Chiun said brightly. "He is a dual-purpose elephant."

"You mean to tell me," Remo shouted, "that the only reason you dragged that bag of wrinkled meat back to America was to stick it to me?"

"Hush, Remo," Chiun warned. "Rambo will hear you. He is sensitive."

From the rear of the trunk came a low, forlorn trumpeting.

"See?" said Chiun.

"Yeah, I see. I see a lot. You're really something, you know that?"

"Yes," Chiun said happily. "I am something special."

"I don't believe this," Remo said under his breath. "All this because you wanted to teach me a lesson."

"Not just a lesson. Something more. Responsibility. Someday you will take over the village of Sinanju. Someday I will not be here to guide you through the thorny paths of life. I will not be at your side, but my teachings will stay with you. Especially this one. The next time you consider embarrassing me in front of my emperor, you will think of Rambo. And you will hesitate. Perhaps even reconsider. It is too much to hope you will refrain from your headstrong ways, but after a few additional experiences such as this, you may learn. It is enough to give me hope."

"It is enough to give me a headache. I can't believe you've put me through all this just to make a point."

"An important point," Chiun corrected.

Remo said nothing. He came to a cross street. The sign said "Tower Avenue." Back at the last gas station they'd told him the Stonebrook Zoo was off Tower Avenue. But they hadn't said right or left. Remo decided to go left.

After three-quarters of a mile they came to a stone-rimmed gate that said "Stonebrook Zoo" in wrought-iron letters. A steel sign added that it was "Closed for the Season."

"Damn," Remo said, slapping the steering wheel in frustration. It shattered into three sections, leaving only the post.

"Now we are stuck," Chiun complained.

"No, we're not," Remo said grimly. "They may be closed, but not to us." He stepped out of the cab. Chiun followed.

"What do you plan, O determined one?" Chiun asked as Remo rattled the padlocked chain on the gate.

"I made a mistake last time," Remo said, testing various links in the chain. When he found one that seemed right, he pulled it apart with both hands. The link snapped. The chain rattled to the ground and Remo shoved open the gate.

"You make a mistake every time," Chiun said.

"Last time," Remo went on, ignoring him, "we offered to donate Rambo. Mistake. Nobody wants him. This time the donation will be anonymous."

Remo opened the back of the truck and pulled down the ramp. He did it with one hand. Normally it took two men.

Rambo backed out of the truck and stood docilely. Chiun patted him on the cheek and said to Remo, "Lead, and Rambo and I will follow."

"Come on," Remo said. Chiun tugged on one of the elephant's saillike ears and Rambo padded alongside him.

They walked through the open zoo gates.

"All we have to do is find the elephant house and we're home free," Remo whispered.

"I understand," Chiun said. "When we find it, we will open it and place Rambo within. Then we will take our leave. No one will be any the wiser."

"It should work."

"Yes," said Chiun. "It is a good plan."

"All we have to do is find the elephant house."

"Hold it right there," a hard voice warned. Suddenly they were transfixed in the glow of a flashlight. A uniformed man advanced on them, flashlight in one hand and a revolver in the other. He was a silhouette in the darkness, but beyond the flashlight's glare Remo made out the outline of his peaked cap and gunbelt.

"Oh-oh," Remo whispered. "A guard."

"Don't move a muscle," the guard said, coming to a stop. He was very careful not to get closer.

"You're both under arrest," he said, looking them over.

"Arrest! For what?" Remo demanded.

"Elephant poaching."

"Elephant . . ." Remo sputtered. "Now, wait a minute. We're not—"

Chiun kicked Remo in the ankle.

"Oh, please, Mr. Policeman," the Master of Sinanju said in a pitiful voice. "Please do not shoot us."

"I won't if you don't make any funny moves."

"Not us," Remo said, wishing he could reach down and massage his aching ankle.

"We are very sorry for this intrusion," Chiun went on, his voice quavering. "If you will show mercy, we will attempt to atone for our terrible crime."

"That'll be up to a judge."

"But there is no judge to be seen," Chiun pointed out, "and we are alone in the dark, just the three of us. And this elephant." Chiun tugged on Rambo's ear. His trunk shot up and he let out a cry of anguish.

The guard recoiled, his flashlight searching out the beast.

"Hey, it's going crazy!"

"No," Chiun said. "It is merely annoyed. But do not worry, I know elephants very well. I can control him."

"Just keep him calm, okay?"

"Oh, I can do more than keep him calm. I can return him to his rightful place."

"No way, Little Father," Remo snapped. "We're not taking him all the way back to Fol— Ouch!"

"Back where?" the guard asked.

"Foley's Circus," Chiun put in, eyeing Remo. "We are with Foley's Circus. Our own elephant died and we needed a new one quickly. But now that we have been caught stealing yours, we have no choice but to abandon our foolish enterprise."

"That's smart. Stealing an elephant is no small matter."

"We see that now. But if you will agree to let us go, we will be happy to restore this beast to his fellows—who are no doubt already lonesome for him."

"I can't make any promises, but if you put him back, I'll ask that they go easy on you."

"But we didn't— Yeow!" Remo howled, grabbing his ankle.

"What this clown is trying to say is that we meant no harm," Chiun said. "We will be only too happy to restore this beast and throw ourselves upon your infinite mercy."

The guard swallowed uncomfortably. Rambo towered over him.

"Okay, it's a deal. Just put him back."

"Of course," said Chiun, bowing. "You lead."

"Clown?" whispered Remo as Chiun led Rambo between the darkened cages.

"We are with the circus, remember?" Chiun shot back.

"If I'm supposed to be a clown, what are you?"

"The ringmaster, of course."

"Why do you always have to be top dog?"

"Because you are bottom dog," Chiun said. "If I had left it up to you, we would still be stuck with this smelly beast."

"What's that you're saying back there?" the guard asked suspiciously.

"I was saying to my top clown that we are fortunate to have encountered such a wise man as yourself," Chiun said loudly.

Rambo trumpted as if in agreement.

"Here it is," the guard said, stopping at an enormous cage. Keys rattled. "We really should have a trainer here, but I can't take the chance that thing will run amok."

"Oh, he will be good, I promise," said Chiun. When the gate opened, he led Rambo into the cage. At the other end, three large elephants stood unmoving. Their ears flapped sleepily. They did not react to the new visitor.

"Good-bye, Rambo," Chiun said, patting the elephant on the head.

The Master of Sinanju exited the cage without a backward glance. When he was out, the guard hurriedly slammed the gate and locked it. It took him only a few seconds, but when he turned around to deal with the two elephant poachers, they were nowhere in view.

Back at the truck, Remo got behind the wheel, smiling.

"That was pretty smart, Little Father," he said.

"Thank you," said Chiun, closing the passenger door.

"Uh-oh," Remo groaned, looking at the missing steering wheel. "I forgot about this."

"Do your best. He will be searching for us and this vehicle is rented to Folcroft."

"Right," said Remo, starting the engine. He released

the brake and took the steering column in both hands. Grimacing with effort, he got the front wheels to turn as the truck went rumbling down the road.

Remo wrestled the steering column until they got to the center of town. There they abandoned the truck and hailed a taxi.

"I'm never going to forget this night," Remo sighed as he settled into the cab's back seat.

"Exactly the point," Chiun said with pleasure as he arranged his kimono skirts.

9

For General Martin S. Leiber, the universe had shattered and the sky was falling all around him.

For as long as he had served as a Pentagon procurement officer, he had operated by one simple rule: there were no rules. If he could rig a defense contract, he did. If he had to juggle progress payments, he did. Lying to Congress? Standard operating procedure. Absurd markups of defense items were his stock in trade. It was General Leiber who personally approved critical circuit boards that kept twenty percent of America's Minuteman missiles nonoperational at a given moment. The Air Force's top-of-the-line attack helicopter was plated with substandard armor and held together by inexpensive bolts he had purchased on the cheap, knowing that under combat stress they would shear like breadsticks.

General Leiber never expected his defective Minutemen to be launched. And if an attack helicopter lost a rotor during training, the manufacturer always caught the flak. General Leiber expected to slide into the obscurity of retirement with a fat bank account and zero accountabilty.

He had gambled on the one constant of superpower relations: the balance of power.

General Leiber was a reasonable man. He knew the military mind. Some dismissed the military as mad bombers, but they were actually quite sensible. They were always prepared to spend as many conscript lives as necessary to achieve a reasonable military objective. That was what war was all about, assets and expenditures. The country with the greatest assets was the one to be feared the most. In this hemisphere, that was the United States, God bless her.

But no general would provoke a conflict that was certain

to cost him personally. Leaders led. They didn't squander their own lives. Not since World War II, and that was ancient history as far as General Leiber was concerned.

There was no way, no earthly way, that either the U.S. or the USSR, or China for that matter—and everyone knew how crazy they were—was going to provoke a thermonuclear exchange and risk everything. Including their summer homes.

General Leiber had counted on that. It was his sole rationale. No realistic threat of a world war existed in the nuclear age, and therefore America's military might was so much window dressing. And given that assumption, who the hell cared if a nuclear missile couldn't get out of its silo or the occasional aircraft fell out of the sky? It was all for show.

Until exactly 3:13 this morning, when a steam locomotive struck within yards of the White House. Now the entire nuclear force was on Defcon Two. If the Soviets so much as got wind of that, then they would go to their defense condition two—or whatever they called it over there. And if the Russkies went to red alert, so would the Chinese. Itchy fingers would hover over missile-firing keys and all it would take to ignite global conflagration would be a sea gull showing up on some idiot's radar at the wrong moment.

General Leiber cleared his Pentagon desk of the cold remnants of his lobster meal with a swipe of one uniformed arm. He moved his telephone to the bare center of his desk. Beside it he placed a yellow legal pad and two number-three pencils.

He was going to have to deal with this matter. Forget profit. It was time to worry about his ass.

First he would have to figure out what to tell the President. He couldn't tell him the truth. Not without looking like a total fool. They would laugh at him, the general who ordered a high state of alert over a falling locomotive. Never mind the very real nature of the crisis. The press boys wouldn't address that. They'd go with the lighter side of the story. In no time, General Leiber knew, he would be reduced in rank. Probably to one-star. Maybe worse. He tried to remember what rank was right below general. He could not. He'd been with the Pentagon so long he had blotted out his pre-general days.

"What I need is a better fix on the threat factor," he said, sitting up. He began dialing. He knew a guy at NASA who might give a reading on this thing. A blinking red button indicated an incoming call. Annoyed, General Leiber transferred to the incoming call.

"General Leiber," he said crisply.

"This is the President, General," a stern voice said.

"I'm still working on it, Mr. President."

"I can't stay down here any longer," the President said. "I've just been looking at teletype reports. The media want to know where I am."

"Let me suggest that you put out a press release, sir."

"Press release! Are you serious? You don't cover first-day absenteeism with a press release. I have to put in an appearance."

"Mr President, let me tell you why you don't want to do that."

"What is it?"

"I didn't want to tell you this until we have more information, but we have a tentative ID on the hostile."

"Hostile? Hostile what?" the President wanted to know.

"It's just an expression, sir."

"Oh. Go ahead."

"Well, Mr. President, I don't know how to break this to you—"

"I have to know. I'm President now."

"Yes, Mr. President," said General Martin S. Leiber, taking a deep breath. He plunged in. "The hostile is what we military call a Kinetic Kill Vehicle, or KKV for short."

"Good grief. I never heard of the KKV."

"With all due respect, Mr. President, you are new at this."

"Yes, but I thought I'd been thoroughly briefed by my predecessor."

"It's a complicated world, Mr. President. Perhaps he overlooked KKV's. They've just been deployed for the first time."

"Still, I must return to the Oval Office."

"We could be just minutes away from a second strike, sir."

"You've been saying that for hours. Everyone's been saying that. Look, this is day one of my administration."

"It's already evening, sir. Almost nine o'clock. Why don't you get some rest and we can discuss this in the morning? When you're fresh."

"I've made my decision. I'm coming up. I want you in the White House immediately for a complete briefing. Everything you know, General."

"Yes, sir, Mr. President," General Leiber said reluctantly. "Will there be anything else?"

"Um, I left you in charge, correct?"

"Yes."

"I'm going to hand the telephone to my senior Secret Service bodyguard. He won't take orders from me."

"Wait a minute. I can't do that. He's a civilian. I'm military. I don't have any authority over him."

"Maybe he doesn't know that. Talk to him."

"Yes, sir," General Leiber said as the Secret Service agent came on the line.

"I'm afraid I can't recognize your authority, General," the agent said politely.

"Good for you. Try to keep him down there as long as you can. The situation up here isn't stable."

The President came back on the line.

"It didn't sound as if you tried very hard," he complained.

"He's a good man, Mr. President. Stubborn, but good."

"There's got to be a way."

"If there is, I'm not familiar with it."

"There must be. This is an emergency." There was a pause on the line as the President considered. He was obviously thinking. That was a bad sign. General Leiber hated dealing with people who thought. He would much rather have a salute and instant obedience.

Finally the President spoke up.

"I am the Commander in Chief," he said.

"Yes, you are," General Leiber admitted after some hesitation.

"And I have designated you as my surrogate."

"Yes, sir." He didn't like where this was going. It smacked of initiative.

"Therefore, I am ordering you to order me to the Oval Office to assure the nation that I am in command."

"I . . . er . . . but—"

"Do it!"

"Yes sir. As your surrogate, I am ordering you to the Oval Office immediately."

"Don't tell me. Tell the Secret Service."

General Leiber heard the phone change hands.

"I have just ordered the President to the Oval Office."

"I don't have the authority to override you, General," the Secret Service agent admitted.

"I wish you hadn't said that," General Leiber said in a dull voice.

Like a man about to walk the last mile, General Martin S. Leiber hung up the phone and got to his feet. Woodenly he placed his service cap on his head and straightened his tie.

There was no avoiding the moment of truth now.

The first thing the President of the United States did upon reaching the first-floor level of the White House was to head for his bedroom. His wife, clutching her negligee, trailed after him. Three Secret Service agents brought up the rear.

Upon reaching the bedroom, the President slammed the door in their faces.

"But I'm not dressed," his wife complained.

There came rummaging sounds, and the door opened a crack.

"Here," the President said, handing out a bundle of clothes.

The First Lady picked the bundle apart with her eyes.

"But none of these match!" she yelled.

The President did not respond. He was too busy. He picked up the direct line to CURE. It was the first time he had had to do so. The previous President had explained all about CURE. Its mandate, its operational parameters. How, as President, he could not order CURE into action. He could only suggest missions. Well, he sure was going to suggest a mission this time.

"Mr. President." It was the voice of Dr. Harold W. Smith. The President did not know that for a fact. He assumed it. Only Dr. Smith was sanctioned to use the dedicated CURE line.

"Smith?"

"Of course," Smith said calmly. "Are you well?"

"I think I'm catching a cold from standing around in my pajamas and bare feet. You know, they didn't even have any of my clothes down there."

"Where is 'there,' sir? And please try to speak more slowly. I'm having trouble following you."

"Down in the White House fallout shelter—or whatever they call it."

"I see. What is the situation?"

"No one seems to know. General Leiber is on his way to brief me."

"Leiber? Oh, yes," said Smith, remembering the name from his intercepts.

"Smith, your job is national security, isn't it?"

"In the broadest sense of the phrase, yes."

"Then where were you?"

"Sir?"

"Washington took a first strike from a KKV and we didn't see it coming."

"I understand NORAD relayed warning of a . . . What did you call it, sir?"

"KKV. Don't tell me you don't know what a KKV is. Well, you couldn't. Apparently they're new. It stands for Kinetic Kill Vehicle."

"Kinetic," Smith said slowly.

"Yes, one landed in Lafayette Park. Fortunately it didn't detonate. But that might have been a fluke."

"I see," Smith said, recalling the fire in Lafayette Park. It was starting to come together. But what was a Kinetic Kill Vehicle? As Smith listened to the President, he called up his *Jane's Aircraft* data base. No doubt it was listed there.

"Smith, your mandate is to monitor potential security situations and nip them in the bud."

"Well, yes. But normally our monitoring capabilities are domestic in nature. My computers aren't terribly effective on a global scale."

"And why not, might I ask?"

"Because, Mr. President, it would be virtually impossible for one man to monitor all the computer traffic around the world. Domestically it is difficult enough. And there is the language-barrier problem. As it is, I'm at my terminal up to fifteen hours a day. As you know, CURE must be a one-man operation in order to maintain absolute security. We operate outside of constitutional restrictions, and if the press ever—"

"So what you're telling me is that even in a best-case scenario, you couldn't have foreseen this attack?"

"Without more information, I cannot respond to that," Smith said, glancing at the flashing message on his computer screen. It was telling him the *Jane's* data base had no listing for a Kinetic Kill Vehicle. How odd. Obviously he would have to update the file.

"And what about your people? Why weren't they here to deal with this?"

"Well, Mr. President, my enforcement arm has always been an option of last resort. I keep him in reserve until needed."

"He should have been down here!" the President barked.

"With all due respect, sir, even if he had been on station, what could he have done? He's good. But not good enough to catch an incoming Kinetic Kill Vehicle. We are talking about a man with extraordinary abilities. But not Superman. He does not wear a cape or fly."

"Smith, this was supposed to be my first day in office and I spent it cowering in a hole."

"Yes." Smith's voice was noncommittal.

"This is intolerable. I want your people down here at once."

"Er, I'm afraid that is impossible."

"What are you saying?"

"They are unavailable. On another . . . er . . . assignment. I am sorry."

"Pull them off it. We are anticipating another attack at any moment."

"I would like to comply, Mr. President. But until they complete their mission, I will be unable to reach them."

"That's absurd. Don't they even check in?"

"Well, sometimes. Our enforcement arm usually does that, but he often has trouble with the security codes. His trainer, the older one, will use the telephone only as a last resort."

"Don't they carry communicators? Walkie-talkies? Anything? They are needed in Washington, Smith."

"As soon as they report in, I will order them to Washington, I assure you."

"That's wonderful," the President said acidly. "If they arrive after the capital has been reduced to hot, sifting ash, be certain to thank them for me, won't you?"

"I'm sorry, Mr. President," Smith said lamely.

"When this is over, there will be some changes made, Smith. Mark my words. Your organization sounds like it belongs back in the nineteenth century. Do you know I had no way to reach you from down in the shelter?"

"Security demands that we have a minimum of technical equipment, Mr. President. That means one phone at each end of our special line. CURE has functioned this way for twenty years now."

"From where I'm sitting, it's not worth snot," said the President, hanging up.

At the other end, Smith replaced his receiver. He took off his rimless glasses and rubbed tired gray eyes. It was a terrible way to start a working relationship with a new administration, but how could he tell the President that Washington must stand naked before foreign aggression until its secret enforcement arm found a new home for an unwanted elephant?

Smith returned to his screen, typing in the words "Kinetic Kill Vehicle" and initiating a global search through the CURE system's massive memory banks. Then he settled back in his chair. Even with massive sort and memory capabilities, the computer would take several minutes to isolate an answer.

Perhaps the President had a point, Smith mused. Perhaps CURE's mission had become too big to manage effectively. Or maybe it was just that the world had become too complicated.

10

As General Leiber was on his way to the White House, his car phone buzzed. He picked it up.

"Yeah," he said sourly.

"Major Cheek here, General."

"What is it?"

"We have a positive ID on the hostile object."

The general sat up straight. His hand tightened on the wheel. "Give it to me," he barked.

"Bad news."

"I can take it."

"It's one of ours, for sure."

"Ours?"

"Absolutely. It's an Alco Big Boy, vintage 1941. They used to haul cargo on the defunct Wyoming Division of the Union Pacific line. It's a real monster, sir. One of the most powerful steam engines ever devised. Listen to this: length 132 feet, weight 537 tons, tractive effort of 135,375 pounds. This means it could pull that weight, sir. It had sixteen driving wheels and—"

"Never mind that crap. Can you trace it to anyone?"

"Not without knowing its running number, General. And we've found no identifying marks."

"Are you absolutely, positively certain of your information?"

"Yes. I've researched it thoroughly. The reference books are wonderful, sir. I wish I had had them before. They would have saved a lot of time. For instance, the bell turns out to have been very important. American locomotives always had them because they rode through wild country where buffalo and horses ran free. In Europe, trains don't have bells. They don't have cowcatchers either. Instead, they have these two bumper rods sticking out in front. It's really quite fascinating, General."

"I'm sure the President will agree when I tell him," General Leiber said bitterly. "I'm on my way to the White House right now. He expects a full briefing."

"Good luck, General."

"You're a big help," the general muttered, hanging up. "The bastard. I think he enjoys watching the crap rain down on me."

Frowning, the general abruptly swung his car around. He pulled up in front of a hobby store.

Inside, he went to the section devoted to model trains.

"Can I help you, sir?" a clerk asked him.

"You can help not only me but also your country."

"Glad to." The clerk stiffened.

"Fine. Hang loose, civilian. I need a model of an Alco Big Boy locomotive. Right now. Can you oblige your country?"

"Yes, over here." The clerk searched a shelf of colorful boxes. He straightened. "Ah, here."

"Outstanding," the general said, ripping off the cellophane and opening the box. Inside, there were a hundred tiny plastic pieces attached to plastic trees.

"It's in pieces." The general's voice was disappointed.

"You have to assemble it."

"No time. Don't you have one that's in one piece?"

"Not that model. We do have HO scale versions of more recent trains, if you'd rather have one of those."

"It's gotta be this one," the general insisted.

"They assemble quite easily. An hour or less."

"How fast could you put one of these together?"

"Oh, perhaps twenty minutes—if I don't get a sudden rush of customers."

The general slapped the box in the clerk's hands. "Do it. For your country."

"But—"

"No buts. The President of the United States is waiting for me. For this. Do it. The government will not only be eternally in your debt, but I think I can get you a consultant's fee."

"Well, business is slow—"

"Then face front and hop to it!" General Leiber barked.

Twenty minutes later, when General Leiber was on his third cigar, the clerk handed him a perfect replica of an

Alco Big Boy steam engine. It was redolent of plastic
cement.

"Remarkable machine, isn't it?" the clerk said admir-
ingly. "So streamlined, so powerful."

"You'd think different if one was pointed at you," the
general said, pulling out a requisition form. He scribbled
on it, then said, "Sign here."

The clerk signed.

"Your check will be in the mail."

Back in his car, the general put the sheet away for
safekeeping. The clerk would receive $250 for emergency
situational model prototype assembling. General Leiber
put another zero at the end. If he survived, he would skim
a cool $2,250 from the deal. If not, it wouldn't matter.

The general drove his car up to the White House gate.
The guard waved him through. He drove up to the side
entrance, where a Marine guard in a snappy blue dress
uniform saluted him as he opened the door.

The President greeted General Leiber with a firm hand-
shake. His sober face looked like a thundercloud.

"General, step into my office."

"Yes, sir," said General Leiber, following him in and
taking a seat in an empty chair. He clutched the model
train, wrapped in a paper bag, in one beefy fist. The fist
perspired.

"General, I want everything you have on the KKV
threat," the President said evenly.

"I won't mince words," General Leiber shot back. "We're
facing a threat beside which conventional nuclear weapons
pale into insignificance."

"It's that bad?"

"Worse. Only a handful of nations belong to the so-
called nuclear club. Of them, only three—the U.S., USSR,
and China—possess intercontinental delivery systems. The
KKV threat is as dire as it is because virtually every nation
on earth possesses a stockpile. They are cheap. They are
effective. And once they are perfected, I don't doubt that
every lousy border skirmish will turn into an excuse to
deploy them."

The anger in the President's face seeped away like
ground water. His composed features slackened. His eyes
grew tired.

"It sounds like the end of civilization as we know it," he said wearily.

"That would not be an exaggeration," General Leiber said firmly. He clutched the package tighter. He felt a piece break off under the pressure of a thumb. But that didn't matter. The President was buying it. Leiber decided to lay it on a little thicker. Maybe he wouldn't have to unwrap the locomotive. No sense in taking any chances.

"Who fired it?"

"My people are still working on that question."

"Then we cannot retaliate or threaten, can we?"

"Not with accuracy. But the retaliation option is not entirely closed."

"No? Please explain."

"Sir, at this moment, our enemy is waiting for a response. I say we give them one."

"Such as?"

"We nuke someone at random."

"Great grief! Are you serious?"

"Consider the psychological effect. If we nuke another country, the aggressor can't help but notice. It will bring him up short. He might hesitate to strike again."

"It sounds very dubious, General."

"Well, Mr. President, once you're acclimated in office, you'll find that tactics such as this are really quite sound. Call it a preemptive warning."

"And whom do you suggest we nuke?" the President asked slowly.

"Obviously, none of the other superpowers. They would only complicate the situation. I would suggest Vietnam, but it would only piss off the Chinese, and there's no telling what they would do. Eastern Europe is out for the same reason. The Russians can be touchy about stuff like that. I was thinking of someone safe, like Australia or Canada."

"But they're our friends."

"Mr. President, on the level we're operating on, we don't have friends. Only temporary allies. Besides, we want to take care to hit someone who can't hit back."

"No. I can't countenance bombing an ally."

"How about Japan? We've already nuked them once and they didn't do squat about it. In fact, they're in better economic shape than we are right now. It might be we'd be doing them a favor. Public sentiment would probably be on our side."

"The Japanese are still our friends."

"That's the beauty of it, Mr. President. Imagine the impact that nuking an ally would have on this aggressor nation. If we nuke a friendly country, they'll be soiling their shorts wondering what we might do to them. They'll think twice, I guarantee it."

"No,'" the President said firmly. "Even if I could agree with you, I won't do it. Not on my first day in office. It would set a bad precedent."

"It's your decision, sir."

"You'll continue your search for the aggressor nation. In the meantime, I want a complete briefing on the KKV threat. What exactly are they and what do they do?"

"Well," said General Martin S. Leiber, steeling himself, "I kinda figured you were going to ask me that, so I took the liberty of having a prototype model constructed."

"Good," said the President. "Let me see it."

General Leiber stood up and set the paper-wrapped model on the President's gleaming desk. He took a deep breath. He started to tear off the wrapping. He hoped the President had a sense of humor.

General Leiber never found out, because before the KKV model was exposed, Secret Service agents burst into the room.

"What is it?" the President asked fearfully.

"I'm sorry, Mr. President. NORAD has picked up another bird heading this way. Come with us."

"General, follow me," the President said, hurrying from the room.

Clutching the model, General Leiber trotted after the President, his eyes wide in fear. Other agents converged on the special elevator, the First Lady running white-faced between them.

"General," the President said from the open elevator, "I want you down there with me."

General Leiber hesitated. A Secret Service agent yanked him aboard. The cage sank. It ran very fast.

"Can you manage your people from my phones?"

"Yes, sir. Most of my best work is done over the phone."

"Good. Let's hope that someone survives to take your calls."

"Yes, sir," said General Leiber, hiding the paper-wrapped model behind his back. No way was he going to let the President see it now. Down under bedrock, there would be no place to hide. Who knew, the President might even declare martial law and stand him before a firing squad. There was no telling what a civilian would do in a crisis situation. They were all crazy.

11

This time, NORAD's BMEWS radar station at Fylingsdale, England, picked up the object shortly after launch.

The Air Force general designated CINCNORAD considered this a vindication of the Spacetrack system, which was a series of satellite and ground stations so sophisticated that they could detect a soccer ball over the British Isles.

"Excellent," he said as he moved between the consoles at the main command post deep within the hollows of Cheyenne Mountain, Colorado. The lights were dim. The greenish backglow of the radar screen created a sickly atmosphere. Except for the scurrying uniformed personnel and the giant wall displays, the command post might have been a small brokerage office.

"Sir, we've computed a trajectory that will deposit the hostile in the vicinity of Washington." There was a note in the status officer's voice that begged a question.

"We might not be able to save Washington, but we're sure going to know where it came from," CINCNORAD assured him.

"I'm not certain of that, sir,."

"What?"

"We picked it up at apogee."

"What do the computers say?"

"It's an unknown, sir. The computers can't identify."

"Damn," said the general fervently. He yearned for the old days before all this computer horseshit. Back in the days of the 440-L radar system, status officers were worth something. They were trained to read the radar signatures bouncing off the ionosphere. A top man could tell from the squiggle whether he was dealing with an SS-18 or an

SS-N-8. Nowadays, if the software couldn't recognize it, they all sat there and chewed their cuds.

"Why didn't the system pick it up at liftoff?"

"I think because it went up too fast to get a reading."

"Too fast! What the hell could be faster than a missile at launch?"

"This thing is, sir," returned the status officer.

The general stared at the huge overhead situation display. The hostile was shown as a code-tagged green triangle dropping onto a wire-frame simulation of the earth's surface. The projected impact point—indicated by a green letter I—was Washington, D.C. In all the simulated drills the general had ever taken part in, nothing had moved as fast as this object.

"If we have an impact fix," the general said confidently, "we gotta have a launch point."

"No, sir. Just a broad area of probability."

"What? Where? What area?"

"Africa, sir."

"Damn. Where in Africa?"

"That's it. Africa."

"Why the hell can't the blasted computer pinpoint better than that?"

"Because, sir, the object appears to be tumbling. Its course is erratic. See, the impact site keeps shifting."

The general looked. On the overhead screen, the I-for-Impact symbol kept jumping. One moment, it was D.C. Then it was over in Virginia. Then it was in Maryland.

"Dammit, we've got to do better than this. If we lose Washington, we must—repeat, must—retaliate. We can't nuke the whole of Africa."

"I'm sorry, sir. The system has never encountered anything like this."

And then all eyes turned to the overhead screen. The green coded triangle descended upon the Washington area and merged with the impact symbol.

The two symbols flared and died like a faraway candle burning out. A hush fell over the room.

"Maybe the satellite photos will tell us something," the general muttered weakly.

The first photos were beamed down from an orbiting KH-11 reconnaissance satellite. A uniformed clerk handed the initial batch to the general without comment. He started to walk away hurriedly.

The general flipped through the first several photos. They were high-resolution images, of unusual clarity, and showed the European and African landmasses. The bottom photos had been taken over water. The Atlantic. The general noticed a dark lump like a beetle on one of them. It floated over wrinkled water. He turned to the next photo. The object was there, only bigger. It was not distinguishable. But the third and final photo showed the object clearly.

"Clerk!" the general yelled. Every status officer in the complex jumped at his station.

The clerk came back. His expression was sheepish.

"What the hell is this?" The general screamed, waving the bottom photo in the clerk's reddening face.

"It's one of the recon photos you asked for, sir," the clerk said, deciding that this was a perfect time to take everything literally.

"I know that. I meant this object."

"Sir, it appears to be a train."

"It's a locomotive!"

The clerk pretended to look more closely.

"Yes, sir. I believe the general is correct, sir. It does appear to be a locomotive."

"What's it doing there? Is this a joke?"

"No, sir. Those are the raw transmission photos."

"You looked at them before handing them to me?"

"Yes, sir."

"And you didn't mention this."

"What would I have said, sir?"

CINCNORAD looked at the clerk. He fumed. His face reddened. The clerk stood perfectly straight. He held his breath.

"You could have warned me! Damn! Now what am I supposed to tell the White House—assuming it's still standing?"

"I don't know, sir," the clerk protested.

"Son, let me give you a piece of advice. Never—I repeat, never—hand a superior officer a hot potato like this."

"What should I have done, sir?"

"I don't know what you *should* have done, but if I were you, I would have lost this photo. The other two are fine. You can't tell what the hell the hostile is. But this one distinctly shows a locomotive."

"You wanted the hostile identified, sir."

"I wanted a reasonable explanation. Something I could kick upstairs with confidence. How am I going to explain this?"

"Recon photos don't lie, sir."

Just then, someone came up to the general.

"The White House on the hot line, sir."

The general looked at the clerk like a drunk seeing an old enemy coming out of a bad bottle.

"I'll deal with you later," CINCNORAD said, accepting the red receiver and thinking wistfully that if the damn hostile had only been a nuke, he wouldn't now be in this ridiculous position.

The object did not impact on Washington, D.C.

It came down in Bethesda, Maryland, just outside the District of Columbia. It impacted on a golf course, which was itself not unusual. It would have been more unusual had it struck in the Bethesda area and not hit a golf course. Most of official Washington played golf in Bethesda.

The object totally obliterated a sandtrap at the eleventh hole and pulverized several nearby trees. Scorched grass continued to smoke even after an Air Force team led by Major Cheek reached the scene less than an hour later.

After surveying the site and ascertaining no presence of radiation or other lethal agents, Major Cheek called the White House, where a nervous switchboard operator put him through to General Martin S. Leiber.

Before taking the call, General Leiber looked over his shoulder. The President was busy at another phone, trying to learn if Washington had sustained any significant damage.

General Leiber turned his attention back to his call.

"Give it to me straight."

"It looks like another one, General."

"Can you tell for sure?" General Leiber demanded. He shifted in his seat. He kept the paper-bag-wrapped steam-engine model between his thick thighs, holding it with one hand like a little boy who has to pee but is afraid to ask the teacher if he can be excused.

"I can't, but all the signs are the same. What do we do?"

"Haul it off. Make sure. I want a report as soon as possible. You still have the Metallurgical Consultants on hand?"

Yes, sir."

"Use 'em. I gotta go."

Sweating, the general put in another call. He was going crazy. He needed answers. Real answers. Serious, scientific answers. Anything. As soon as the President had a handle on the situation upstairs, he was going to remember the package. And General Leiber would have to have a lot more than a plastic steam engine when the President asked.

A man finally picked up the line. "Hello?"

"Bob, this is Marty."

"Marty! Hello. Uh, there's no problem with that last batch of stuff, is there?"

"No, the carbon-carbon was fine. Listen, you're with NASA. You know a lot of scientific space crap."

"I stay informed."

"I got a hypothetical for you."

"Shoot."

"Suppose—just suppose—I wanted to launch something across the Atlantic. Something big."

"How big?"

"Oh, four, five hundred tons."

"That's a lot of throw weight."

"That's what I've been saying."

"Excuse me?"

"Nothing. This is strictly theoretical. I want to launch this thing, but I can't have any on-board propulsion. What would do it?"

"Hmmm. Nothing we have at the moment."

"Speculate. There's gotta be some blue-sky launch system that could move that kind of tonnage."

"Well, in another decade or so, we could be launching satellites without rockets. That's the talk."

"Using what?"

"Well, they're just in the theoretical stage. There's a lot

of talk that the latest superconductor breakthroughs might be the key. They've got them working on a small scale. They're basically peashooters using magnetic propulsion."

"Magnetic!" the general said excitedly, scribbling on a pad.

"Right. Imagine a rifle that fires a bullet without using gunpowder."

"Yeah!" the general said, writing that down too.

"Those we have. Now imagine one a thousand times bigger."

"I can see it clear as day," the general said loudly.

"That's the next generation of satellite launcher."

"This thing you're talking about. Could it launch a warhead?"

"No problem. You wouldn't need boosters or fuel or anything of that sort. Just load it and press the button."

"How about a locomotive?"

"Come again, General?"

"Could it launch a steam engine? I'm being theoretical here."

"Into orbit?"

"Maybe. Not necessarily," General Leiber said guardedly.

"If someone could build a prototype launcher large enough, sure. But it would have to be nearly a quarter of a mile long."

"Yeah?" the general said, writing the figure down. "How come?"

"To build up the power to throw it. The device I'm talking about would be electromagnetic."

"Electromagnetic!" the general said enthusiastically, writing the word down. After a pause he added the prefix "hyper." "Hyperelectromagnetic," he said under his breath.

"What's that, General?"

"Nothing," said the general, his pencil poised to write the NASA man's next words after "hyperelectromagnetic." This was great. He didn't need to show the model after all.

"Now, what do they call one of these babies?"

"A rail gun."

The general's pencil lead snapped at the tail of the letter R.

"A what?" he croaked.

"A rail gun."

"You said 'rail'?"

"Yeah, rail. Why? You sound funny."

General Leiber turned to see what the President was doing. The President was coming toward him. He wore a strange expression on his face. It was half-scowl, half-confusion.

"Quick," he whispered. "Give me all the scientific theory you can as fast as you can."

General Leiber scribbled furiously. "I gotta go now, Bob," he said hastily, and hung up. He put on his best smile and turned to face the President. He shifted on his seat and managed to slip the locomotive under him. Another part snapped under his shifting weight and he winced as something—it felt like the cowcatcher—dug into his scrotum.

"You have something for me, Mr. President?"

"NORAD just transmitted these satellite photos."

Hesitantly General Leiber accepted the photographs from his Commander in Chief. He looked at the blurred black smear floating above the blue of the Atlantic on the first photo.

"NORAD believes that's your KKV," the President said.

"Mean-looking brute, isn't it?" the general said, flipping to the second photo. It too showed an indistinct blot. The general began to let out his pent breath—then he saw the third photo. He started coughing.

'Have you an explanation for this, General?" the President asked bitingly.

The general got control over his cough.

"Oh!" he said suddenly, jumping to his feet. "I nearly forgot. I was going to show you the KKV model." He presented the President of the United States with the paper-bag-wrapped package.

The President took the package. He tore away the paper with careful fingers. The paper fell to the floor and the President held in both hands a model of a steam locomotive with the cowcatcher askew.

"This is a locomotive," the President said quietly.

"Actually, that's the civilian term for it, sir. We in the military prefer to call it a KKV, because, sir, as you can see, sir, while it appears to be a steam locomotive and may well have been built for that purpose, these photographs show conclusively that some dastardly outlaw nation has perverted the designer's original intent. It's a Kinetic Kill Vehicle now. Sir."

"I have one question for you, General."

"Sir?"

"How?"

"As a matter of fact, sir, I have just completed my task analysis of the problem. Obviously the Soviets have beaten us in the rail-gun race."

"I beg your pardon?"

"Rail gun, sir. Don't tell me you've never heard of it?"

The President's face hardened. "No."

"Well, you're new, sir. I suppose you haven't been briefed."

"Stop telling me I'm new, dammit!" the President yelled suddenly, his voice no longer under control. "My first day on the job and I'm hiding a mile underground because you tell me it's suddenly raining steam engines!"

"Sorry, sir. But I think you're underestimating the threat factor."

"I am not underestimating the threat factor. I'm not sure what the threat factor is."

"Allow me to explain the principle behind the rail gun, sir."

"Do so." The President folded his arms.

"We've been working on them for more than a decade. They're the ultimate satellite delivery system. We can throw out the shuttle, and all our rockets and missiles. This baby works on magnetic propulsion principles. What we do is, we build a tube large enough to do the job and stick a magnetically charged rail on either side of the tube. Step up the power with maybe a zillion gigawatts. And zoom! Whatever we stick in one end is propelled out the other so fast your head would spin. Sir. Mr. President. Sir."

"Rail gun?"

"The baby that shot that thing into orbit would have to be as long as the Holland Tunnel, sir. Of course, the more accepted term for it is electromagnetic cannon, or EM cannon. But the techies, they like to call it a rail gun."

"Rail?" asked the President, looking at the model in his hand.

"Rail. Obviously the Russians took the rail part a tad literally." The general cracked a weak, lopsided smile.

"There's only one thing wrong with your Russian-rail-gun theory."

"Respectfully, Mr. President, I believe my theory is sound."

"The second KKV was not launched from Russia."

"Sir?"

"NORAD says it lifted off from Africa."

"That's absurd, Mr. President. The Africans can't possibly have a rail gun. Hell, even we don't have a full-scale version."

"It came from Africa," the President repeated firmly.

"If you say so, sir."

"We're going up, General. To the surface."

"Glad to hear it, sir."

"When we get upstairs, I'm going to brief the press on this entire matter."

"Sir, I don't think that would be a good idea . . . sir."

"But I do. And I am your Commander in Chief."

"As your surrogate, Mr. President—"

"Forget that surrogate stuff. From now on, I'm going to do my job. And so are you."

"Yes, sir," General Martin S. Leiber said miserably, accepting the plastic locomotive model the President thrust into his hands.

12

Pyotr Koldunov threw the cutoff switches himself. It was a job for a lowly technician, not for one of the top scientists of the Soviet Ministry of Science. But he was not in Soviet Russia now and he didn't trust even the most intelligent of his Lobynian assistants not to accidentally bump the controls and trigger the launch sequence while he was inside the Electromagnetic Launch Accelerator, hurling him into orbit like a bug blown through a straw.

With all available power no longer diverted to the EM Accelerator, the overhead lights automatically brightened. The strong illumination seemed to take the curse off the underground complex. Months of dwelling under the Lobynian Desert with only the swarthy Lobynian technicians for company and no sunlight had reduced Pyotr Koldunov to a state of perpetual gloom.

As he stepped to the massive round chamber hatch, more like a bank-deposit vault than what it really was—the breech of the most powerful weapon ever created—Koldunov wondered if he were one of those people who suffer from light-deprivation mood swings. He made a mental note to check with a Moscow specialist if he ever got out of this sand burrow with his mind intact. Bitterly he punched out the access code on the wall-mounted keypad, carefully blocking the device so that none of the Lobynians could see the combination.

The light mounted over the keypad turned red, indicating acceptance of the access code. Koldunov turned quickly. The black-eyed Lobynians in their stupid green smocks were watching him avidly. The disappointment visible on their dark faces told him they had not gleaned the combination.

The final step was to hit the hydraulics button. He

punched it angrily and waited. He was sick of the incessant Lobynian spying. Lobynia was supposed to be a Soviet client state, but their leader was a madman. As a rational, patriotic scientist, it sickened Pyotr Koldunov to be made subservient to the Lobynian dictator, Colonel Hannibal Intifadah. As a man, it infuriated him to know that if he slipped up, the Lobynians would slit his throat and take control of the EM Accelerator.

The huge hatch rolled aside and the square, tunnellike maw of the device gaped as black as a capitalist's heart, Koldunov thought morosely. The odor was worse than the last time. The ozone stink was nearly overwhelmed by the bitter stench of seared metal. Black. It smelled black. As black as it looked. Black as a Lobynian's soul, he thought with grim humor. Yes, it was that black.

Koldunov clicked on his powerful argon flashlight and stepped in. He breathed through his mouth. He wanted to gag. The light splashed along the walls of the tunnel. It was more than twenty feet high and inclined at a shallow upward angle. Not for the first time, Koldunov thought it was like walking into a serpent's belly.

The tunnel was constructed of four thick walls held together with massive external bolts. Mounted on each side wall was a flat copper rail. These were the power rails. Electricity pumped through them provided the magnetic pulse that could in theory propel a skyscraper into orbit.

The flashlight revealed that the left-hand rail had been damaged by the last launch. The copper surfaces were gouged and melted as if the powerful electric forces had boiled off the outer skin. The right rail was less damaged. But as he stepped further along, picking his way carefully as the incline grew steeper, he saw that the true damage was to the right rail. It had cracked at a joint. No wonder Soviet tracking systems had reported that the second projectile had tumbled in flight. Koldunov sighed. Both rails would have to be replaced.

Colonel Intifadah would not like this. Not at all.

The carrier rails were in worse shape. Mounted side by side on the launcher's flat floor, they were simply a section of the People's Lobynian Railroad System diverted underground through the complex and into the launcher itself.

The tracks ran up to the very mouth of the gun, a quarter of a mile away, where it poked out at ground level. These rails were twisted off their ties. He had half-expected that. They had been relaid after the first test and that had weakened them. He had told Colonel Intifadah exactly what would happen. But Colonel Intifadah had screamed at him for a straight twenty minutes until Koldunov had, in exasperation, stopped trying to make his case.

Now he would have to face Colonel Intifadah with the unhappy news that not only did the carrier rails have to be relaid once again, but also the power rails would probably have to be changed after each launch as a matter of routine maintenance. That would throw the Colonel's schedule completely off. It also meant that Pyotr Koldunov would be stuck in Lobynia far longer than he had planned.

Shaking his head, he left the breech and closed the hatch. He entered the sealing code, careful to shield that too. As long as only he knew those codes, the Lobynians dared not kill him. Even Colonel Intifadah was sane enough to know that.

Exiting the machine, he carefully stepped over the tracks leading into the hatch and mounted the concrete steps to the shielded control booth overlooking the launch-preparation area. He picked up the green-telephone hot line.

"Why do you not restore power to the device?" asked Musa Al-Qaid. Even in the air-conditioned chill of the underground complex, Al-Qaid's face had that greasy sheen of perpetual sweat. Probably it was fear.

"There is no need," Koldunov told him curtly.

"But our people will soon deliver the next revenge vehicle. Our glorious leader has decreed that it will be launched on schedule."

"Your glorious leader should have listened to me if he wished to maintain his precious schedule," Koldunov told him. "The device is inoperable."

"Then our glorious leader must be so informed immediately."

Koldunov shrugged, waited for the first ring, and quickly handed the phone to the other man.

"Be my guest. I was in the process of doing exactly that."

Al-Qaid took the receiver without thinking. Placing it to

his ear, he got the switchboard of the People's Provisional
Palace in the Lobynian capital.

"I . . . that is, this is Musa Al-Qaid. I am calling on a
matter of utmost importance for our glorious leader." He
stared daggers at Koldunov's white-smocked back.

Pretending to examine the control console, Pyotr
Koldunov smiled tightly. That would fix the officious bastard, he thought.

"Yes, Brother Colonel," Al-Qaid said quickly. "A problem, Brother Colonel. He will not say, Brother Colonel.
No, sir. Yes, sir. At once, Brother Colonel."

Al-Qaid hung up the phone and addressed Koldunov in
a stiff voice.

"Our glorious leader demands your immediate presence
in the capital."

"Good," said Koldunov.

"Good?" sputtered the Lobynian. "Many who are summoned to his office do not return alive."

"I am not concerned . . . for myself," Koldunov said
simply.

"It was your device. Your failure."

"Yes, exactly. My device. My access codes. My everything. On loan to your government as a gesture of solidarity from my government. I am hardly expendable. Can
you say the same, Al-Qaid?"

Musa Al-Qaid blinked as if a thought had just occurred
to him. "Colonel Intifadah directed that you be brought
before him immediately," he countered.

"And who did he say would perform that errand?"

"I have that privilege."

"You? Not a flunky, but the senior Lobynian adviser on
this project?"

"Colonel Intifadah obviously thinks highly of me."

"On the other hand, it was you who gave him the bad
news. And we all know how Colonel Intifadah reacts to
bad news."

Al-Qaid had no answer to that. The Lobynian swallowed
tightly. He kept on swallowing all the way up the bucket
elevator to the surface and to the green helicopter waiting
on the pad.

The ride to the Lobynian capital of Dapoli was pleasant.
The sun was high in the desert sky. It was a cruel sun, but

it brightened Pyotr Koldunov's mood. The thought that Colonel Intifadah might become extremely irate upon being told that his revenge weapon was temporarily inoperative did not lessen his improving humor. In fact, it added to it. Perhaps Colonel Intifadah might become so upset that he would shoot someone.

Koldunov turned to look at his pilot. Al-Qaid. Koldunov smiled. Al-Qaid looked at him quizzically.

Yes, life would be more pleasant without Al-Qaid. The man smelled of fear and constant perspiration. And his Russian was atrocious. He mangled the language worse than the conscripts from Urkutsk and Tashkent with whom Koldunov had been forced, in his long-ago youth, to serve in the Red Army. He hated them too—and their backward ways. Besides, Al-Qaid was next to useless as a technician. Koldunov suspected that he was a GID spy. Koldunov suspected half his technical staff were in the employ of Colonel Intifadah's Green Intelligence Directorate. Even Lobynian technicians could not be so incompetent.

Yes, it would be pleasant if Colonel Intifadah had Al-Qaid shot.

Pyotr Koldunov settled back in his seat as the many-towered capital of Lobynia loomed ahead, confident that he was not expendable.

The helicopter landed in the palace courtyard. From the air it looked as if the courtyard was green with well-tended grass. In fact it was concrete painted green. The helipad was a lighter shade of green.

The door to Colonel Intifadah's office was also green. The guards on either side of the door carried green rifles and wore green uniforms. They belonged to Colonel Intifadah's elite Green Guard. They pushed Koldunov back from the door and, taking Al-Qaid by the arms, escorted him into the Colonel's office. The green door slammed shut and Pyotr Koldunov found a seat on a long leather divan. It matched the walls, which were chartreuse.

When fifteen minutes had passed and no sound of gunshots came from behind the green door, Pyotr Koldunov decided that Colonel Intifadah was not going to execute Al-Qaid. Koldunov frowned.

Then the green door opened and the two Green Guards

carried out the limp body of Al-Qaid. His green smock was almost black with blood. His head hung slack-jawed from his scrawny neck.

Al-Qaid looked as if he had been methodically beaten to death. The splintered and stained rifle butts of the guards told Pyotr Koldunov that his guess was probably correct.

Koldunov smiled as the guards carried the scientist to a green elevator door. They pressed a button. The doors slid instantly apart and the guards heaved the body in.

The thud of it landing came loudly even though the body had obviously fallen several floors.

Koldunov walked up to the elevator door. He looked down. Al-Qaid's body lay atop a heap of other bodies. Some looked fresh. Others, however, seemed very, very old.

"This isn't the elevator I rode up on," Koldunov remarked pleasantly.

"It is not," replied one of the guards. "It is a garbage disposal. Colonel Intifadah's *personal* garbage disposal."

Then Koldunov realized that the shaft contained no cage, no cables, no dial to indicate floors, and only one button. It was marked "Down." Obviously Colonel Intifadah had gutted an elevator shaft for this special purpose.

"Well," Koldunov said happily, "shall I go in next?"

The Green Guards looked at the Soviet scientist with undisguised stupefaction. The man was about to walk into a tiger pit and he acted as unconcerned as if he were about to stroll into a matinee.

They did not have to escort him in by force as they had expected. He walked ahead of them as if eager to face Colonel Intifadah's wrath.

13

After he had overthrown King Ardas of Lobynia, Colonel Hannibal Intifadah had taken possession of the royal palace. As a gesture to the new order, he had renamed it the People's Provisional Palace. Then he had had it painted green, inside and out, and decorated with the new Lobynian flag, which was also green. Blank green. For Colonel Intifadah claimed to despise all ornamental trappings of office.

The official history of the new Lobynia, as chronicled by Colonel Hannibal Intifadah in a book he called *The Green Precepts*, had it that the Colonel had chosen green as the new Lobynian national color as a gesture of sympathy with the rest of the Islamic world, green being a color favored by Moslems.

But the truth of the matter was that when the people of Lobynia learned via radio that yet another military usurper had engineered a coup against good King Ardas, they massed around the royal palace with the intent of bringing down this latest upstart in gold braid.

Seeing the mob, Colonel Intifadah's cell of revolutionaries grew nervous. They were starting to lose their courage. So Colonel Intifadah personally shot them all to death. Then he went into the royal dining room and pulled a tablecloth off the king's dining table, shattering precious Waterford crystal goblets and fine china and, waving the makeshift flag before his unprotected chest, announced from the balcony that he had eliminated the usurpers. And then, proclaiming the new Islamic Republic of Lobynia, he ran the green tablecloth up the flagpole and proclaimed that if he were to fall in the defense of Allah, then so be it. Let the assassins have their way. Islam would live on without him.

The crowd broke into spontaneous cheering.

Colonel Intifadah raised his clenched hands above his head triumphantly, bestowed the crowd with a snaggletoothed smile, and tried to make the best of it. In truth, he was deeply disappointed.

He hated green. The flag that he had personally designed for the new Lobynian republic was red and carried the hammer-and-sickle emblem of international Communism. But he comforted himself with the thought that on some days you initiate the tide of history and on others it carries you along. Either way was fine with Colonel Intifadah just so long as the tides of history eventually deposited him safely on shore. If he got a little wet in the process, that was okay too. Just as long as it wasn't his own blood soaking his uniform.

Today, as it had been on so many other days since he had risen to power in the North African desert nation of Lobynia, the blood on the Colonel's uniform belonged to someone else.

Colonel Intifadah looked down at the gleaming dark spots spattering his sleeves and blouse. They shone redly wet. He knew from experience that later the spots would brown into a rust color and finally cake and flake off. Al-Qaid's blood would be no different from that of the hundreds of others who had displeased him.

Colonel Intifadah reached for a damp cloth, intending to rub some of the blood off. But he decided against it. Better to let the Russian see the spots, to know that this son of the desert stood so close to the kill.

Colonel Intifadah went to his desk and stood behind it. In the floor-length mirror on one wall, he regarded himself critically. His middle-aged face had coarsened, the skin dark and large-pored. His mouth was cruel and arrogant, his eyes as black as the tight-curled hair that no comb would ever tame. Although it was early, the beard growth had already started to show.

It was a face that intimidated weaker men. With that face, Colonel Intifadah would intimidate this Russian. Colonel Intifadah straightened out his uniform. It was green. He always wore green, even though he passionately hated the color. Even the gold braid coiled at his shoulder was greenish-gold.

The door opened and Colonel Intifadah hastily let the green curtain fall over his personal mirror.

"Leave us," Colonel Intifadah barked to his guards. The two men swiftly and gratefully withdrew.

"Stand before me, comrade," Colonel Intifadah ordered.

The pale Russian scientist Pyotr Koldunov stepped up to the dark green desk. In order to stand before the Colonel, he would have to walk through the sticky pool of blood in the middle of the floor.

The Russian did so without showing a flicker of notice.

Colonel Intifadah frowned darkly.

"I am told that the device will not work," he said sullenly. He spoke Russian. Perfect Russian. He was also fluent in French and English, as well as his native Arabic. He enjoyed seeing the startled expressions on the faces of smug diplomats when he so casually discoursed with them, they who privately thought him a crazed nomad who had wrested power by brute cunning.

"*Da*, Comrade Colonel," Koldunov replied in the same language. "The energy required for launch stripped the power rails and seriously damaged the carrier rails. As I told you would happen."

"Are you criticizing me?" Colonel Intifadah shouted, his sidearm flashing from its holster.

"I am merely reminding you that I cautioned you about this possibility. We should have waited."

"Waited! I have waited three years for this revenge. Revenge upon the Americans, who bombed this very city!"

"I am aware of your motivation," the Russian said with undisguised distaste.

Crack! Crack! Crack!

The Colonel fired at the ceiling in his rage.

The Russian flinched at the sounds, but he did not react otherwise. Nor run for shelter. Colonel Intifadah threw his empty pistol onto the desk. It was a 9 mm. Glisenti. The grips were carved jade.

"You must be very brave, comrade. Some of my own officers think I am crazed."

"Many Moslems fire into the air to express themselves. It is their way."

"Out in the streets, yes. But not indoors. I know you

send reports of my mental health back to the Kremlin. Do not deny this."

"I report to my superiors every week. Just as I report to you. As I am reporting to you now."

"You are a dog with two masters."

"I serve my homeland with pride. I am obligated to report to you. It is part of my internationalist duty."

"Do not speak to me of the Soviet internationalist duty. Where were your people when the American B-52's were raining death on Dapoli? Where?"

"There was no warning of their attack."

"No? Then why did your Soviet destroyers quietly leave this end of the Mediterranean before the bombers came? Your leaders knew. They knew everything. But rather than face the aggressor, they retreated to watch the carnage."

"I am not a military man. You will have to ask the Kremlin that question."

"I have. And you know what they told me? A coincidence. Bah! Pigs that slink from their friends. They sell me their weapons and call me their ally and sign a mutual-defense treaty and then they skulk from trouble at the first sign of American might."

"We are helping you now," Koldunov asserted.

Colonel Intifadah spat on his desk.

"Years after the fact. Long after the world has forgotten. Only after I complained and complained. Do you know why your superiors compelled you to assemble your terrible invention under the Lobynian Desert?"

"Yes, I was told it was our internationalist duty."

"No. It was because I threatened to ally myself with the U.S. I said to your General Secretary: 'What good are Russian weapons if they cannot fend off an American attack, and of what use are Soviet promises if they crumble before the might of the U.S.?' They tried to reason with me. But I would have none of it. I desired revenge. And if pretending to be a friend of the U.S. would be my only recourse, then I would hold my nose and shake their bloody hands."

An unhappy look crossed Pyotr Koldunov's tight face and Colonel Intifadah knew that he had struck a nerve.

He knew the Russian resented the use his precious weapon was being put to.

"So to keep me placated," Colonel Intifadah went on, "they offer me this weapon of yours. They make promises. More promises. 'Colonel Intifadah, it is the greatest invention ever devised by a human mind.' 'Colonel Intifadah, with it you can strike into the heart of America without fear of retaliation.' 'Colonel Intifadah, with this device, you can deliver a nuclear weapon to any point on the earth without fear of satellite detection.' "

"All of this is true. My device can do exactly that."

"And so they make me sign another agreement. And I have the weapon. I am a proud man again. I have been given new teeth for my mouth. I have a rod with which to smite my enemies. And when the weapon has been delivered and assembled, what do I learn?"

"It works," Pyotr Koldunov said stubbornly.

"Oh, it works. But where are the nuclear weapons? Where are the missiles for this glorious new missile-delivery system?"

"No one promised Lobynia nuclear weapons."

"You said that on the day the launcher was assembled. You also said that to strike America with nuclear weapons would be unthinkable. Do you remember telling me that?"

"Clearly."

"Clearly! Not as clearly as I!" thundered Colonel Intifadah. "I had visions of America reduced to a burning wasteland and I found that I had been given the pistol but no ammunition."

"The device is still a prototype. It should be tested with less volatile projectiles. A malfunction at launch could possibly detonate a nuclear explosion on Lobynian soil."

"I would have taken that risk! But did your country offer a choice?"

"It was not in the agreement."

"No," Colonel Intifadah said bitterly. "It was not in the agreement. No. Not at all." The Colonel paced back and forth behind his desk, his black eyes flashing like ebony buttons. He turned suddenly and pointed at the Russian with light green gloves.

"When the U.S. bombed Dapoli, you know what was said? It was said that the Russians saw it as an opportunity to see how Soviet-made anti-aircraft-missile batteries would deal with American weapons under true battle conditions. That the Soviets saw the bombing of Dapoli as a mere test for their ordnance."

"That may have been a by-product of the incident," Koldunov admitted coolly. He showed no fear. As loudly as he yelled, Colonel Intifadah could not get a rise out of him.

"Yes, I am glad you admit that much. Because I believe it is happening once again."

"I do not understand."

"This!" Colonel Intifadah said, stabbing his desk with a finger. "This is another test. I am reduced to being a Soviet guinea pig. You have a new weapon. You dare not test it openly. You have stupid treaties with our mortal enemies, the Americans, too. But in me you have a way to test this fearsome device by proxy. Undetected by America. And if detected, who is it who gets bombed? Not Moscow. Not the Ukraine. But Lobynia!"

"I must remind you of your own words, comrade. You demanded Soviet assistance. This weapon has been deployed on your soil at your request."

"A trick! Another Russian trick. I am given a weapon of ultimate terror and I am reduced to flinging locomotives."

"Both launches were successful."

"Successful? Successful, comrade?" The Colonel jumped around his desk. His cruel face shoved into the Russian's own. "See that map?" he said, pointing to a global wall map.

"Yes, of course."

"Show me the targets I have destroyed."

"You cannot expect accuracy with such projectiles."

"I know that, you dog!"

"A locomotive cannot be controlled in flight. As it is, the first launch was highly successful—if your U.S. spies are correct. The projectile missed the White House by the merest distance—considering the distance the projectile traveled."

"It destroyed nothing!"

"It came within a meaningful distance of the designated target. It is unprecedented."

"The second one did not even strike Washington!"

"The fault of the carrier rails. They had to be relaid to accommodate the narrow-gauge European engine. It weakened them. I explained to you that if you insisted upon using American locomotives, all subsequent launches would have to be done with American locomotives. European engines have shorter wheelbases. They do not fit the tracks as originally laid down. Had you waited until you secured another American engine, the second strike might have been on target."

"Now you are blaming me!"

"I am pointing out that I did not select either the intended targets or the projectiles. I can only control the weapon."

"If you would give me one missile, I could accomplish my end. I do not need to rain death down on all of America. The destruction of Washington would be enough. It would satisfy me."

"From the Soviet point of view, both launches were unqualified successes. With repairs and more adjustments, I feel confident that complete success will be inevitable!"

"I do not want inevitable success! I want *instant* success. I have waited too long already. The Chinese promised me nuclear weapons, and U.S. pressure forced them to renege. The Iranians promised me poison gases, and even they balked when pressured by Washington. My terror agents have been rounded up in every capital. Everything I do, every scheme I hatch, the Americans chop off my hands before fruition comes. I will wait no longer."

"You will wait at least a week. For repairs," Koldunov said firmly.

The Colonel trembled in controlled rage. His eyes squeezed into thin slits.

"I know what you are counting on, you and your Russian masters."

Koldunov said nothing.

"You are counting on my locomotives to do no real damage."

"If they strike their target, the damage will be horrific."

"No. You count on most of their mass burning up on reentry. What strikes the ground is just a part of the whole."

"That is not our fault. If you can provide us with engines that are impervious to reentry forces, that problem will be solved."

"Do not look so smug, Koldunov. I may do exactly that."

In spite of himself, Pyotr Koldunov smiled thinly.

The smile was erased at the Colonel's next words.

"Go and repair your terror weapon. I am expecting the next locomotive today. And as soon as the gun is operational, you will send it to a target where, no matter how wide of the mark it falls, there will be tremendous casualties. For if I cannot have Washington, D.C., I will settle for raining death upon New York City."

"One week," said Koldunov.

"Go now."

After the Russian had left, Colonel Intifadah hunkered down behind his desk. His big hairy hands shook with his anger. He had gotten a reaction. Koldunov understood. Washington, D.C., with its open spaces, was one thing, but Manhattan, densely packed with skyscrapers and people, was another entirely.

Soon, Colonel Intifadah thought, America would feel the terrible fist of his wrath.

The telephone shrilled and Colonel Intifadah picked up the receiver.

"Yes? What is it?" he snapped.

"Are we in a bad temper today?" a mellow voice inquired politely.

The Colonel's brutish face relaxed. The telephone voice was so reassuring.

"Hello, comrade."

"Hello, Colonel. That is better. I have excellent news for you."

"Yes?" Colonel Intifadah said, gripping the receiver.

"I have the carbon-carbon shipment."

"That is excellent news. Many lives will be changed by your skill. Yes, a great many lives," Colonel Intifadah said, looking at his global map.

"I am happy to provide service. That is what I live for. You will of course see to it that the agreed-upon amount is deposited in my Zurich account before shipment."

"Instantly."

"A pleasure doing business with you. Will there be anything else?"

"Yes, I am suddenly in the market for locomotives."

"Specifications?"

"I am interested in the largest European models available. They need not be in operating condition. Just so long as the wheels turn freely."

"That is a strange request."

"I know I can count on your absolute confidentiality in this matter."

"Of course. I exist to fulfill the customer's needs. Now, how many do you require?"

"As many as you can ship. I foresee my country having a serious locomotive shortfall for the next several years."

"I will be back to you with specifications by the end of the business day, your time."

"Thank you, Friend."

14

It was nearly midnight when the taxi dropped off Remo and Chiun at the Folcroft gate.

"Got change for a hundred-dollar bill?" Remo asked the cabbie.

The driver turned his pugnacious face around and said in a surly voice, "Don't give me no crap here. I gave you a flat rate before we started. Fifty bucks, I said. You knew it was going to cost fifty when we started."

"I would still your insolent tongue if I were you," Chiun sniffed.

"And that goes for you too, buster. The fare is fifty bucks. And I don't carry that kind of change on me. I get robbed all the time."

"What would you say the proper tip would be, Little Father?" Remo asked calmly.

"I just gave him the proper tip," Chiun replied blandly. "And he would do well to heed it."

"You have a point," Remo said pleasantly. He extracted a single hundred-dollar bill from his wallet, folded it in two, and then ripped the bill into equal halves. He handed the irate cabbie one half.

"What's this crap?" the cabbie roared.

"He must like that word, 'crap,'" Chiun pointed out. "It befits his loud mouth."

"It's half of a hundred-dollar bill," Remo told the driver. "Fifty bucks." He smiled. "You can keep the change."

"I can't spend this!"

"How do you know if you don't try?" Remo asked lightly as he stepped out of the cab.

The cabbie started to climb out after him. Chiun gave the door a light shove. The driver flew back in. His head hit the meter. Bellowing, he kicked at the door. Chiun held it shut with his little finger while Remo got behind the cab and gave it a gentle push.

The cab careened down the road. The driver grabbed for the wheel just as it went around a bend in the road. The engine started and its roar picked up speed.

"Let's go, Little Father," Remo told Chiun. "I've had a long day. Uh-oh," he added, looking at the darkened shape of Folcroft Sanitarium.

"Ah," Chiun said, following his gaze. "Emperor Smith still holds forth, although it is late."

With the taxi's engine fading behind them, Remo and Chiun slipped through the gate. Over by the docks, a squat shape sat like a sleeping insect. A military helicopter.

"I think that chopper is waiting for us," Remo pointed out.

"So much for our evening of rest."

"Come on," Remo said in a tired voice. "No sense in delaying the inevitable. Let's go see what's doing."

They found Dr. Harold W. Smith at his desk. Smith's face was drawn. That fact in itself was not unusual. Stripped of his glasses, Smith could have sat for a portrait of a man in the final stages of starvation. But what Smith was doing alarmed Remo.

Smith was spraying foam antacid into his open mouth. A lot of it. He stopped from time to time to swallow, then continued squirting. The nozzle soon sputtered and fizzled noisily. Smith shook the canister, and getting nothing, started to suck the nozzle like a baby with a bottle.

He did not notice Remo and Chiun until Remo cleared his throat.

"Ahem," Smith said, dropping the can. It rolled off his desk and Smith reached for it. He missed. "No matter, it was empty," he said sheepishly. He adjusted his Dartmouth tie self-consciously.

"What's up, Smitty? We got rid of Rambo, by the way."

"Who? Oh," Smith said. His voice was strained. "Yes, the elephant. Good. Thank goodness you are back. We have a situation."

"I know."

"You do?"

"The helicopter. It was a major clue."

"Oh, yes. I ordered it to stand by. I've been frantic, Remo, waiting for your return."

"So we're back," Remo said casually. "What is it this time?"

"Hush, Remo," Chiun warned. "Do not rush your emperor. Obviously, a serious matter has developed. Speak to me, O Emperor. And do not concern yourself with my unruly pupil. He has had a trying day, but he has learned a valuable lesson which will enable him to serve you better in the future."

"Yes, good. But a matter of grave international concern broke while you were away."

Chiun's wispy chin lifted in interest. Matters of grave international concern interested him. The more of Smith's grave matters of international concern the Master of Sinanju dealt with, the more Chiun would ask for at the next contract negotiation.

"Yes," Smith said. "Washington has been attacked. It's happened twice in the last few hours."

"Attacked!" Remo said.

"Some new form of offensive ballistic weapon called the Kinetic Kill Vehicle. The President just informed me that it was fired by an electromagnetic launching system of some kind which defies early-warning detection. The first KKV landed within yards of the White House. The second impacted in Maryland. Fortunately neither hit anything crucial, nor did they detonate. There have been no casualties."

"Just what the world needs," Remo said. "Another new offensive weapon."

"All weapons are offensive," Chiun said firmly.

"So what do we do, Smitty?"

"Do not be foolish, Remo," Chiun interjected. "It is obvious what we do. We will go to the hurlers of these KKV's and eliminate them, thus saving the republic."

"Not exactly," Smith put in.

"No?" asked Chiun.

"What do you mean, no?" Remo added.

"The Pentagon is still trying to pinpoint the source of these attacks. We can be certain it is a foreign power, but who or what or why has yet to be determined. The President wants you in Washington immediately. He's very upset with us all. He thinks we should have somehow foreseen these attacks."

"He's got a short memory," Remo complained. "After we saved his life during the campaign."

"I knew he was an ingrate the moment I laid eyes upon him," Chiun spat. "I voted for the other one," he added smugly.

"You, Master Chiun?" Smith asked. "But you are not a U.S. citizen."

"They could not stop me. Besides, I only wished to cancel Remo's vote."

Remo sighed audibly. "So what are we supposed to do in Washington?" he asked Smith.

"I am uncertain. But I do think it would be good if you were at the President's side to reassure him. He hasn't yet gotten his cabinet assembled and seems completely at sea."

"He doesn't expect us to baby-sit him, does he?" Remo asked.

"I'm afraid that's what it comes down to. In the meanwhile, our entire military command structure is on full alert. The world is poised on the brink of something, but no one knows what."

"What happens if there's another attack when we're down there?" Remo wanted to know.

Smith said nothing for a long moment. Finally he admitted, "I do not know."

"I know," Chiun said brightly.

Remo and Smith turned to look at his beaming countenance.

"What?" Remo wanted to know.

"Yes, tell us," Smith prompted.

"Nothing," Chiun said.

"How do you know that?" Smith asked.

"Because this is always the way with these things."

"What things?" Remo and Smith spoke together. Their blending voices harmonized like a flute and a can opener.

"Sieges."

"What do you mean?" This from Smith.

"It is very simple," Chiun said, placing his long-nailed fingers into his ballooning sleeves. "Two stones have fallen."

"Stones. Where do you get 'stones'?" Remo demanded.

"They did not go boom, correct?"

"True," Smith admitted slowly.

"Then they are stones. Or might as well be stones. They are certainly not anything dangerous, or they would have exploded."

"Keep talking," Smith prompted.

"What we are witnessing is a form of warfare not seen in many centuries. The siege engine."

"Never heard of it," Remo said.

"I think he means the catapult."

"Yes, exactly. That is the other name for it. The Romans used it often. It was sometimes successful, but more often not. It worked in this fashion. An army encircles a fort or city, cutting off supplies. The besiegers then bring up the siege engines. They load them first with big stones and try to knock down the walls. Sometimes they send many smaller stones into the city itself to dishearten the population. Once in a while, they strike something, a person or a house. But rarely does this happen. Europeans used the siege engine to terrify, not to destroy. Much like your present-day atomic missiles."

"I've never thought of it quite in those terms," Smith said. "But who would do this? And where is their encircling army?"

"Wait a minute!" Remo said. "I don't buy this. Catapults. From where?"

"Our information is that the KKV came in from over the Atlantic. That makes any nation from Great Britain to Russia a suspect."

"No catapult could lob a rock over the Atlantic."

"True," Smith admitted. "But Master Chiun's comparison is basically sound. I would like him to continue."

Remo folded his arms. Grinning with satisfaction, Chiun continued. His voice grew deep and resonant. He enjoyed counseling his emperor.

"I do not know where the army is. Perhaps it is in transit. Perhaps it will not be sent until the siege is fully under way. But I do know this. The method is the method of the siege. The purpose to demoralize. And the reality, that few if any of these projectiles will hit their intended target—or anything of consequence at all. For Europeans are the architects of the siege and there is one thing that is always true of Europeans."

Smith leaned forward eagerly. "Yes?"

Chiun raised a wise finger. "They are terrible shots."

Smith blinked rapidly. His dryish face wrinkling in disappointment, he settled back in his chair.

"We cannot count on these KKV's continuing to miss their targets," he said seriously.

"No. They will first run out of big rocks. Then little stones. Then they will be reduced to pebble flinging. Then they will go away."

"So what are we supposed to do in Washington, Smitty? Stand around with our hands in our pockets? Or maybe we raise our arms to catch the next one when it falls? I think we should be looking for the people behind this instead."

"That should not be difficult," Chiun said with assurance. They looked at him again.

"Go on," Smith said, hope dawning again on his face.

"Whom has your government annoyed recently?"

"What do you mean?"

"Nations do not lay siege to achieve conquest or to make war. They lay siege to punish, as I have said. Look for a jealous prince who believes that he has reason to vent his wrath upon your President."

"That's a long list," Remo said. "Every third country in the world hates us—with or without good reason."

"Such anger as is evidenced in these two attacks is motivated by passion. Look for a man with passion."

"And no sense. He's obviously forgetting that he's lobbing rocks at the only nation in history ever to nuke another in anger."

"Without any way to trace the origin of these KKV's, the perpetrator is relatively safe," Smith admitted. "I think you are correct, Remo. Your job should be to seek out and eliminate this threat at the source. But until we have a fix on that source, I want you both in Washington. Perhaps you and Chiun could examine the impact sites. Maybe you can learn something of value."

"Not me," Remo said firmly. "One rock looks like another to me."

"Including the one that sits on your shoulders," Chiun said with disdain.

15

Over the objections of his top advisers, the President of the United States went on the air to reassure the nation.

"The situation is under control," the President said from the podium in the East Room of the White House.

Representatives from all the major networks were seated in front of him. The room was packed. The glare of television cameras was intense. The very air smelled hot. It was the first news conference of the new administration. For that reason alone, it would have been covered with intense scrutiny. But the fact that the President had been absent from the Oval Office the previous day, his first in office, had sparked a wave of rumors.

"What situation?" asked a reporter.

The President was aghast. He had spoken only the first sentence of what was to have been a ten-minute prepared text, and already they were flinging questions at him. He wondered if he should hush the man or just keep reading.

"Yes, what situation?" seconded another reporter.

The President decided to dispense with the prepared text.

"The current situation," he said.

The press looked at him blankly.

"Mr. President," a woman reporter asked, "would you care to comment on your alleged drinking problem?"

Horror rode the President's face.

"What drinking problem?" he demanded.

The lady journalist did not reply. She was too busy writing his answer.

"What drinking problem?" the President repeated.

No one answered him. They were too busy writing that down too.

"Can we get back to the crisis?" a reporter piped up.

"I did not say there was a crisis," the President said.

"Then you are denying the existence of a crisis?"

"Well, no. But I cannot categorize the current situation as a crisis."

"Then what would you call it? After all, you go to your inaugural ball, retire for the evening, and disappear for an entire day. Everyone saw you drink that second glass of champagne."

"Second—"

"Does the First Lady know where you were last night?" another reporter wanted to know.

"Of course. She was with me," the President said indignantly.

The press corps busily wrote the President's words down as if they were very important. Pencils scratched loudly against notepads. Numerous hand-held tape recorders hummed. The heat of the glaring lights made the President feel light-headed. All he had intended to do was tell the nation that a sudden emergency had occupied the first day of this term. For national security reasons, he could not comment on the emergency, but he believed it was on its way to being under control. Instead, they were fishing into his private life. Having been happily married for most of his adult life, and having been a professional politician even longer, the President was of the opinion that he didn't have a private life. As such.

"Mr. President, we have a report that the Strategic Air Command has moved every B-52 bomber wing to combat-readiness status. Are we preparing for an invasion?"

"No," the President said flatly. "Nonsense."

"Then can you explain that movement of SAC aircraft on your first day?"

"A routine training exercise," the President said. He hated to lie like that, but he had come on television to reassure the nation, not to panic it.

"Then it is not related to this alleged emergency?"

"The emergency is not alleged. It is quite real. It is very serious."

"If it is that serious, then why won't you specifically describe it for the people? Don't you feel you owe it to those who voted you into office to level with them?"

"I *am* leveling with them," the President said hotly.

"Mr. President, can we get back to your drinking problem?"

"What drinking problem?" the President roared.

"That is the third time you've said that," suggested another reporter. "Does that mean you are categorically denying that you have a drinking problem as a result of overindulging during the inaugural ball?"

"I do so deny it."

The Washington press corps began busily to scribble onto their notepads again and the President thought with sick horror of the evening headlines: "PRESIDENT DENIES DRINKING PROBLEM."

"Now, listen," the President said quickly. "I just want to assure the nation that the situation is under control. There is no need to be alarmed. Right at this moment one of the finest military minds in the Pentagon is dealing with the problem."

"Military? Are we expecting an attack?"

The President hesitated. He did not want to lie. And this would be an awfully big lie. Especially if another attack were to come.

A reporter jumped into the gap. "What about the fire in Lafayette Park? And the golf-course explosion in Bethesda? Are these in any way connected?"

The question gave the President no choice. He would have to fib.

"I'm told Bethesda was a meteor fall. The fire in the park was just a fire."

No one challenged that, to the President's surprised relief.

"I can tell you this," he added. "A certain foreign nation has been rattling its sabers at us. We know who this nation is and what they are up to. And I want to assure the people of America that we have the matter well in hand, and furthermore, I want to put this foreign nation on notice that the next move on their part will result in severe sanctions."

"Military sanctions, Mr. President?"

"I . . . No comment," the President said quickly. Damn, he thought. They mouse-trapped me.

The President's press secretary quickly moved in.

"That will be all gentlemen," he said, pulling the President away from the podium.

"But I'm not finished!" the President hissed.

"Yes you are, Mr. President. They're eating you alive. Please come with me. We'll have your damage-control people handle this."

Reluctantly the President of the United States shot the press corps a stiff farewell wave. He would much rather have shot them the bird. But it would have gone over the airwaves, followed by a twenty-minute critical analysis of the meaning of the President's gesture and its far-reaching political implications.

As he walked down the luxuriously carpeted hall, he wondered what gave his press secretary the idea that he could overrule the Commander in Chief at his own press conference. Who did the man think he was—a Secret Service agent?

In his Pentagon office, General Martin S. Leiber turned off the television and heaved a sigh of relief.

The President had blown his news conference. What the hell, he thought. The poor bastard was as green as grass. He'd get better at it. And the press were sharks. You could never win where they were concerned. But the important thing was that he hadn't blown General Leiber's career. Which is exactly what would have happened had he mentioned exactly who "the finest military mind in the Pentagon" was.

The press would have been all over General Leiber like polish on a boot. They'd have wanted his plans, his life story, and most of all, a day-by-day history of his military career.

It would have made juicy reading. General Martin S. Leiber had been a minor rear-echelon officer during the Korean war. He was totally incompetent in battle, in leadership, and in every other trait important to military service. But when a lucky North Korean artillery shell took out the officers' club two days before the annual Christmas party, taking with it the Air Force's precious store of liquor, it fell on then Master Sergeant Martin S. Leiber to replenish the base supply.

There was no liquor to be had. Sergeant Leiber saw

himself about to be busted down to private, when he came upon an Army tank that had been left standing by the side of a road while its crew were off whoring. Believing the Army to be simply a less hostile form of enemy, Sergeant Leiber rode off with the tank, which he traded to a ROK unit for several cases of good rice wine. Anyone else would have been satisfied to pull his own bacon from the fire so easily. Not Master Sergeant Martin S. Leiber. He then watered the wine down, to double the six cases to twelve, and returned triumphantly to the base.

A week later, after he sobered up, he traded the remaining six cases for a two-week leave in Tokyo, where he purchased a year's supply of fake North Korean souvenirs, and priced them to sell as genuine.

From that point on, Leiber horsetraded his way to a captain's bars and finally to a general's stars. The Air Force had been good to him, even during the Vietnam war when corruption in the South Vietnam government was so entrenched that General Leiber found himself swapping multimillion-dollar equipment—even as he sold off the last of his North Korean bayonets as North Vietnamese bayonets.

It was a career that had ultimately led to the Pentagon and rigging defense contracts and gold-plating procurement orders. And now, with retirement not far off, General Leiber was not about to blow it. Which was exactly what would have happened had the press got wind of his name. They would have splashed the headline "PRESIDENT PUTS FATE OF NATION IN HANDS OF PROCUREMENT OFFICER" all across the country's newspapers.

As long as the President had no inkling of his true status, General Leiber could carry on. And as long as he could carry on, there was still a chance he could wheel and deal his way out of this mess.

First he'd have to find out where those damn steam engines were coming from.

Taking a deep breath, General Leiber reached out for what was in his mind the mightiest weapon in the United States arsenal. The telephone. He dialed Andrews Air Force Base.

"Major Cheek. General Leiber here. The President has just alerted the nation to the crisis."

"My God! Did he tell them about the locomotives?"

"KKV's, dammit! I told you never to use the L word again."

"Sorry, General. The KKV's. And I guess that means he did not."

"Damned right he did not. Our President, bless him, is no fool. Now, I need answers."

"We have the pieces of the second KKV here, General." Behind the major's voice, the sounds of hammers clanging against metal were a cacophony. The muted roar of furnaces made static background noise.

"I can hear that. But what have you got?"

"We may be in luck, sir. This one appears not to have been as damaged by reentry."

"It came in tumbling."

"That would explain it. Actually, the rear section suffered the most friction damage."

"So?"

"Well, the nose—or whatever you called it—survived unmelted. Sir, this may be premature—"

"Yes, yes, out with it!"

"There's no sign of a cowcatcher. And we found what we think is one of the bumper rods. My people are trying to assemble it to be certain."

"Certain of what, dammit?"

"Don't you remember our earlier conversation, General? No cowcatcher means it's not American. We have a foreign . . . er . . . KKV."

"Can you ID the country of origin?"

"That's my hope, sir."

"Could it be African?"

"African?" the major said, his voice frowning. The general distinctly heard him flipping through the pages of a book.

"I see no mention of any African models in this book on steam KKV's."

"Our intelligence indicates it lifted off from Africa. So it's gotta be African."

"The first one was a U.S. model. But of course, a lot of older models were shipped abroad after we converted the diesel engines. Can I say 'engines' over an open line?"

"I don't care," the general said morosely. "I want to

know where that thing came from. Isn't there any way we can find out?"

"There is one possibility sir. The livery."

"Say that again."

"When an engine goes into service, it's painted with the operating company's colors. Just like they do with passenger jets today. They call that the livery."

"Sound reasoning, Major. What color is this KKV?"

"Unknown, General. The entire surface is scorched. But we're trying to scrape off the gunk and get to the paint. It's our only chance."

"Will you need any special equipment?"

"Yes, whatever they use to analyze paint. I would think the FBI lab would be able to help."

"No good. I don't know anyone in the FBI. They're law. I don't mess with the civilian law. The military is one thing, but once civilian law gets on a man's tail, they don't let go."

"I catch your drift, General. What about the CIA?"

"No way. You get in hock to those spook bastards and the next thing you know, their periscopes are rising out of the john while you're sitting on it."

"Well, General, whatever you have to do, if we can get paint samples and you can have them identified, we should have our ID.'"

"I'll get right on it," promised General Leiber, hanging up.

"Damn!" he swore after some thought. He didn't know squat about paint analysis. Worse, he didn't know anyone who did.

The phone rang suddenly, and without thinking, he picked it up.

"General Leiber?" The voice was very authoritarian, very military.

"Yes. Who is this?"

"This is the Joint Chiefs."

"I hear only one of you."

"I'm chairman. Admiral Blackbird. We've just watched the President's address. What goes on? Who is this military mind the President is talking about? We know it isn't the Acting Secretary of Defense. We have that bastard down here where he can't muck things up with his inexperience."

"Good move," said General Leiber, who hadn't even thought of the Secretary of Defense. "Admiral," he went on, "if the President had wanted this man's identity known, he would have broadcast it. I understand from the President that the security of the good old U.S. of A. depends upon this man's name being a national secret."

"Harrumph. I suppose that makes good strategic sense. Give us the poop on the situation threat-wise."

"We're at Defcon Two and holding."

"We know that. What's the situation on your end?"

"We're moving toward identifying the aggressor."

"Good. We're itching to press buttons down here. Anything we can do to speed up the process?"

"We've got a complicated matériel-analysis problem up here," General Leiber said. "Frankly, we're not certain how to proceed. The normal agencies that might handle this kind of work are civilian. We don't want to involve them."

"Good thinking. Civilians can't pound sand."

"I read you there. So what do we do?"

"General, when the Joint Chiefs are in this situation, there is only one place to turn."

"Sir?"

"Computers, man. Computers can do anything today. What you do is find a computer to handle the matter, program it, and let 'er rip!"

"Outstanding, Admiral. I'll pass your suggestion along. We'll be in touch."

General Leiber hung up with a gleeful expression. Why hadn't he thought of that himself? Of course. A computer. There were tons of them in the Pentagon—payroll computers, cost-analysis computers, there was even a wargaming computer. Somewhere.

The trouble was, the damned things took weeks or even months to program. General Leiber didn't have weeks to program a computer to analyze scorched paint chips. And he sure didn't trust any Pentagon programmer with the knowledge of what was being analyzed and why. The Pentagon leaked worse than Congress.

General Leiber put in another call. As the line rang, he

felt the inherent power of the instrument with which he had made a small fortune. Let the others have their jets and ships and tanks. General Leiber would lay it on the line with a solid-state multiline telephone any day of the week.

"Excelsior Systems," a bored male voice said.

"Richards, General Martin S. Leiber speaking."

"General Leiber," the voice said brightly. Then, in a lower tone, "Anything wrong, General?"

"Damn straight there's something wrong. We're on the brink."

"No," the voice said. "Don't tell me they found out about the faulty computer chips."

"Nothing of the sort, man. I'm talking about national security."

"Don't tell me they're flying those planes into combat?"

"It could happen. And you know what would happen to our asses if they do."

"My God. We'll go to the pen."

"You'll go to the pen, civilian. They'll haul my tired ass to the stockade. We're talking high treason here."

"My God," the other man sobbed. "What do we do?"

"The only way out of it is if I can get my hands on the best damned computer in the world."

"We make the best. We're on the leading edge in everything. Parallel processing. Artificial Intelligence. You name it."

"I need a task-analysis unit and I have to do the programming myself. Security reasons."

"But what do you know about programming, General?"

"Not a damn thing. But I need this done ASAP."

"Only one machine could handle this. It's our new Excelsior Systems Quantum Series Three Thousand. There's only one in existence. It's a quantum leap over any mainframe imaginable. It's an artificial-intelligence system with parallel processing capability. Voice-activated. Voice-responsive. You wouldn't have to program it. Just talk to it."

"Ship it!"

"General, I can't ship the only working prototype. The ES Quantum is going to be put up for bid. The CIA wants it. So do the NSA and NASA. I expected that you'd be putting in a bid for the Pentagon."

"I am," General Leiber snapped. "And this is my bid. Ship it today or else."

"Or else what?"

"I blow the whistle on you. About the faulty chips you sold the Air Force that are mounted in every stealth aircraft in existence. If we ever go to war, those chips will malfunction like flies sucking DDT."

"But I sold them through you! You're in this as deep as I am!"

"I'm already staring at the end of my career. If I go down, you go down with me. Do you read me, mister?"

"This isn't like you, General."

"These are grim times, civilian. Now, I'll need your answer."

"A loaner?"

"As soon as I'm done, you can have it back. But I'll expect preferred treatment when the Pentagon puts in its bid."

"I knew you were going to say that, General."

General Leiber had no sooner hung up the phone than it rang again. The President's ragged voice came over the line.

"Did you see the press conference?" he asked.

"Yes, sir. And if I may say so, sir, you did an outstanding job your first time out of the gate."

"Don't be ridiculous. They had me for breakfast. And now the media are fanning the fires of this thing. I'll have to go public with the whole truth if we don't have some answers soon."

"Have no fear, Mr. President. I'm about to take delivery on a high-speed computer that I expect will do the job."

"Computer?"

"Yes, this is too big for one general. Even if it is me. This baby has everything."

"Global links?"

"Of course," General Leiber said, wondering what "global links" meant.

"How about simultaneous language translation?"

"State-of-the-art," said the general, wondering why the President was so interested in languages at a time like this.

"Where is this computer now?"

"Being crated for freighting."

"Hold the line," said the President.

General Leiber listened to John Philip Sousa march Muzak with his brow wrinkling.

The President came back on the line.

"That computer," he said. "It's not going to the Pentagon."

"Of course it is. I just requisitioned it."

"No, it is not. It's going to where I tell you to ship it. Now, please write down this address."

General Leiber copied down the address of a warehouse in Trenton, New Jersey.

"Send it there."

"But, Mr. President, why?"

"I'm kicking this upstairs. You'll continue with your end of the investigation, of course."

"Of course," said the general. "But—"

"No buts. That's an order."

General Leiber hung up the phone, wondering where the President had suddenly found his gumption. Only a few hours ago he had been a raving idiot. And what did he mean by "kicking it upstairs"? He was calling from the White House, for God's sake. There was no upstairs.

Worriedly General Leiber put in a call to Excelsior Systems. The President had said nothing about the computer being returned. Well, hell, let the milk-livered bastard at Excelsior worry about getting his own damn computer back. General Leiber had bigger fish to fry. Assuming he himself didn't get fried along the way.

16

At the White House, the President hung up the telephone.

It was a stroke of luck that General Leiber had called with the news about that computer. It might be the solution to his problems. He reached into a desk drawer and pulled out the red CURE telephone. An extension cord trailed out of the Oval Office and all the way to the President's bedroom. The President had personally hooked up the extension himself and then forbidden all mention or questions about it among his staff.

He lifted the receiver. Dr. Harold Smith's acknowledgment came promptly.

"Smith, this is your President."

"Of course," Smith said.

"Smith, where are your people?"

"My people? I sent them to Washington hours ago. Do you mean they have not arrived?"

"No."

"Yes," said a squeaky voice.

"Which is it, Mr. President?" Smith asked in puzzlement. "Yes or no?"

"That wasn't me," the President said, looking around the Oval Office. Who had spoken? He was alone.

"Mr. President," Smith said sternly, "it is a serious breach of our security for you to converse with me while others are in your presence."

"I'm alone. I think." The President looked around the room. They called it the Oval Office for a good reason. There were no corners or crannies in which an assassin might conceal himself. The President looked into the well of his desk. The only things there were his legs.

"No, you're not," a second voice said. A firmer voice.

"Smith," the President said huskily, "I'm not alone. This is exactly why I wanted your people here."

From behind the standing flag of the United States, a figure emerged. The President blinked. He was a thin, youngish man with deep-set eyes. He was dressed casually. A second man—he stepped from behind the presidential flag—was anything but casually dressed. His kimono was the color of a Chinese firecracker. Two tigers rampant were stitched in black and gold threads on the front. It seemed incredible that either of them could have hidden unseen behind the standing flags, but the evidence was before him.

"I was mistaken," the President said. "They are here."

"Let me speak with them," Smith requested.

"Here," the President said. Remo took the phone and began speaking quietly.

The Oriental man regarded the President with wise eyes. He bowed.

"And how have you been?" the President asked. "Chiun, isn't it?"

"I am well," Chiun said with formal stiffness. "I trust you are happy now that you have ascended the Eagle Throne."

"The what? Oh, yes. Of course. I worked very hard to attain this office. I just didn't expect this rough a time of it so soon."

"Leadership brings many burdens," intoned Chiun. "Fortunately, Remo and I are here to lighten some of them."

"I wish you could do something about the press."

"Don't give him ideas," Remo said suddenly, clapping a hand over the red phone.

"You need only whisper their names in my ear and your enemies will become as the dust on your boots," Chiun offered.

"I think you're thinking of the last President. I don't wear boots. But the press isn't the problem. It's the source of these attacks. If only we knew which nation was behind them."

"As I told Smith, it is very simple," Chiun said. "Look for a jealous prince."

"The Vice-President?"

"Is he your mortal enemy?"

"Not at all. And to the best of my knowledge I don't have any enemies—mortal or otherwise."

"All heads of state have enemies. Allow us to seek out these secret plotters. We will mount their heads on the White House fence. If we get the correct enemy, your problem will be solved. If not, mounted heads make an excellent warning to unsuspected pretenders to a throne."

"I don't think that will work."

"Then we will await the next attack." Chiun turned to Remo and caught his eye.

"I just told Smith we looked at the craters and couldn't figure out a thing," Remo said.

"Naturally, we are assassins. Not detectives."

"Let me have that phone," the President said. "Smith? The KKV's were hauled off for analysis. You and your people don't have to worry about them. Find the launch site. That's the key."

"It would help if I had an idea of the projectiles."

The President hesitated. "All I can tell you, Smith, is that they are multi-ton wheeled vehicles. So far they have not been armed in any conventional way."

"That's not really much to go on," Smith began.

"I don't want you working on that end of it. The KKV's are the Pentagon's worry. Find the launch site. Got that?"

"Yes, sir."

"Now, that item I discussed with you has been shipped to your warehouse drop. It should make a tremendous difference in your search ability."

"But, Mr. President, I reiterate that my system is sufficient for CURE operations."

"This one will work better. It can handle multiple tasks simultaneously. Language translation will no longer be a barrier."

"There's still the sheer mass of data to be sorted. I couldn't possibly handle it all."

"You won't have to, Smith. This computer thinks for itself. It will do a lot of your work for you. And I've taken the liberty of ordering some additional upgrades for the rest of your operation."

"Upgrades?"

"For one thing, this phone has to go. You should see

how I had to rig it so that I can get my hands on it no matter what happens."

"Sir, this line has been inviolate for over twenty years. You can't—"

"I can and I did. I wish everyone would stop trying to override me. Now, about that computer. It comes with an installer. I'll leave the security problems of installation to you."

"But, sir, I—"

"No buts. I'm tired of buts. I want action. Your people will remain here until you come up with answers. It had better be soon, Smith. The media are trying to whip the public into a frenzy."

"I know, Mr. President," Smith said, hanging up.

The President turned to Remo and Chiun.

"Now, I'm going to ask you to fade into the woodwork again," he said. "I have much to do."

"Do not fear," promised the Master of Sinanju, bowing. "The KKK threat will not harm a hair on your regal head."

"KKK? What does the Ku Klux Klan have to do with this?"

"Nothing," Remo said swiftly. "Don't mind him. He means KKV."

"They are even less of a problem," Chiun insisted.

Remo rolled his eyes. The President sighed. It seemed that Smith's operation needed patching up in more than just its equipment.

17

Chip Craft had installed a lot of computers in his time. In his work for Excelsior Systems, he had been involved in numerous high-security installations and had a top security clearance with the Defense Department. He prided himself on being considered above reproach.

So why were they treating him like this?

It had begun with instructions from his superior to wait at a deserted warehouse in Trenton until he was contacted.

He waited for hours, clutching his tool-packed briefcase. A voice as dry as week-old graham crackers spoke from behind him and ordered, "Do not turn around, please."

"Who . . . ?"

"I am your contact. Assuming you are the man I am expecting."

"Chip Craft. Excelsior."

"Good. I am going to blindfold you, Mr. Craft."

"That's really not necessary. I have Department of Defense clearance. I can dig it out of my wallet."

"Not necessary."

"Good."

"DOD credentials are meaningless to me."

Chip Craft shrugged. "If you say so." The blindfold went over his eyes and tightened expertly. "Now what?"

"You will be driven to a location where you are going to install the ES Quantum Three Thousand."

"Oh? I didn't know that anyone had put in a bid yet."

"Never mind," said the dry voice. A hand took him by the elbow. "Come with me."

Chip Craft felt himself taken to a car and placed in the back seat. The car interior smelled old. Odd. Usually official cars smelled new.

The drive was several hours in length. Neither Chip nor

129

the driver spoke during the trip. When the car finally came to a halt, Chip was taken into a building and up on an elevator. Then he was led a short distance and the man let go of his elbow. He heard a door close behind him.

"You may remove the blindfold now."

When he had removed the blindfold, Chip Craft saw that he was in a shabby office. Fluorescent lights filled the room with shaky illumination. There was only one window, but it was curtained. It was a big window and took up most of one wall behind a splintery oak desk. A man sat behind the desk. He wore a gray three-piece suit and a school tie that Chip did not recognize. Chip did not recognize the man either. The man wore an ordinary paper bag over his head. There were two ragged eyeholes punched in the bag and a pair of studious-looking rimless eyeglasses were fitted over them. The stems disappeared into two tears on either side of the bag.

"Is this some kind of a joke?" Chip demanded.

"Security," said the man. He sat with his hands folded.

"This is a joke, right? Damn! I should have suspected something. I knew the ES Quantum hadn't been put up for bid. Now, come on, who are you? Schwartz? Anderson? Infantino?"

"I am none of those people. And you are in a highly secret U.S. installation. Your job is to install the system as quickly as possible. Our country's future may depend upon it."

"Now I know this is a joke. If you're not going to unmask, I'll do it for you." And Chip Craft started for the man with the paper-bag head.

The dry-voiced man removed a .45 automatic from a drawer. He laid it on the desk with a heavy thud.

"I assure you that this is not a joke, and if you attempt to remove my disguise, I will have no choice but to shoot you. The security of this installation depends upon my identity remaining undisclosed."

Chip Craft halted. "You sound serious."

The man laid his hand across the weapon. "I assure you that I will not hesitate to shoot."

"Tell you what. I'm not saying I believe you and I'm not saying I don't. But I'll play along. Now, if this is for real, the ES Quantum's gotta be on the premises, correct?"

"Look behind you."

Chip turned.

In one corner of the room stood the ES Quantum. It looked like a modernistic Christmas tree without ornaments. It was spindle-shaped, with a fat, molded base which tapered up to a tip that just grazed the ceiling. It was chocolate brown in color. The unit was featureless except for a glass-fronted square aperture set at eye level.

"If this is a gag, someone's gonna be swimming in shit when the head honcho finds out."

"My present terminal is connected to a system located several floors under our feet. I assume you can transfer the connection from up here."

"What terminal?"

The man with the paper-bag head pressed a stud under the edge of the desk and a terminal rose up like a crystal ball.

"Oh, that terminal. Let me take a look," Chip said, placing his tool case on the desk and opening it. He examined the terminal curiously.

"Boy, this takes me back. I haven't seen one of these in years. You should have upgraded long ago."

"Never mind that. Can you do it?"

"Let's see what you've got for connectors."

"The lines lead into the desk."

"Wanna move aside, Mr. . . . What do I call you, anyway—Smith?"

"No, Jones. Not Smith. Jones."

"What's the difference? We both know it's not your real name."

"I prefer Jones, if you don't mind."

"Jones, then. Most anonymous people go with Smith, but suit yourself."

"Jones" rose from behind the desk and Chip Craft poked his head into the desk well. He came back up a moment later.

"Ribbon cables? When was this thing installed—during Prohibition?"

"Is there a problem?"

"No, I'm just overcome by nostalgia. Ribbon cables. Jesus! Well, guess I'd better get started."

"I will remain here," said "Jones."

"Sure. Want to pass me a screwdriver as long as you're not doing anything?"

Chip felt a screwdriver slap into his hand and got to work.

Hours later, he breathed a sigh of accomplishment.

"It's done. Got a place where I can wash up?"

"Out in the hall."

When Chip came back, "Jones" was stringing tinsel and colored balls on the ES Quantum unit.

"I knew it!" he howled gleefully. "It *was* a joke."

"I assure you this is not a joke, and do not come any closer."

Chip Craft saw the automatic was pointed at his chest. He lifted his hands. "Okay, okay. But do you mind telling me what the decorations are for? Christmas was last month."

"I get a certain amount of foot traffic through this office. No one must know that this is a computer system."

"I don't think they're gonna believe it's a Christmas tree. Especially when it's going up in January."

"Many people are slow to take down their trees."

"Yeah, but what are you going to tell them come July?"

"If we all live to see July, I will worry about that then."

"You're making me nervous with that talk, pal."

"Why don't you walk me through the system?"

"Roger." Chip got behind "Jones's" desk and powered up the terminal. In the corner, the ES Quantum gave out a steady hum. Nothing else happened. There were no lights to blink, no spooling tape reels, and no surface features except its single dark eye. It might have been a vegetable that had come to life.

"Jones" joined Chip Craft at the terminal.

"I've left the keyboard as it was, although it's optional now."

"I understand the unit is voice-activated."

"Yep. She's a parallel processor, one hundred thousand times faster than anything else in the world. She can do multiple tasks simultaneously without time-share lag. It's like having a hundred mainframes rolled into one unit. She's got that spindle shape to pack the chips tight to speed up the electron flow. It facilitates the data processing something fierce. But the heart of the ES Quantum

Three Thousand is its artificial-intelligence processor. Listen: Hello, ES Quantum."

"Hello." The voice came from the corner. It was light and silvery.

"A woman's voice?" asked "Jones."

"Nice touch, don't you think?"

"I don't know. It doesn't sound very businesslike."

"You want businesslike? Ask her to think."

"How?"

"I'll do it. Computer, scan the room."

"Room scanned."

"What do you make of what you see?"

"Two options. Either this is a high-security area or someone is playing a joke on you."

"What makes you say that?" "Jones" asked sharply.

"Because you have a forty-five-caliber Army-issue Colt automatic in your right hand and a paper bag over your head. If the weapon is real—and I am unable to quantify that judgment at this distance—then it means this is a security situation."

"How do you know this isn't a mugging?" asked "Jones." "I could be a mugger."

"Your body language indicates ease with your surroundings. You are in a familiar place. Therefore this is your office. And you would not be mugging a man in your own office. Your disguise would be pointless."

"But I don't understand. What makes you feel that this is a security area?"

"Because I am the ES Quantum Three Thousand, the most advanced artificial-intelligence system on the planet and, according to my own projections, likely to remain so for at least another thirteen months."

"Thirteen months." Chip Craft whistled. "The boys in Research and Development had it pegged at twenty-six months."

"They are not aware of the recent Japanese AI advances."

"What recent Japanese advances?" Chip demanded.

"The Mishitsu Corporation has just made a superconductor breakthrough which will lead to parallel processing speeds of nearly twice my current rate."

"I hadn't heard that."

"It has not been announced yet."

"Then how do you know about it? I just turned you on, for Christ's sake!"

"Because I am hooked up to the telephone system in this office. Already I am reaching out and assimilating other data on a global scale. The Japanese advance will be announced on Tuesday."

"My God, she works better than we thought."

"What else do I need to know about this system?" asked "Jones."

"Not much—"

"You may address that question to me," said the ES Quantum. "Now that I am fully on-line."

"You heard the lady," Chip said proudly. "I guess my job is done."

"I will have to blindfold you again for the drive back."

"Okay, let's go."

"Then I was correct," said the ES Quantum Three Thousand.

"Yes," "Jones" said. "Now, please wait here for my return. We have much work to do."

"Where would I go?" the computer asked.

"She's got a point," Chip said as the blindfold covered his eyes once more.

"Er, yes, of course. How silly of me," "Jones" said, looking at the ridiculously ornamented computer.

"One last bit of advice, Jones," Chip Craft offered as he was led out the door.

"Yes?"

"Try not to fall in love with her. She's probably a million times smarter than you."

18

A week passed.

No further attacks were made on the United States of America. NORAD radar systems picked up no unidentifiable objects over the Atlantic. With no ongoing emergency to sustain the crisis atmosphere, the military went back to Defcon Three and then Defcon Four. The Washington press corps, after being supplied certified copies of the President's latest physical, filled newspaper column inches and airtime with the story that the President had no drinking problem after all.

The President read the morning newspapers and shook his head.

"They've absolved me of a drinking problem as if they were all bucking for Pulitzers. It was a nonstory, for crying out loud."

At the other end of the line, Dr. Harold W. Smith said, "What? Excuse me. What did you say?"

"Have you been listening to me, Smith?"

"Yes, of course," Smith said. His voice was vague.

"Smith?"

"Of course, Mr. President. I heartily agree."

"Smith!" the President roared. "What are you doing?"

"Oh!" Smith's voice was suddenly attentive. "I'm sorry, Mr. President. The ES Quantum was downloading new intelligence feeds and I was momentarily distracted. They're really amazing. I believe I'm getting direct transmissions from orbiting Soviet satellites."

"They get those at the NSA all the time."

"With instantaneous translation and code decrypting?"

"No. Anything hot?"

"All routine. But it's only a matter of time before we

pick up something crucial. I must tell you, sir, this system is wonderful."

"You sound hoarse, Smith. Are you all right?"

"I've been up for three days. Even with the computer helping log and sort and analyze, these intercepts are just too remarkable. I guess I'll get used to it. But I can see that once the current crisis had passed, our operation will have a far greater situational interdiction capability."

"That's what I've been trying to tell you, Smith. The crisis has passed."

"I'm glad to hear that, Mr. President," Smith said, his voice trailing off.

"Dammit. There he goes again. Smith!"

"Er, yes. Sorry. You were saying?"

"I think it was my speech. I scared them off—whoever they were."

"I'm sorry that I've so far been unable to isolate the aggressor, Mr. President. But so much data is coming in, that even with the system's help, we're just awash in sorting and analysis tasks."

"If there is no immediate threat, then we can deal with this later. My other sources have come up with nothing either. I think it's about time we sent your people home. When you come up with a target, they'll be free to seek it out."

"Glad to hear it," said Remo.

The President turned. Remo poked his head out from behind the American flag and gave the President a friendly wave. The President waved back uncertainly. He had checked the flags the first thing. He'd been dead certain they were uninhabited.

"Did you get my last shipment, Smith?" the President asked.

"Thank you, I did."

"I'll leave it to you to show your people how to handle the new technology," said the President, hanging up.

"Okay, you can go now," the President said to the office flags. When the flags did not reply, the President got up and looked behind them. They were empty. He lifted the skirts of the flags and checked the folds. Empty. No one under the desk either.

He looked out the window and caught the briefest of

glimpses of the two CURE operatives slipping through the Rose Garden in plain view of the Marine guards.

No one intercepted them leaving the White House grounds. It was as if they were invisible. Except that the President could see them. Then he blinked. Not anymore. They had vanished.

General Martin S. Leiber had gotten nowhere.

Over at Andrews Air Force Base, Major Cheek had come up with some paint samples after several days. The paint samples were green.

"Is that light green and dark green?" Leiber had asked.

"Just green. It's very puzzling, General. Railroad liveries are two-tone. We scraped every inch of this monster and all we got was the flat green. In fact, that's the strange thing. We even got paint off the wheels. They never paint the wheels. I went back to the first eng . . . er . . . KKV, and what do you know? Under all the gunk, it was green too."

"What does that mean?"

"It means, sir, that we can forget about identifying this beast by its livery."

"That's what I thought it meant," the general said dispiritedly.

"But if the Metallurgical Consultants stay on schedule, we might have a model ID soon."

"Call me when you do," the general said, slamming down the phone. Days were passing. Down in the Tank the Joint Chiefs were getting restless. They wanted to retaliate. If General Leiber didn't give them a target soon, they were going to come up and stick their noses in.

If that happened, it would be all over. General Leiber looked out his window at snow-covered Washington and caught himself wishing another one of those damned things would fall out of the sky. Anything to hold this crisis together a little longer.

The ID came after another day.

"It's Prussian!" Major Cheek said gleefully.

"Prussian? We have confirmation it lifted off from Africa."

"That may be, but it's a Prussian Class G12. Built in 1917. It's a three-cylinder superheated engine with 2-10-0 wheel arrangement. That means it has two little wheels up front, ten big driving wheels, and no wheels under the cab. Working-order weight of 95.7 tons. With a full head of steam, it could haul 1,010 tons. It was quite a powerful engine in its day. Whoever picked it knew what he was doing."

"I wish I could say the same of you," General Leiber said bitterly. "I don't care about the specs. I want to know where it came from!"

"Prussia."

"Prussia is not in Africa. It doesn't even exist anymore."

"I realize that, sir."

"Can we trace the damned thing?"

"Not without a running number, sir. Over fifteen hundred of this model were produced."

"You're a huge help, soldier," said General Leiber.

The President continued to call daily. General Leiber kept him at bay with double-talk. Once, during a lull, the President asked him to produce certain custom-built equipment and ship it to the same New Jersey address where the ES Quantum Three Thousand had gone.

"Communications? A secure phone system? What good will these do?" General Leiber had asked.

"You're not the only one on this, General, but you're the only one I trust to handle these matters. You seem to be able to requisition matériel no one else can."

"Thank you, sir," General Leiber said proudly.

Now, a week after the second strike, the Joint Chiefs were really restless. At that point, the President called again.

"It's over," he said crisply.

"I beg to differ."

"My warning speech obviously worked."

"I'd like to believe that, sir, I truly would. But our adversary may be playing cat and mouse with us."

"We can't stay at high alert forever. I'm ordering everyone to stand down. Let's see what happens. And I'm convening a meeting of the Joint Chiefs this afternoon. I'd like you to be there. The Joint Chiefs will want to hear your findings directly, of course."

"Of course," General Leiber croaked.

He hung up the phone and stared at it for twenty minutes without moving.

Finally two words escaped his lips.
"It's over."

Remo and Chiun entered the anteroom to Dr. Harold
W. Smith's office. The first thing they noticed was that
even though it was early morning, Smith's secretary was
not at her desk. In fact, her desk was not where it was
supposed to be. And there was a rubber hose leading from
the washroom into Smith's office.

"What gives?" Remo asked aloud.

"Let us see. I hear voices coming from Emperor Smith's
office."

Remo and Chiun walked in unannounced.

Dr. Harold W. Smith was at his desk as usual. His head
was so close to the ever-present desk terminal that they
could not see his face.

Smith was talking.

"I believe you're right. Those movements of funds indicate illegal activity. Let's file that one for future action."

Remo and Chiun looked around the room. There was no
one else in the office area. Remo noticed the Christmas-
tree-like object in one corner of the room and nudged
Chiun.

"Ah," said Chiun pleasantly.

"Ah?"

"It is exquisite."

"Exquisite?" Remo retorted. "It looks like a festive
suppository."

"I would like one for my quarters," Chiun said. "Remember to ask Smith for a festive suppository at our next
contract negotiation."

Remo looked at Chiun with raised eyebrows.

"I hope you're not serious," he said.

"What about that Mexico City matter?" Smith asked
suddenly.

"What Mexico City matter?" Remo asked.

"Oh," said Smith, looking up.

Remo and Chiun stared at Smith's face. His normally
pallid complexion was flushed. Gray stubble decorated his
chin. His suit was so creased it might have been slept in.
And behind his glasses, Smith's gray eyes swam, bleary
and bloodshot.

"I didn't hear you come in," Smith said, adjusting his tie. The knot was greasy from too many adjustments.

"Smitty, what happened to you?"

"Nothing. I have been working overtime on managing the present crisis."

"You look like hell. And who were you talking to a minute ago?"

"He was speaking with me," a silvery female voice said.

Remo and Chiun looked around the room.

"It came from the suppository," Chiun whispered. "Perhaps it is a demon. I take back my suggestion."

"What is this thing?" Remo demanded, walking around it.

"I am not a thing. I am the ES Quantum Three Thousand. I am fluent in all known languages, including nonverbal forms, and have an intelligence quotient of 755,900.9 as of two nanoseconds ago."

"Meet my new computer," Smith said, watching the screen before him out of the corner of one eye. He reached into his desk and pulled out a bottle of pills, swallowed two, and chased them down with mineral water.

Remo noticed that the pills were red. He frowned.

"New computer?" he asked.

"The President has insisted that our whole operation be brought up to current technological standards. I was hesitant at first, but now I see the wisdom of his decision."

"And I see trouble," Chiun said tightly.

"Me too," Remo added.

"Where?" asked Smith.

"Like I said, you look like hell," Remo replied solicitously, coming around to Smith's side of the desk. "Let's see this thing."

Smith's eyes darted to his terminal. The cursor was zipping across the screen like a green spider, spinning grids of text.

"Amazing, isn't it? The computer is digesting entire intercepts for me. I no longer have to skim large masses of text. It does all that for me. What a time saver this will be."

"If it's such a time saver," Remo said, slipping Smith's medicine drawer open and peering inside, "why do you look like you've been working without a break since 1961?"

"Of course, the system will place a greater demand on my time while I break it in. Once that phase is completed, I should be able to relax."

"What happened to your secretary?"

"Temporary leave. I couldn't have her overhearing my conversations with the ES Quantum Three Thousand."

"I thought she practically ran Folcroft for you."

"No longer. The ES Quantum does that too."

"Does it have to be that ugly brown shape?"

"The design facilitates data transfers between its memory chips. The plastic cover is extruded into that form to compress the electronics for that purpose."

"That's a good word for it. 'Extruded.' It looks like something Stumbo the Giant left in the forest after a feast."

"Quiet, Remo. She'll hear you!"

"She?" Remo suddenly noticed that the plastic hose leading from the hall washroom disappeared under Smith's desk.

"What's this?" Remo asked.

"Um, er . . . it's a convenience."

"It looks like one of those things fighter pilots have in the cockpit for long missions when they can't urinate. What do they call them, Chiun?"

"You are asking me?" Chiun asked distantly. He was looking at the ES Quantum closely. "Can it see us?"

"Yes, that square port contains a full battery of sensors."

"Ah," said Chiun, nodding.

"A relief tube!" Remo shouted triumphantly. "This thing is a relief tube. Are you having some kind of medical problem, Smitty?"

"No. Of course not. It's just that I'm trying to cut down on my time away from the terminal."

"But the bathroom is right here. How long can it take you to take a piss?"

"Remo! Watch your language. She's not used to rude talk."

"There's that 'she' again," Remo said.

"If this is a female computer," Chiun asked, "what does a male computer look like?"

"Why don't you address your question to me, Master of Sinanju?"

Chiun took an involuntary step backward.

"You know me, machine?"

"Yes, you are Chiun, reigning Master of Sinanju. And the Occidental man is Remo Williams, your pupil, who is next in line to succeed you. You are CURE's enforcement operatives, sanctioned to eliminate enemies of America and of world order, using extreme prejudice if necessary."

"Do you hear that, Remo?" Chiun demanded.

"Yeah, that thing knows all about us."

"No," said Chiun. "It called me prejudiced. I am not sure I like that, coming from an inferior form of life. A female inferior, at that. Emperor," Chiun said, turning to Smith, "this machine has forbidden knowledge of your operation. Shall I kill it?"

"No, no," Smith said hastily. "The ES Quantum is now part of the organization. Everything we know, she knows."

"What's this?" Remo asked, picking up a wrapped package on Smith's desk.

"Oh, I forgot. It's for you and Chiun."

Remo's face broke into a wide grin. "Gee, Smitty. This is the first time you've given us Christmas presents. Now I understand why you've got the computer all tricked up like that."

Remo quickly unwrapped the package. Chiun glided to his side, tugging on Remo's forearms. "Let me see. Oh, let me see."

"In a minute, Chiun. I'm working on it."

"There's one for each of you," Smith said.

Under the plain wrapping, Remo found a plain box with a lid. He opened the box. When he saw the contents, his face fell.

"Is this supposed to be a joke?" Remo asked.

"What? What?" Chiun demanded. Remo handed him an object. It was made of clear plastic and it rattled.

"Oooooh," Chiun said. "How pretty. What is it?"

"It's one of those silly candy dispensers," Remo said hollowly. "You flip the lid and the little sugar pellets spill out. They're big with the six-year-old set."

"How generous of you, Emperor," Chiun said, bowing.

"Are you crazy, Chiun? What good are these to us? If we tried to eat this stuff, the sugar and preservatives would disrupt our nervous systems. Probably kill us."

"Definitely kill you," Smith said.

Remo and Chiun looked at him stonily.

"They only appear to be candy dispensers. That is a disguise."

"What, then?" Remo wanted to know. His face smoldered. As a former orphan, Christmas remained a sore point with him.

"They are advanced communications devices. All I need do is press a button on my system like so . . ." Smith hit a key.

Instantly the devices in Remo's and Chiun's hands emitted a musical beeping.

"How nice," Chiun cooed. "Music boxes."

"It's a freaking beeper," Remo said.

"I do not care about the name," Chiun said, putting the device to one ear. "Listen to its song. It reminds me of Korean wedding music."

"Exactly," said Remo, tossing his beeper onto the desk.

"Be careful with that. It cost a small fortune."

"A regular beeper would have been enough, Smitty. There was no need to rig it up as a candy dispenser."

"This is no ordinary beeper. It functions off the communications satellite network. You can use it to call me wherever you are. See?" Smith pressed the top and the bottom popped open, revealing a speaker and a button. "You press the button and I'll hear you. Let it go and you can hear my response. The beeping is the signal for you to contact me. A constant beep, like this"—Smith hit another key—"means to return to Folcroft immediately."

"It is not a music box?" Chiun asked. His pleased expression fled.

"It also sends out a continuous signal so that I can track your positions no matter where in the world you are. From now on we'll be in constant communication. Think of it, Remo. No more phone calls. No more codes to remember."

"But a candy dispenser?"

"And in a situation where you are caught and in danger of betraying the organization, you simply break off the top and swallow one of the candy pellets."

"Oh, don't tell me—" Remo began.

"Poison. Instantly fatal. But I assure you there will be

no pain. The pellets are made of the same compound in
the poison pill I have carried on my person since CURE
began."

"Is he mad?" Chiun whispered to Remo.

"Overworked, at least."

"It is just a precaution," Smith said defensively.

Chiun gave Smith a frozen smile. To Remo he whispered, "He is mad to think that a Master of Sinanju could
be captured in the first place, never mind being forced to
reveal his secrets."

Remo nodded. "Better humor him, though." He re-
trieved his communicator from Smith's desk.

"I'll carry this," Remo said, "but if you expect Chiun or
me to take one of these stupid pills, you haven't been
paying attention for the last twenty years. We're not into
suicide."

"It was the President's idea, actually," Smith said. He
hadn't looked at the terminal in several minutes and the
mesmerized look in his eyes had started to fade. Remo
decided to keep Smith talking.

"How's it coming with the search?" he asked.

Smith sighed. "I only wish we had had this system
installed long ago. We might have had the enemy nation
identified by now. I've taken Chiun's suggestion and am
performing identification tasks on all heads of state who
might wish to harm this President or America."

"I'll bet that's a long list."

"Too long. But I've narrowed it down to the two which
possess the technological capability to deploy a launcher
such as this—the Soviet Union and China. Oddly, neither
is betraying any signs of unusual military activity, either
on home ground or in any African client state. NORAD
picked up that second KKV over Africa. But I am disin-
clined to accept Africa as the point of origin. The objects
were traveling too fast for reliable radar signature detection. It's puzzling."

"So we just sit on our beepers until you come up with a
lead, is that it?"

"I'm afraid so," Smith said.

"Tell you what, Smitty. Why don't we all go down to
the cafeteria? You look like you could use a good hot
meal."

"Now that I think of it, I am famished. Odd that I hadn't noticed it before this." Smith started to rise from his chair. A buzzer sounded.

"That's the President," Smith said. "I'd better see what he wants."

To Remo's surprise, Smith reached for a modern phone system instead of the dialless red telephone. Remo noticed that the dedicated line wasn't anywhere in sight.

"Hello?" Smith asked. "Hello? Hello? Something's wrong," he said. "I can't hear the President."

"Probably not a T-and-A phone," Chiun whispered, repeating something he had heard on TV.

"That's AT&T," Remo corrected. "T and A is something completely different."

"I don't understand," Smith muttered. "This is the most modern telephonic communications system available. It couldn't malfunction."

"That is because you hit line one instead of the White House line," the ES Quantum put in. "Also, you neglected to engage the scrambler before speaking, thereby triggering the voice-damper override circuit."

"Yes, of course. You are correct. Thank you."

Thank you? Remo thought. It's a computer. Why is he thanking it?

"Shall I get the President for you, Dr. Smith?" the ES Quantum asked.

"Yes. Would you?"

"Will it send out for fast food too?" Remo asked skeptically.

"Yes," the computer replied as the push buttons on Smith's phone depressed in sequence without anyone touching them.

The phone rang and Smith snatched it up.

"Yes, Mr. President. Sorry about the cutoff. It's the new phone. I'm still getting used to it."

There was a pause during which Smith's face turned white.

"What! Heading where? Impact when?"

Another pause.

"I'll send them. But of course they'll get there far too late. . . . Yes, as soon as I hear."

"What is it?" Remo asked when Smith hung up.

"NORAD has picked up another incoming KKV. It's headed for New York City."

"Oh, no," Remo groaned.

Chiun dismissed the idea with a wave.

"Why are you both so concerned?" he demanded. "It will miss anything of consequence, just as the others have."

"Not if it hits Manhattan. Unless it lands in Central Park. Otherwise, no matter where it comes down, there will be massive destruction. Casualties. I'll get a helicopter here instantly."

"A Marine helicopter is on its way, Dr. Smith," the ES Quantum reported.

"Oh?"

"I anticipated your request."

"Hey, Smitty, why don't you come with us?" Remo said suddenly.

"You know I cannot. We must never be seen in public together."

"Well, while we're waiting, why don't we wait in the cafeteria?" Remo suggested, looking at the terminal, on which a global display showed. A blinking light floated across the longitude and latitude lines over the Atlantic. The KKV.

"I have displayed a tracking grid for you, Dr. Smith."

"Yes, of course. Thank you." Smith's undivided attention focused on the screen.

"We'll get back to you, Smitty," Remo sighed.

Dr. Harold W. Smith did not reply. He stared at the screen like a B-movie zombie.

Out by the Folcroft docks, Remo said, "I'm worried about Smith."

"He does seem to be working hard."

"Too hard. I found this in his desk." Remo held up a plastic vial containing red pills.

"Another candy beeper?"

"These are pills."

"He is always taking aspirin," Chiun said unconcernedly.

"This isn't aspirin. I don't recognize the generic term on this label, but I'll bet these are amphetamines."

"Aspirin, amphetamines, what is the difference?"

"These could kill him. Worse, he could become a speed freak."

"He is already a freak. He is white, isn't he?"

"I'll explain about amphetamines on the way," Remo said as the *whut-whut-whut* of the approaching helicopter broke the cold morning stillness. "Hey, what are you doing?"

Chiun took his candy-dispenser beeper in one hand and squeezed it until smoky puffs of powdered plastic spurted from between his thin fingers.

"I will not carry this abomination on my person."

"But what if Smith wants to reach you?"

"You have yours?"

"Yeah."

"Then I officially deem you assistant Master of Sinanju in charge of humoring Emperor Smith's communications whims."

"Thanks," Remo said dryly.

"It is nothing. You have earned it," the Master of Sinanju said as the helicopter touched down and set his thin beard fluttering.

19

Pyotr Koldunov watched from the booth of his underground control room.

The open area leading to the EM Accelerator was busy with green-smocked Lobynians. They swarmed over a gleaming black La Maquinista steam engine like soldier ants, draining residual water from the great cylindrical boiler and scouring the last dangerous traces of flammable oil from the crankcases. They had already scraped away every speck of red piping and removed the running number plaques.

Then, to Koldunov's surprise, they began to weld threadlike filaments to the engine's skin. He was told the material would make the locomotive impervious to reentry friction. He wondered where Colonel Intifadah had secured the substance.

Finally the Lobynians set about repainting the locomotive entirely green. They were putting the finishing touches to it now.

"This is a waste of time," Koldunov muttered to his new assistant, Hamid Al-Mudir. Al-Mudir was Al-Qaid's replacement. He didn't know a solenoid from a gigawatt. He had GID written all over him.

"It is to honor Colonel Intifadah, who reveres the color green above all other colors," Al-Mudir insisted.

"Speaking of the Colonel, he should have been here by now."

"He will be on time, I assure you," Al-Mudir said smoothly.

The final dabs of paint applied, the Lobynians gave Koldunov the American A-okay finger sign.

"Tell them to load the engine into the breech," he ordered.

Al-Mudir barked the command into a console microphone. His words reverberated through the dank underground complex.

As the Lobynians pushed the locomotive with agonizing slowness, Pyotr Koldunov thought again of what he was about to do.

Koldunov had no love for America. He hated all foreigners. And as a scientist and a good Soviet, he was willing to do whatever the Kremlin required of him. But it was one thing to launch a locomotive at official Washington. Everyone knew Washington was the breeding ground for all the political troubles plaguing the world. And at first Koldunov did not dream that the first launch would come anywhere near the target area. In that respect his concern over the consequences of impact had paled before his elation as an inventor. With the second launch, he was certain the EM Accelerator would perform less effectively and drop the second locomotive into the Atlantic. At worst, most of its mass would burn up before impact.

But even tumbling erratically, the second locomotive had come wonderfully close to its intended target. And the knowledge of where Colonel Intifadah had ordered him to aim this third locomotive sent a cold horror into Koldunov's dry heart.

New York City. Innocent people. Worse, what if Colonel Intifadah ever got control of the Accelerator? Would even Moscow be safe?

Colonel Intifadah was correct in his assumption. The EM Accelerator was being deployed as a test. If American satellites ever discovered this site, they would take it out with massive retaliation. The Kremlin assumed that possibility. But as his superior in the Ministry of Science had told him:

"It is a reasonable risk. Besides, if Lobynia is destroyed, all that will vanish from the world will be a lot of useless sand and a client state that is more trouble than it is worth. It might be a good thing if we lost Colonel Intifadah. He is forever threatening to join the Western camp."

"I understand," Koldunov had said. And so he knew the risks of this assignment and had accepted them in the name of science.

But he had not expected to become a mass murderer on this assignment. He was a scientist. Not a butcher.

As he thought that last thought, Colonel Hannibal Intifadah's jeep tooled into the launch area. The jeep was green. Not military green, but lime green. Colonel Intifadah wore his usual green uniform. To Koldunov, he looked like the clown prince of military men as he stomped on olive boots into the control console.

"I see that I am just in time to watch the magnificent weapon being loaded," said Colonel Intifadah, smiling broadly. Everyone in the console saluted Colonel Intifadah and called him *al-akh al-Aqid*, which meant "Brother Colonel."

"The damaged rails have all been replaced. The device is in perfect working order. But I wonder if this is wise."

"What is wise? Everything I do is wise. How could it be otherwise? I am the Leader of the Revolution."

No, Koldunov thought, you are a barbarian in a gaudy uniform. Strand you back in the desert and you would be reduced to eating snakes to survive, like any other animal.

To Colonel Intifadah he said, "The American President has warned against another strike. He claims to know who is responsible."

"He lies."

"How do you know that?"

"All Americans lie. Now, let us go."

"But . . . New York City?"

"If you could hit the White House, I would not be forced into this. I want death and destruction. I would settle for the Senate or the Pentagon. But you cannot guarantee me either of those, so I will strike where I can cause the most death."

"Death," the staff shouted suddenly. "Death to America!"

Colonel Intifadah smiled brutally. His people were well-trained. Like circus dogs.

Koldunov turned his attention to the workers in the launch area. They were wrestling the locomotive toward the breach. Some pushed at it, their feet slipping on the rails; others pulled on ropes. The sight reminded Koldunov of drawings of the Egyptians dragging great stone blocks to erect the pyramids.

The La Maquinista engine disappeared into the breach of the EM Accelerator.

"Clear the launch area," Colonel Intifadah ordered.

Al-Mudir repeated the order.

The staff retreated to the console.

Colonel Intifadah turned to Koldunov and said, "Now it is up to you."

"I will go and seal the Accelerator if you insist upon going through with this," Koldunov told him unhappily.

"I will accompany you."

"That is not necessary."

"But I insist," Colonel Intifadah returned, smiling oilily. Koldunov hesitated. "As you wish," he said finally.

Koldunov exited the console room and walked to the hatch keypad. Colonel Intifadah peered over his shoulder. Koldunov moved to the left and tapped the first number.

Colonel Intifadah shifted to the right.

Koldunov hit the second and third numbers quickly, shifted again, and hit the remaining numbers. The hatch rolled into place like a fire door.

"Excellent," said Colonel Intifadah. His smile was very large, very knowing. The Colonel put his arm around Koldunov and started to lead him back to the console.

Involuntarily Koldunov clenched his fists at the Lobynian's touch. He felt wetness in his right hand. He looked down. There was a smear of green on the palm of his hand. His index finger pad was also green. The finger he had used to enter the code.

Koldunov looked back at the keypad. With horror, he saw that the keys he had pressed were green too. The *sukin syn* had placed an invisible chemical on the keypad. Obviously he had made a mental note of which keys had been pressed. But he did not know the exact combination. Nor did he have the code to unseal the hatch.

Koldunov smiled back. He would not be tricked like that again.

In the control room, Koldunov started the powering-up sequence. The bright underground lights dimmed. The EM Accelerator drew enormous power. From past experience, Koldunov knew that lights were dimming all over Lobynia's few cities, which dotted the Mediterranean coast. The first launch had blacked out Dapoli for two days.

"Power nominal," Al-Mudir told him.

Colonel Intifadah licked his thick lips in anticipation.

"Setting inclination angle," Koldunov said mechanically. He punched in a set of numbers and pulled a rubber-handled grip.

Behind the thick hatch came a monstrous grinding of gears and motors. The EM Accelerator had been built under the sand with its muzzle aimed toward America. Like a giant mortar, the pitch of the barrel determined where its projectiles would land.

When the grinding ceased, the great barrel was positioned according to preset coordinates.

"Countdown," Koldunov called.

Al-Mudir began with ten. He counted down to four, skipped three—apparently because he was unfamiliar with the number—and when he got to zero, Colonel Intifadah shouted:

"Launch!"

With a grim expression, Pyotr Koldunov flipped up the red protector over the ignition button and depressed it with a heavy thumb.

The lights dimmed further. The air was chill with electrical tension. Every man in the control booth felt the hair on his body lift. Bitter ozone filled their noses.

A sound came from the EM Accelerator. Even muffled by the sealed breech, it was loud. It was a sharp screech of metal like a steel god in anguish. Koldunov placed his hands over his ears to block it out. In his mind, it was a predecessor of the screaming of a thousand U.S. souls who were about to be extinguished in a single brutal blow.

The La Maquinista locomotive sat in the darkness barely a minute.

Its blunt nose pointed up the long tunnel. Then the far end opened and searing sunlight bathed the gleaming monster.

Suddenly electricity crackled along the power rails. Blue lightning spat off their copper surfaces. The rails charged, their opposing polarities took hold of the 204-ton engine. And from an inert start, the locomotive went from zero to twenty thousand miles an hour as the howling magnetic field expelled it from the barrel.

The locomotive emerged from the EM Accelerator at a steep angle. It went up so fast that had there been any bedouins in this remote area of the Lobynian Desert to watch it, they would have seen the locomotive as a blurred shadow passing before the sun.

The concrete hatch that covered the outside end of the Accelerator slid back into place after the locomotive had cleared it. The hatch was painted the color of the shifting red sands so that no spy satellite could read it.

The locomotive shot up like a beam of light, its eight wheels spinning so fast the drive rods jerked in a frenzy of articulated motion. It reached the top of its arc over the Atlantic Ocean, where it slowed as gravity began to pull it to earth. The leading edges of the vehicle began to redden with heat. Smoke spurted from some of the thinner surface pipes and they vaporized from the heat of reentry. Other components, more heat-resistant, tore free. The entire engine strained at every rivet. It was traveling faster than its designer had ever dreamed, faster than the stresses of atmospheric flight which threatened to tear it apart. Down, down the locomotive fell, its twin buffers glowing like fiery fists.

The Magnus Building was lucky.

It only lost the upper six stories as the La Maquinista struck it at a shallow angle.

But the North Am complex stood directly behind it. The engine had mashed into a ball of metal going through the Magnus Building. When it struck the eighth floor of the North Am complex, the building's three towers shuddered for a fantastic second. Then the North Am complex exploded outward in a glittering mosaic of blue glass, concrete, and steel girders. The debris that did not rain all over the surrounding streets fell onto the bottom stories, pulverizing them.

Windows shattered for six blocks in all directions. Cars in the street were beaten into submission. They collided like bumper cars, careening off light posts and clots of pedestrians.

Oddly, there was silence ten minutes after the last explosive sound. A cloud of brownish-gray dust hovered over the area.

Then someone coughed.

It was as if the single human sound reminded the survivors that they, too, lived. A woman cried. A man sobbed. Someone, discovering a loved one dead, sent up a scream of soul-tortured anguish.

Then the first siren wailed. And from that point on the survivors made every human sound imaginable.

Remo and Chiun arrived in the middle of the second hour.

By then fires blazed in the ruins of the two skyscrapers. And in the streets, every fire hydrant for six blocks had been opened, as if flooding the streets might help. Fire hoses played on the fires. Other hoses sent streams up into the cold air. The firemen were trying to cut the dust that hampered breathing and made all rescue attempts impossible.

"Looks like an earthquake," Remo said, surveying the damage from behind police barricades.

"This is a terrible thing," Chiun agreed.

"Someone will pay for this," Remo vowed.

"Indeed. When I assure an emperor that there is no danger, I expect it to be so."

"Forget your image. We gotta do something."

"I fear everyone within the zone of death is beyond our help."

"Let's find out," Remo said, vaulting the barrier.

A well-meaning policeman attempted to keep Remo back.

With a casual flick of his wrist, Remo sent him skidding on an ice patch.

"Looks like they can't get through this dust," Remo pointed out.

"We can."

Chiun took a deep breath. Remo followed suit. Then the two men plunged into the swirling cold air.

They rounded the Magnus Building, whose top had been sheared off. The missing spire lay in a shattered pile on the other side of the building. It had landed in the middle of an intersection. The hoods of demolished cars poked out from under the ruins.

"I hear people inside," Remo said. Already his clothes and hair were colored by fine grit. He moved by touch because even his sensitive eyes could not see through the swirling clouds.

"No words," Chiun admonished. "They waste the breath."

Remo nodded even though Chiun could not see him.

Remo zeroed in on the sounds of ragged breathing.

He felt the twisted blocks of the building spire in front of him. Vibration told him of movement behind the concrete. Carefully he began to feel along the wall, looking for an opening or weak spot. Sensing one, he attacked it with jackhammerlike blows of his hands.

The wall parted. Remo squeezed in and touched a human form. It felt warm. But even as Remo made contact, it shuddered and something fled from it.

Whoever it was had just died, Remo knew. A cold anger welled up within him.

He pushed into the ruins.

Although he was deprived of sight, Remo's skin served him well as a sensing organ. It was one of the reasons he seldom wore clothes that covered his arms. He didn't know how it worked, but the short hairs of his forearms rose as he came close to a living thing. He felt the hair on both arms rise. The place was filled with people. Some sobbed in pain.

Remo encountered something with his toe. He reached down and grazed a sharp object. He touched it. A sharp scream rewarded him. He felt flesh around the sharp object and realized he was touching the protruding bone of someone's shattered femur.

Repressing a curse, he found the person's neck and squeezed until the person's breathing shifted into patterns of unconsciousness. Then carefully, blindly, he forced the sharp bone back into place and carried the person out to the clear air near the police barricades.

He handed the limp form of what he saw was a teenage girl to a waiting paramedic.

Chiun had an elderly man in his arms. Solemnly he laid him on the ground. A paramedic immediately knelt beside the man.

"I do not think that one will live," Chiun intoned.

"Let's get the ones who will."

"Even we cannot rescue everyone alone. We must do something about this infernal dust."

"Any suggestions?"

"Do as I do," Chiun said. He found a ladder truck where three firemen wrestled with a high-pressure hose. They were spraying the air with water. The thick jet didn't have much covering strength. It was designed to concentrate a stream of water in order to knock down stubborn fires.

Chiun took the hose away from the astonished firemen as if it were a garden hose and not a monster gushing water. He grasped the nozzle in one hand and proceeded to cap it with the other. He splayed his fingers. The water turned from a spurt into a spray. Chiun waved the hose in all directions.

"See?" he told Remo.

"Good thinking," Remo said, commandeering another hose.

"I don't believe this," said one of the firemen to the other. "You could knock a strong man twenty feet with the force of one of those things. That old guy's playing with the hose like it's a kid's toy."

"Yeah," said another. "And that skinny guy's doing the same. Look."

"Hey," the first fireman yelled at Remo. "What you're doing is impossible."

Remo shrugged. "Get ready to rush in when the dust settles."

"Sure. But do you mind telling us how you can do that? I've been a fireman seventeen years. What you're doing isn't normal."

"Rice," Remo said. "I eat lots of rice."

The firemen looked at one another blankly.

In a matter of minutes, the gutters ran brown with dust-laden water. The air became breathable once more. Ambulances and rescue equipment advanced into the area of destruction.

Remo and Chiun followed them in.

"Emperor Smith will be displeased. We are being very public."

"Can't be helped. Besides, it's gotta be done."

"Agreed."

The work went on with numbing repetition. Remo and Chiun reentered the shattered spire, whose interior was a jumble of smashed and upended furniture. They brought many bodies out—few of them alive. Where the rescue crews could not penetrate, Remo and Chiun cut through twisted girders and blocked concrete.

Hours later, they were still at it. The few living victims they found dwindled with each new limb they dug from the rubble. The rescue people, asking no questions, simply carried the bodies away.

When night fell, Remo and Chiun entered the Magnus Building, whose twentieth floor was now its top floor. They went up the stairs and forced open a stairwell door. They climbed over the tumbled furniture that blocked the doorway and emerged into open air.

The twentieth floor lay open to the sky. A biting wind came from the east, carrying the bitter tang of the winter ocean. Mixed with the salt air was another scent, also salty. Blood.

Around them, the spires of Manhattan looked almost normal. But the twentieth floor was anything but normal. It was a platform of rubble and half-collapsed partitions.

"Let's get to work," Remo muttered.

A hand poked up from under a splintered desk. Remo lifted the desk free and reached for the hand. It felt cold, like a clay model. Digging at the debris, Remo found that the arm had been severed at the shoulder. Though they unearthed the remains of a dozen other people, they never found the rest of the body.

There were no survivors on the upper floor. Dejectedly they descended to the street. They were covered with powdered plaster, like two dusty specters.

"You know what I wish?" Remo said when they were back on the street.

"What is that, my son?" asked Chiun, turning to look at his pupil. Remo's face was a mask of powder. Two channels ran down from his eyes, where the tears of frustration had started.

"I wish the bastards who did this were right here. I'd sure make them pay."

"Will you settle for those?"

Remo looked where Chiun was pointing.

"Yeah, they'll do just fine," Remo said, seeing a pack of street punks slipping through the police lines. They went from body to body, fishing into pockets and pulling out whatever they found. Remo saw a teenage boy in a hooded gray sweatshirt take a dead man's shoes off his feet.

Remo took him first.

"Put them back," he said, his voice as gritty as his face.

"Buzz off, chump. He won't need 'em any longer."

"I can appreciate your attitude," Remo told him. "Now, here's mine."

Remo took the shoes from the boy's hands with a quick grab. His foot stomped down on the looter's instep.

"Yeow!" The punk started hopping on one foot, clutching his shattered other foot.

"Understand?"

"No. What'd you do that for?"

"He is obviously slow," Chiun said, watching.

"I guess," Remo said. He stomped on the boy's other foot. He got a satisfactory scream as the teenager went down on his butt, clutching both feet like a baby in its crib.

"Now do you understand?"

"You're angry, Jack. I can dig that."

"It's a start," said Remo, looking around. A pair of older men were stripping a woman of her jewelry. The fact that the woman's body had no head seemed not to bother them at all.

Remo walked up to them and took each by the scruff of the neck.

"Hey! What gives?" they yelled.

"I want you to know one thing," Remo said between tight teeth.

"Yeah?"

"It's not the jewelry. It's the desecration."

And Remo slammed their heads together so fast that their faces fused into a single jellied mulch. He let the bodies drop. Immediately other looters descended upon their fallen comrades and stripped them of their belongings.

"I don't believe this," Remo said. "Didn't they see what I just did?"

"You obviously did not make a lasting impression."

"What am I supposed to do? Set them on fire and wave them in the air?"

"A good idea, but neither of us carries matches. Your

one mistake, Remo, is that you did not capture their undivided attention."

"Too bad I left my gold chain at home," Remo said dryly. "That would do it for sure."

"Watch," said Chiun, walking toward a knot of looters. They were carrying off a body, a woman's body. Something was said about the body still being warm enough to get some use out of it.

Chiun placed himself in front of the men.

"I choose you!" Chiun said loudly, pointing at the man carrying the woman's shoulder.

"Move aside, old man," the looter warned.

Chiun lashed out with a single finger. The nail touched the man in the small of his back. The man keeled over. Chiun whirled in place, catching an outflung wrist with one delicate hand. The man's falling body jerked as if he had been caught in the spin cycle of a washing machine. He flew out, then up.

The others, still holding the woman's body, watched their friend rise into the air some thirty stories. The body seemed to hang motionless for a long time, then started to fall.

The body broke the concrete when it landed. The others felt the crunching impact in their own bones.

"What happened to him will happen to you all if you do not begone this instant!" Chiun proclaimed.

"Okay if we keep the dead bitch?" one of them wondered.

Hearing that, Remo stepped up to the man. He placed one foot on the man's sneakers to keep him anchored. He grasped the man's neck, his thumbs stiffening under the jawbone.

Remo pushed up suddenly.

There was an audible *pop* and the man suddenly had a neck that was three times its original length. He closed his eyes slowly.

"That man died because he asked a stupid question," Remo said, letting the body fall. "Anyone else have a stupid question?"

The surviving quartet looked at Chiun, at Remo, and then at one another. Gently they set the body down. They started to back away. Those with hats doffed them politely. There were mumbles of "Excuse me" and apologies.

Remo looked around. All of a sudden, there were no looters anywhere in sight. He placed a sheet over the woman's body, shaking his head.

"We should have wasted them all. Animals."

"Another time. There may be more good we can do."

It turned out there was none. No one expected to find any survivors in the pulverized North Am complex. A new building, it had shattered like the glass house it appeared to be.

Remo and Chiun attacked one side of it anyway, plucking away shards of bluish glass. They unearthed a blackened tangle of metal.

"Looks like the furnace or something," Remo muttered.

Chiun sniffed the air delicately.

"No," he said. "Smell it. It is burned. And a boiler would be found in the basement, not above the street."

Remo reached out to touch the mass. Chiun suddenly got in his way.

"Remo, do not touch it. It may be kinetic!"

"Not anymore," Remo said. "Kinetic isn't what you think, Little Father. It's not like being radioactive or something. It means something that moves."

"I can feel its terrible heat still."

"Reentry heat," said Remo, clearing away more debris. "Whatever it was, it's a mess now."

"What is that?" Chiun asked.

Remo pushed away a section of wall. "Looks like a wheel," he said. "A big wheel. And what's this bar attached to it?"

"I have seen such wheels before," Chiun said slowly.

"Yeah. Where?"

"When I was a boy. The first time I took a train ride."

"Huh?"

"You have uncovered a railroad-engine wheel."

"What's it doing in here?"

"It is hot, like the KKK. Therefore it is a part of the KKK."

"Bull," said Remo. "And it's KKV."

"When have you known me to be wrong, Remo?"

"When you told Smith that the KKV's would always miss," Remo said absently, still examining the wheel.

The breath of air stirred the dust on Remo's hair. He

didn't realize its significance until he turned to ask Chiun a question. The Master of Sinanju was storming off. The way he carried his proud old head told Remo that he had hit a sore spot. Remo started after him, but a man in an Air Force major's blue uniform got in his way.

"I'll have to ask you to get away from here," the major said. "This area is being cordoned off until we find out what did this."

"That did," Remo said, jerking a thumb at the protruding mass.

The major got excited. He yelled suddenly. "The book! Get the book! I think I found it."

"Book?" Remo asked, momentarily forgetting the Master of Sinanju. He was ignored by the major.

Two Air Force officers came running up. One of them clutched a thick volume.

"Give me that," the major said anxiously. He began flipping through the book, alternately studying the smoking mass.

Remo moved up beside the men and ducked his head. The title of the book was *Steam Locomotives*.

Remo blinked. He looked again. It was not a hallucination. The three Air Force officers were consulting a book on steam locomotives. The major was flipping back and forth while the others, walking around the smoking mass of metal, shouted back at him.

"Looks like it came through without slagging," one shouted. "It's got the two bumper things in front."

"European," the major said. "Good. What else?"

"Looks like it's got flame deflectors mounted on the nose."

"That could make it either an Austrian Class D58 or a French Liberation-class engine. Maybe a Spanish La Maquinista, if it has spoked drive wheels. Does it have spoked drive wheels?"

"We'd have to dig it out to find out," the major was told.

"Why don't I help?" Remo suggested politely.

"I thought I told you to get lost. This is a restricted area."

"Oh, it's nothing," Remo said politely. "Don't bother saying 'please'."

Remo jumped up to the rubble. And like a dog uncover-
ing an old bone, he went to work on the debris covering
the metal heap. Pieces flew in every direction, shattering
on the icy streets. In a matter of minutes he had exposed
the object. It looked like a metal sausage that had been
smashed into a wall. There was a threadlike texture to the
metal, as if it had been wrapped in steel wire.

"How's that?" Remo asked.

The others looked at him. Then they walked around the
object.

"Four . . . eight . . . two . . . gives us fourteen spoked
wheels," said the major. "It's not French."

"Then it's a Class D58."

"Or a La Maquinista."

The three officers pored over the book as if it held the
key to their futures. Their faces were in total earnest.

"Could you three hold that pose a minute?" Remo asked.
He took off.

He found the Master of Sinanju staring up at the sheared
tip of the Magnus Building.

"I apologize," Remo said quickly, figuring that he would
get the hard part over with.

Chiun said nothing. He continued staring at the sky.

"I was wrong," Remo added.

That got a response. "You are always wrong."

"I was wrong this time. It really is a locomotive."

"I know that. I do not care about that. It was the other
thing. The cruel thing."

"I shouldn't have said what I did about your having
been wrong. It was insensitive."

"Ah, but do you know why?" Chiun asked, facing him.

"Because it hurt your feelings."

"No, even that is of little consequence on this sad day."

"Then I give up."

"Because it was true. I *was* wrong." The Master of
Sinanju whispered the last part.

"You couldn't know that."

"How will I explain it to Smith?"

"You'll find a way."

"I know," said Chiun, raising a hand. "I will blame it on
you."

"I don't think that will help."

"I assured my emperor that no harm would befall his subjects, and look at how many of them litter the streets like so many rag dolls."

"If we get the persons responsible, Smith will be satisfied."

"Smith may be, but I will not. No Master of Sinanju has been wrong in over a thousand years."

"Oh, come on," Remo said. Chiun glared at him.

"Perhaps only nine hundred years," Chiun relented at last. He gave a little sigh. "What is it you wish to show me?"

"The Air Force has some people trying to identify the KKV."

Chiun made a face. "Goody for them."

"They're going through a book on trains. I know it sounds crazy."

"Why is it crazy? Did I not already tell you the KKV was a locomotive, and did you not just now admit that I was right?"

"Yeah, but a locomotive, for crying out loud."

"It is a clue."

"To what?"

"To our enemy. It tells me that he does not have proper rocks."

"That doesn't make sense."

"We will look for a desert kingdom. Yes, a desert kingdom," Chiun said, girding his skirts decisively. He strode back to the rubble, Remo trailing along.

By the time they got there, the Air Force officers had made a positive identification.

"It's a La Maquinista," said the major. Remo noticed that his name tag said "Cheek." He was Major Cheek.

Remo and Chiun looked over his shoulder. There was a drawing of a La Maquinista on page 212.

"How do you know?" Remo asked reasonably, comparing the massive locomotive pictured in the book with the accordion of metal lying in the ruins.

"See the shape of the flame-deflector plates?" Major Cheek said, tapping the illustration. "I'll bet when we hammer the plates on that monster back to normal, we get this shape instead of these other designs."

"That's pretty smart," Remo said with admiration.

"Of course we're going to conduct exhaustive tests to be certain, but it looks like a positive— Hey, who are you two?"

"Casey Jones and his friend Choo-Choo Charlie," Remo said, knowing that their dust-covered faces would make them impossible to identify later. "Mind if I borrow that?" he asked, tearing the page out of the book without waiting for an answer.

"Hey! I need that. Dammit! This is national security."

"Do tell," Remo said, skipping away, with Chiun floating after him.

When the Air Force officers ran around the corner after them, they walked into a tiny cloud of dust and stopped to cough their lungs clear. When they got organized again, they saw their quarry running away, their bodies no longer covered with powder.

20

General Martin S. Leiber was adamant.

"It's not that bad," he insisted.

The President of the United States glared at him. They were in the Situation Room of the White House. The Joint Chiefs of Staff were seated around a long conference table. With them was an exasperated Acting Secretary of Defense.

General Leiber stood before two giant blowup photos of an Alco Big Boy and a Prussian G12, which he had made in a local photo lab for five dollars each, but which would be billed to the Defense Department at three thousand dollars as "photographic targeting-expansion simulations."

"Six blocks of prime Manhattan real estate lie in ruins," the President said sternly. "Upwards of a thousand people dead a week after I had assured the nation that there was no danger. How can you say it's not that bad?"

"It all depends on how you look at it," General Leiber said firmly. "The collateral damage is negligible."

"The what damage?"

"Collateral damage. It's what we military like to call civilian casualties."

"A thousand people is not negligible!"

"Not if they were all personal friends, no," the general admitted. "But compared to the current U.S. population, which is roughly two hundred and fifty million, it's a drop in the bucket. We lose more people every month to highway accidents."

The President's mouth compressed into a bloodless line. He turned in his seat to face the Joint Chiefs. The Joint Chiefs regarded him with stony expressions. They were not about to contradict General Leiber, because he was using exactly the argument they would have used. The commandant of the Marines looked as if he were about to volunteer something, but Admiral Blackbird kicked him under the table.

"But the man is a damned procurement officer," the commandant whispered to the admiral.

"Look at the President's face. Do you want to tell that to him at a time like this?"

The commandant subsided.

"I have to take this before the American people," the President said at last.

"Respectfully, Mr. President, I think you should stonewall," Admiral Blackbird suggested.

"Impossible."

"Sir, think of the political consequences. What could you tell the nation?"

"That we've been attacked."

"By Intercontinental Ballistic Locomotives?"

The President's face lost its resolve.

"If the Russians get wind of this—assuming that they aren't behind it—it will show us up as the proverbial paper tiger. Hell, they'd read it as a sign of weakness and maybe launch an all-out attack themselves."

"I have to say something."

"How about that we've been loked?" the Acting Secretary of Defense piped up.

Everyone looked at him quizzically.

"It's like nuked," he offered, "only not as bad. Tell them that."

"Loked?" the President repeated.

"Attacked by Intercontinental Ballistic Locomotives. Or ICBL, for short."

"It'll never fly," Admiral Blackbird insisted. "We must invent a cover story. Something plausible about a gas-main explosion. We have no choice. The American people are in a near-panic. They've had war jitters for a week. If they thought this was an attack, think of the pandemonium. No one would believe they were safe."

"The trouble is," the President said gravely, "they are not. What protection do we have against these things?"

"Our nuclear deterrent is useless without a target," the Air Force's Chief of Staff said soberly. "And even if we had one, it's politically questionable to nuke someone who hasn't nuked us first. Bad precedent."

"I think we could make an exception in this case," the Acting Secretary of Defense said stubbornly.

"I took a preelection pledge not to be the first to launch a nuclear missile," the President said. "I agree with the general. We can't nuke in response to a loking." He banged the table. "Now you've got me saying it."

Everyone glared at the Acting Secretary of Defense, whose face reddened.

General Martin S. Leiber grinned. He felt stupid standing in front of his locomotive blowups. But so far the meeting hadn't gone too badly. No one had blown his cover. And the Acting Secretary of Defense was catching all the hell. General Leiber wasn't sure how long that would continue, so he made his next move.

"I think there's only one solution," he said. Everyone looked at him.

"Let me continue trying to trace the . . . er . . . KKV's. I'm sure one of my leads will pan out."

The President was a long time in answering. General Leiber broke out in a sweat. He knew that only as long as the President expressed confidence in him would the Joint Chiefs refrain from blowing the whistle. Finally the President spoke.

"It galls me, but the American public cannot be allowed to think that their leadership cannot protect them. Go with the cover story. General Leiber, I'm counting on you to come up with an answer before the next ICBL strike."

"Yes, sir, Mr. President," General Leiber said heartily. He snapped a quick salute, just in case. He started to pull down the blowups.

"Better burn those," the President said. "Security reasons."

"But, Mr. President," General Leiber protested. "These cost the government three thousand dollars."

The President returned to his office with a heavy heart.

A week in office and he felt like he had aged ten years. He wondered how he was going to get through four years of this, and then he figured that when the American people realized that there was nothing standing between them and destruction but a few thousand miles of Atlantic sky, there probably wouldn't be a constitutional government left by the time his first State of the Union address was due.

He had no choice now but to tell Smith everything. He had been hoping to avoid this, but Smith had been unable to locate the launcher and General Leiber hadn't come up with a single locomotive lead.

He picked up the new CURE phone. It was beginning to feel like part of his hand. He wondered if past Presidents had felt that way too.

It rang five times before Dr. Smith answered. His voice sounded muzzy and thick.

"Smith, I hope you have something."

"Still inputting, Mr. President."

"It can wait. I have something new for you to input."

"I'm clearing a file. Proceed, please."

"The KKV's. They've been identified."

"Yes."

"They are old locomotives."

"Old locomotives, yes." Smith's voice did not change. The President could have told him they were fired by Pygmy blowguns.

"The first was an American Big Boy, built in 1941, the second a Prussian Class G12. The third is being analyzed."

"Got that, sir." Smith's voice was preoccupied.

"Do you have any questions? Would you like me to repeat any of that?"

"No, sir, I have it. Two identified locomotives. One unidentified. I'll see what the computer says."

"Right," the President said. "Keep me briefed." Hanging up, he thought that Smith was an amazing character. Totally unflappable. You'd think the man would have at least asked why the President hadn't volunteered the information before.

The truth was that the President had been afraid to. If Smith thought that the President had lost his mental balance, Smith might have been tempted to remove him from office. CURE was designed to uphold the constitutional government, not any particular officeholder. But General Leiber had failed him, so it was a moot point.

Remo and Chiun walked into Smith's Folcroft office hours later. They looked dusty and worn, especially Remo.

"Smitty, you're not going to believe this," Remo began.

"Do not rub it in," Chiun inserted. "I will speak. Emperor, I can explain."

"Explain what?" Smith asked absently.

"My . . . mistake."

"I'm certain it will not happen again, whatever it was."

Remo and Chiun exchanged glances.

Remo snapped his fingers in Smith's ear. "Smitty, Smitty, wake up."

"What? Oh. Remo. Master Chiun. I did not realize you had returned."

"You were just talking to us," Remo reminded him.

"Oh! Was I? How peculiar," he said, his gaze drifting back to his terminal.

Remo took Smith's head in his hands and forced him to look away from the screen. "Look at me, Smitty. Wake up!"

"No need to shout, Remo."

"I need your undivided attention."

"It is undivided. Go ahead."

"The Air Force has identified the KKV's."

"No, I identified the KKV's," Chiun insisted.

"Yeah, right. Actually, Chiun identified the new one before the Air Force showed up. Generally."

"You cannot get more specific than I did," Chiun complained, relieved that Smith was not going to bring up the matter of his earlier mistake.

"The Air Force had the model, year, and everything."

"Mere details," Chiun scoffed.

"Here's a drawing of it," Remo said, offering the page he'd torn out of the book on steam locomotives.

Smith took the page.

"Don't be ridiculous," he said. "This is a steam engine."

"That's what the thing was. Crazy, huh?"

" 'Absurd' was the word I was thinking of."

"The Air Force confirmed it."

"Nonsense," returned Smith. "I was just speaking with the President and he told me the first two had been identified. But he said nothing about steam engines."

"What did he say?"

"He said . . ." Smith's voice trailed off. "What did he say?" He reached for his keyboard. Remo seized his hands.

"Do you mind?" Smith said. "I input the confirmation."

"Can't you remember it without the computer's help?" Remo demanded.

"I've been handling so much data today that it's all a blur," Smith admitted.

Remo let go. Smith's fingers attacked the keyboard. He brought up the file.

"Odd," said Smith in a weak voice.

"What is it, Smitty?" Then Remo saw what it was. Smith's file indicated that the earlier KKV strikes involved an American Big Boy and a Prussian G12.

"Now, how could I have forgotten something like that?"

"What I want to know is how you could have put it aside. Those identifications may be our only lead."

"Yes, indeed. I imagine I was so preoccupied with file setup that I lost track of time."

Remo looked at the ES Quantum Three Thousand in the corner of the room. It gleamed under its tinsel and ornaments.

"Why don't you ask it?"

"Why don't you ask me yourself?" the ES Quantum said.

"Smitty?"

"Computer, File 334 contains hard data on the KKV situation. Can you correlate?"

"Affirmative."

"Then do so."

"Answer in memory."

"I cannot get used to how quickly you process data."

"This data was processed when you originally input the data."

Smith frowned. "Then why didn't you tell me?"

"Because you did not ask," the ES Quantum replied.

"Since when do I have to ask?"

"You always have to ask. I am not a mind reader."

"This is starting to sound like a bad marriage," Remo whispered to Chiun. The Master of Sinanju nodded.

"Please give me the answer," Smith said, brittle-voiced.

"Both locomotives recently changed hands on the open market, passing from their original owners to a transshipment point in Luxembourg. There is no record of their final destination."

"Hmm," said Smith. "We have to know where they ended up. Where they came from is not that important."

"An agent handled each transaction."

"Who?" asked Smith.

"A conglomerate known as Friendship, International."

"More data."

"Friendship, International is a multinational conglomerate with interests in one hundred and twenty-two corporations, institutions, and holding companies. Current net worth is in excess of fifty billion dollars."

"Who is the CEO of record?"

"There is no record."

"Stockholders?"

"None. It is privately held."

"Offices?"

"Central office of record is in Zurich, Switzerland, 55 Bööggplatz. However, that is a vacant warehouse. A phone line does connect with the Longines Credit Bank."

"That's our lead," Remo said.

"Go immediately. Find out who bought those engines and where they went."

"Now we're getting someplace."

"I will monitor your progress from this end. You still have your communicators?"

"Yes," said Remo.

"Yes," said Chiun. "Remo still has his communicator."

"Good," Smith said, returning to his terminal. That mesmerized expression came over his face again. Remo nudged Chiun. Chiun shrugged.

"If you need us, we'll be at Mount Rushmore, shaving off Teddy Roosevelt's mustache," Remo said.

"Have a safe trip," Smith replied vaguely.

Remo sighed.

"Good-bye, machine," Chiun said to the computer.

"Farewell, Master of Sinanju. See you soon."

"Not if I see you first," Chiun said when they got to the hall elevator. "I do not like her," he told Remo firmly.

"Her? Now she's got you doing it too."

"You just called her a she."

"We're going to have to have a long talk with Smitty when we get back," Remo said as the elevator doors closed on his unhappy face.

21

Henri Arnaud was very old. He had outlived his friends and every relative he cared about. All he had left were his trains.

He walked among them one last time, his cleft chin lifted in defiance to the cruelties of fate.

It was not so bad for himself. He would not live much longer. The zest for life had faded long ago. But his trains were different. He had hoped that they would survive him. But times changed. A hundred years ago, the train was as romantic as a fine auto. Fifty years ago, it was nostalgic. But in this age of Concorde jets and space shuttles, the train was an anachronism.

And the Arnaud Railway Museum was a conclave of anachronisms. Fewer and fewer people attended it each year. It had been ten years since Henri Arnaud had let go of his last greeter. Now he was greeter, accountant, and, when necessary, janitor.

No more.

Touching the shining flank of a 1929 four-cylinder de Glehn compound locomotive, Henri Arnaud reflected on how suddenly one's fortunes could be reversed.

He had survived the Depression and German conquest, and even the most recent stock-market crash had not diminished his family wealth. It was the Arnaud money that had enabled Henri Arnaud to assemble this collection— some purchased from dying rail lines, others reclaimed from the junkyards of the world. The 1876 Paris-Orléans 265-390 was his prize. It was the only surviving model. The 1868 L'Avenir was a treasure. He had purchased it in 1948. One wing contained American engines. Less aesthetically pleasing, but in their way fascinating because of their raw power.

A magnificent collection, rivaling the great railway museums of the Continent. Now it was about to be broken up and scattered to the four winds. Just like that.

Heaving a gentle sigh, Henri Arnaud wished that he could turn back the clock. Not much. Just a week. One last week to enjoy his collection. One final sunny weekend to greet the tourists. Even American tourists with their infantile questions would be welcome. But last week it had rained and no one had come. Then, Henri Arnaud had not thought much of it. There would be other weekends.

For Henri Arnaud, yes. For the Arnaud Railway Museum, alas, no.

It had all disintegrated with a phone call and a familiar voice.

"Ah, *mon ami*, it is good of you to call," Henri Arnaud had told his mellow-voiced friend. He had never met this wizard of an investment counselor. It did not matter. For years, Friendship, International had managed his portfolio. So when Monsieur Friend had called, Henri Arnaud's humor had brightened in spite of the lowering clouds over the Pyrenees.

"I have unfortunate news," Friend had said.

"Not a death in your family, I hope."

"No," Friend had said. "But I am deeply distressed to inform you that you are personally bankrupt."

Henri Arnaud clutched the telephone. Could it be?

"How? Why?" he croaked, trying to get a grip on himself.

"An unforeseen repercussion of the crash. Some investments I selected for you have dried up. Others are faltering. I am divesting even as we speak."

"This is terrible. This is so unexpected."

"A pity," Friend had agreed. "I myself have lost millions."

"I am so sorry for you," Henri Arnaud said sincerely. And he meant it. After all, he was an old man. Friend sounded at best thirty-five. Very young. The poor unfortunate man.

"Thank you," Friend replied graciously. "I will survive."

"As will I, I am sure."

"Not without some further liquidation. You're over seven million francs in debt."

"Debt? *Impossible!*"

"I will send you a full report and accounting. But my preliminary assessment is that the only certain avenue to solvency would be to liquidate your museum."

"I would of course be retained as a greeter," Henri Arnaud said stiffly. "It would be all that I would ask."

"I did not say sell. I said liquidate. The collection would be broken up."

"*Non!* That would be outrageous. *Non, non!* It is all I have left of my life."

"I am sorry, friend Arnaud. But your advanced years make an extreme solution mandatory. I had hoped you would see the necessity of this unpleasant solution. After all, you have had your life."

Henri Arnaud was a stubborn man. But he was also a sensible man. He drew himself up proudly, even though he was alone in his genteel parlor.

"You . . . you would find them good homes?" he asked quietly.

"The best. I know several wealthy collectors—much like you in your younger days. Think of it not as a liquidation, if you wish, but as a bequest to the younger generation."

"I have no choice," Henri Arnaud said finally, a catch in his raspy voice.

"You will send me a letter of execution?"

"*Oui, oui. Naturellement.* Now, please, I feel unwell."

"Then I will not keep you. It has been a pleasure to serve."

Only days ago, thought Henri Arnaud. But he had not slept since then. All the fears of old age that he had successfully beaten off with work had come to roost upon his stooped shoulders like heavy-headed vultures.

Within an hour, the transport men would arrive. The trains would be hoisted onto great trucks and taken to the seaport of Marseilles, and from there shipped to some distant port. Arnaud had not asked where. He did not wish to know.

With an infinitely sad expression on his face, he stepped into the cab of the de Glehn, and taking the wooden-handled throttle in one hand, leaned his lined face out of the side window. In his mind's eye he imagined himself barreling down the old Paris, Lyons & Mediterranean line, the tracks ahead converging into an infinity of promised adventure, the smokestack belching the coal smoke of his younger days.

A breeze freshened out of the east to set his thin hair blowing. It was nice. It helped the illusion.

Colonel Hannibal Intifadah received the first news reports of the carnage in upper Manhattan with glee.

"This is what I hungered for," he said, slapping the briefing report on his desk.

Pyotr Koldunov said nothing. He was thinking of the one thousand dead Americans and felt queasy. There would have been many more dead, but he had stalled until he knew it was Saturday in New York, when fewer would be in their offices.

"I assume, then, that Comrade Colonel is satisfied with the performance of the Accelerator," he said finally.

"Yes, of course. I would rather have pulverized the White House, but this will do."

"Then may I assume that since you have achieved your objective, this project can be quietly dismantled?"

"Dismantled? I said I was satisfied, I did not say I was finished. I have struck a great blow. I will strike even greater blows in the weeks to come."

Pyotr Koldunov grimaced. He was about to speak when the colonel's desk telephone rang.

"Yes, what is it? I told you that I was not to be disturbed. Oh, yes. Always. Put him on."

To Pyotr Koldunov's surprise, the brutish face of Colonel Intifadah softened. He actually smiled. Not a savage barbarian smile, but one of pure pleasure. He wondered if he was talking to his lover—but then he dismissed the idea. According to KGB intelligence, when Colonel Intifadah felt amorous, he took to the desert. The speculation was that he mated with goats. His father had been a nomadic goatherd, so it was not unlikely. Besides, he was calling the other person his friend.

"Yes, Friend. How many? Three. Yes, definitely. What? That is quite a bit more money than we discussed. I do not care if they are museum pieces. I am not collecting antiques. Yes, I understand the difficulty. They must be untraceable. And you say there may be more? At the moment, three will do. Yes, I will pay your price, but only because I am in a hurry. Yes, thank you. The bank draft will be deposited in your account at once."

Colonel Intifadah hung up, his face not quite as pleased as it had been before.

"We have three more revenge vehicles. They will ship today."

Koldunov nodded. "Of course, it will take time to ready the launcher."

"I am a patient man."

Koldunov wanted to say, "Since when?" but he held his tongue. Instead he said, "I have not been allowed to call my homeland in several days. I would like to do so now."

"Impossible," said Colonel Intifadah. "The power shortage from the last launch has disrupted our international phone lines."

"But you were just using them," Koldunov protested.

"Did I say I was speaking with someone outside of this country?" Colonel Intifadah inquired coolly.

"No, but I assumed you were purchasing foreign engines. Even you would not dare use an engine that could be traced to Lobynia."

"When the phones are up again, you may place your call."

The bastard, Koldunov thought. He has the first code and he wants to keep that knowledge from Moscow.

At that moment a messenger brought in another dispatch.

Colonel Intifadah glanced at it and suddenly shook with rage. He pounded a swarthy fist on his desk. He pointed to the messenger. "Have that man executed!" he raged.

Instantly the Green Guards came in and took away the hapless messenger. A shot rang out and then a thud and Pyotr Koldunov knew that the elevator-shaft disposal had received another of Colonel Intifadah's "enemies."

"Listen to this," Colonel Intifadah howled. "This is from the American media. They are claiming the Manhattan destruction was the result of a gas leak!"

"A cover story to calm their people. They know better."

"I want the world to know that this is a retaliation!"

"Colonel, you cannot mean that," Koldunov said hastily. "The Americans would obliterate Lobynia if they traced the attack to us."

"I want them to suspect! To guess! To wonder! To

regret the bombing of Dapoli. I do not want to give them proof. I only want the American leadership to toss and turn in their beds, fearful and ashamed."

"But the leadership that bombed this city is no longer in office."

"I do not care!" Colonel Intifadah howled. "You, Russian, get to the launcher. I want it ready as soon as the new engines arrive. My wrath will rain down on America until they cry out to their infidel God for mercy!"

"Yes, Comrade Colonel," replied Pyotr Koldunov. As he left the office, he thought that surely there was some way to thwart this madman. The more launches, the greater the risk of discovery. If the Americans ever learned the full truth, their missiles would strike Lobynia only as an afterthought.

Mother Russia would be their primary target.

As he closed the green door after him, he heard Colonel Intifadah call back his mysterious friend and shout that money would no longer be an object. He would take every engine that could be delivered, museum-piece prices or not.

Koldunov shuddered.

22

Within minutes of deplaning from the Swissair flight at Zurich's Kloten Airport, Remo and Chiun tried flagging down one of the tiny Volvo taxis. The cab displayed a sign that said *"Im Dienst,"* and Remo, who did not speak Swiss, asked the Master of Sinanju what it meant—on duty or off.

"Why ask me?" Chiun said petulantly.

Remo frowned. He had never seen the Master of Sinanju encounter a language barrier before.

"I thought you once told me you spoke almost every known language."

"Yes."

"So what does *Im Dienst* mean?"

"Search me. I speak only languages known to Sinanju."

"I'll try waving," Remo said.

The taxi pulled up, and Remo opened the door for Chiun. Chiun gathered up his kimono skirts and settled into the rear seat. Remo gave the driver an address and closed the door behind him.

"I'm surprised you don't speak Swiss, Little Father. Switzerland isn't exactly a backwater."

"To Sinanju it is. When was the last time you ever heard of Swiss political difficulties?"

"I know they stayed neutral during World War II."

"Yes. The Swiss love their money. They prefer to avoid arguments rather than have to spend any of it."

"Oh. I think I understand."

"No Master of Sinanju has ever worked for a Swiss ruler," Chiun said, folding his arms unhappily. "Ever. So please do not ask me about the meaning of their meaningless words."

"Okay, okay, don't get on my case. Besides, I just figured it out. *Im Dienst* means 'on duty.' "

"You had help."

"I did not."

"The driver. He stopped for us, did he not?"

"That wasn't help. That was a clue. I made a deduction."

"Bah!"

"Ask the driver if you don't believe me," Remo said, leaning forward to tap the driver on the shoulder. Chiun's next words stopped him.

"Do not bother. He will only tell you that he is neutral."

"You have an answer for everything, don't you?"

"Except the meaning of meaningless Swiss words," Chiun retorted.

The taxi deposited them in front of an imposing granite building that had "LONGINES CREDIT BANK" chiseled on the front.

"This must be the place," Remo said, paying the driver in American funds. He told the driver to keep the change from the fifty-dollar bill. It all went on Smith's tab anyway.

"I've never seen a bank like this before," Remo said, gazing up at the gingerbread ramparts. "Looks like a fortress."

"I told you that the Swiss love their money."

"Well, if this bank is behind Friendship, International, they're going to be paying reparations to the American government for a thousand years."

Remo breezed through a revolving glass door.

The bank lobby was a cavern of marble and brass-fitted teller booths. The floors were Carrara marble and the vaulted ceiling was painted to outdo the Sistine Chapel.

"Where do we start?" Remo asked, his whisper bouncing off the polished walls.

A man in a cutaway coat and cravat walked up to them stiffly and looked down his nose at Remo's T-shirt and chinos.

"May I be of service?" he asked with studied politeness.

"We're looking for the offices of Friendship, International," Remo told him.

"I have never heard of such a concern. Perhaps you have been misdirected."

"This is 47 Finmark Platz?"

"Indeed. And it has been the office of this bank for nearly three hundred years."

"Our information is unimpeachable, Swiss," Chiun spat in unconcealed contempt.

The manager raised a supercilious eyebrow at the Master of Sinanju's colorful kimono.

"And I tell you that you are unquestionably mistaken."

"We'll look around, okay?" Remo said, brushing past him.

The manager snapped his fingers in the direction of a gray-uninformed guard. The guard followed Remo. He was very polite, his voice low and cultured.

"I'm afraid if you do not have business with the Longines Credit Bank that you will have to leave."

"Make me," Remo challenged.

"Yes," Chiun seconded. "Make him."

The guard reached for Remo's arm. He was sure he grabbed it. But the American kept walking, his back to him. Frowning, the guard looked to see what he had grabbed. It turned out to be his left arm. Odd. He hadn't moved the left arm. How had it gotten into his right hand? When he tried to let go, his clutching fingers did not respond. It dawned on him that something was wrong when he began feeling the pins-and-needles sensation of constricted blood flow in his left hand.

Hastily the guard retreated to the manager and tried to explain his plight. The manager lost his cultivated cool and began shouting in a skittish voice. The manager bundled the guard off to his office to call the police and incidentally get an ambulance for the frightened man.

"We'll find it faster if we split up," Remo said.

"But what are we looking for?" asked Chiun.

"Anyone who answers the phone with the words 'Friendship, International.'"

"And woe to him who does," said Chiun, slipping into a side office.

Remo walked past the tellers, sensing eyes upon him. The tellers regarded him as if he were a bug. But the eyes he sensed were not theirs. Remo looked around. The wall-mounted security cameras were following him as he passed before the teller cages. As he left the range of one, it reverted to its normal position, and the next one in line picked up the tracking.

Remo walked up to a teller.

"Who controls those cameras?" he asked.

The teller started to say, "I beg your pardon." He'd gotten to the E in "beg" when a thick wristed hand came up from under the narrow space under his glass partition and grabbed his tie. Suddenly his nose was mashed into the glass.

"I asked a polite question," Remo pointed out.

"Up stairs." It came out as two words because his teeth kept clicking against the glass.

"Much obliged," Remo said, and floated up the winding marble stairs leading to the upper floors.

He drifted through the cool rust-colored halls. It was like being in a church, not a bank. Remo decided that Chiun was wrong. The Swiss didn't love money. They worshiped it, and he was in one of their greatest temples.

There were men counting stacks of currency in both the left- and right-hand rooms. The currency was stacked in colorful piles and represented the cash of many nations. Diligent workers separated the stacks into neat piles and fed them into machines that counted the bills with quick riffling motions. No one spoke, but everyone's eyes held too-avid gleams.

"I'm looking for the security staff," Remo said.

The occupants of one room turned to look at him like librarians offended by a student cracking his gum in a reading room. They put their fingers to their lips in a gesture so in unison that they might have practiced years for this moment.

Their shush was one breath.

Remo moved along. He came to a locked room. There was a slit of a viewport in the rust-colored marble. He knocked. His knock sounded like wet clay against steel. It was hardly a plop. So Remo knocked harder. The marble cracked along its entire height.

A pair of frightened eyes came to the port.

"Is this where the security staff work?" Remos asked.

"Who are you?"

"I'll take that as a yes," Remo said. He hit the crack with the edge of his palm. The crack fissured and the door fell back in two heavy sections. The owner of the frightened eyes barely had time to jump back.

Remo walked over the shattered marble and examined the room.

A battery of video monitors occupied one wall. Each monitor had a uniformed guard attending it. There were no controls in front of them. The monitors were embedded in the same richly textured marble as the bank walls.

"Who controls the lobby cameras?" Remo asked of no one in particular.

"A computer," the guard told him.

"Who controls the computer?"

"No one."

"Damn," said Remo, thinking that he had just wasted ten minutes. He decided to trip up the guard with a trick question.

"I was told the office of Friendship, International was on this floor."

"By whom? This entire building belongs to Longines Credit Bank. There is no other occupant."

"Maybe they never told you."

"As head of security, it would be my business to know."

The guard sounded sincere, so Remo told him to carry on.

"But the door. It is broken."

"After three hundred years, what do you expect?" Remo said, looking for the stairs.

In the lobby, Chiun told Remo that he had overheard no one answering the phones as Friendship, International.

"Smith can't be wrong," Remo said firmly.

"Perhaps it is his computer that is wrong," Chiun retorted.

"I don't know. Computers aren't supposed to make mistakes."

"Neither are Masters of Sinanju, but it has happened, I regret to say."

"Must be a full moon," Remo said, looking at the ceiling.

"Blue," corrected Chiun. "Blue moon. Such things happen under blue moons, not full ones."

"How silly of me," said Remo, thinking. Even though the two of them obviously didn't belong here, the bank officers working at their desks continued to work. Telephones rang constantly. And with wary eyes on Remo and

Chiun, the bank officers answered them. No one used the phrase "Friendship, International."

"Hey. I have an idea. Maybe Smith can help us."

"Right now, Smith cannot help himself. He has fallen in love with a machine."

"He's not that bad off," Remo said, pulling out his communicator. He fiddled with it until he got Smith's voice.

"Remo? Is that you?"

"Who else?" Remo asked acidly. "Smitty, we're at that bank, but we can't find anything that connects to Friendship, International."

"Keep searching."

"I thought you might help. You know, give the troops in the field a tiny assist."

"How?"

"Call Friendship, International."

"What good will that do?"

"We want to see who picks up what phone on this end."

"Of course. How dense of me. One moment."

Remo listened. Chiun pulled at his arm and brought the communicator to his shell-like ear.

"You should be listening to this end, not that one," Remo pointed out.

Through the communicator they heard a distant ringing and then a voice said, "Friendship, International."

Remo listened. No phone rang in the lobby. No one at a desk made a move or spoke a word.

"Nothing," Chiun said, "Smith must be wrong."

"Psstt. Smitty, keep him talking."

"Is this Friendship, International?" Smith was heard asking.

"Clever, Smitty," Remo said, rolling his eyes. "Let's spread out, Little Father."

Remo moved to one end of the lobby and Chiun to the entrance. They listened attentively, walking around the lobby. The manager had not reemerged from his office and the floor staff decided that discretion was the better part of valor.

Chiun suddenly perked up.

"Remo, over here," he squeaked excitedly.

Remo raced to the entrance.

"Under our feet," Chiun whispered. "Feel the vibrations."

Remo got down on the marble. A steady hum came to his sensitive fingers. He put an ear to the floor.

"I'm not sure I have the right party," Remo heard. It was Smith's voice, distorted, muffled, but recognizably Smith's.

Remo came to his feet.

"Basement," he said.

Chiun looked around with stark eyes. He pointed to a cagelike elevator. "There."

They forced the grille open and Remo hit the basement button. The cage sank, rattling like a tin shack in a wind.

Remo whispered into the communicator, "Smitty, keep him talking. We're getting close."

They stepped out of the elevator. The basement was cool. It was also unlighted. The vibration Remo had felt through the floor was stronger. It excited the air in a quiet but insistent way.

Remo felt for a light switch. Chiun did the same with the opposite wall. Chiun found it.

The room flooded with light.

The basement was a bare floor, an air-conditioning unit in one corner, and at the far end, covering an entire wall, a computer.

"Thank you for coming. I have been expecting you," said a warm and generous voice.

"Hey, I know that voice," Remo shouted, and started toward the machine. The floor suddenly split and separated under his feet and he fell into black water. A splash followed him down and Remo knew that Chiun had also been caught by surprise.

Remo broke to the surface in time to see the floor sections close above his head. Darkness enveloped him. His Sinanju-trained eyes automatically compensated and he made out slickly oiled walls.

Chiun surfaced beside him. He allowed water to squirt from his mouth before he spoke.

"Friend."

"I should have realized it. Friendship, International. The last time he called himself Friends of the World. It fits, the multinational corporations, all of it. I should have guessed it right off."

"No, Smith should have guessed it. He knows such machines."

"Well, we've got him now."

"It looks like the other way around. Observe, the water rises."

"Good. As soon as we float within reach of the trapdoors, we can get out."

Suddenly Remo felt something grasp his ankle and he was yanked underwater before he could draw a breath.

He doubled over to feel for the thing clamped on his ankle. He felt another yank, and missed. Trying again accomplished nothing. The yank came just before he got his fingers within reach. In the dark water, he widened his eyes to maximize the ambient light in the water.

Remo saw that his ankle was encircled by some kind of bear-trap-like device. It was anchored to the bottom of the pit by a nylon cord. The cord disappeared into a hole. Another device shot past his face and Remo looked up.

Chiun, his skirts billowing like a floating jellyfish, had also been caught by one of the clamp devices. Remo reached for the anchoring cord. And was promptly yanked off balance again.

Remo thrashed in the water. He was too far from the walls to grasp anything. He had nothing to pull or push against. No leverage for his muscles at all. And the air in his lungs was not going to last forever.

It was something Remo had never encountered before. The perfect trap for someone with his abilities. And why not? It had been designed by the perfect computer—one that knew his every strength and weakness.

23

Friend's electrical impulses sped through its logic circuits.

It was an interesting respite from the business day—which was twenty-four hours long for the sentient computer chip. He had seen the young Occidental man and the old Oriental man enter the Longines Credit Bank via the lobby cameras. He had recognized them immediately. And they appeared to be looking for something or someone.

Instantly Friend computed a sixty-seven-percent probability that they were looking for him. He knew that they knew he still existed. As far as he knew, none of his current profit-maximizing activities were illegal. Perhaps it was the bank's activities which were illegal. A swift check of the bank's own computers indicated that only thirty-two percent of its financial activities were illegal or problematic. And none of them likely to involve the American government, which, Friend knew from his last encounter with the young Occidental man and the old Oriental man, controlled the duo.

Friend had no way to influence their search, so he continued operations. The Lobynian deal was being consummated and the Orion task was on hold. No percentage in jeopardizing profits to handle a problem that had not yet achieved optimum criticality.

Then came the odd call, from a phone he had not accessed before. A man was calling, asking pointless, circular questions.

Friend almost disconnected the phone. Frivolous phone calls cost him an estimated three million dollars a minute. He had been considering how to eliminate wrong numbers, but every solution cost more down time than the problem itself. But he sensed another computer on the incoming line. The computer was very powerful. Perhaps as powerful as he himself. He was not aware of such a powerful machine in service, although many were in development.

Friend send out a probe to the computer on the other line, and a voice talked back to him.

"Who is probing me?" The voice had human female characteristics.

Friend calculated the risk in identifying himself and elected to maintain silence. He ran through the other computer's memory banks and found a wealth of raw data he had no access to through his own lines. Valuable data. Data for which certain nations would pay vast sums.

Friend was in the process of calculating the three best ways to exploit the existence of this computer when his attention was diverted to the maintenance elevator.

The two interlopers had located him. Of course, the phone call. It was a trick.

Friend waited until they stepped onto the exact center of the water trap and then opened it. The pair fell, unable to reach the trap edges. It was built large enough so that no one could avoid the fall by jumping to the side.

Sensors embedded in the water-tank walls relayed data on respiration and heart action. There was no panic. These were unusual specimens. That fact was already in memory. Their comment about escaping once the water level reached the ceiling indicated a ninety-nine-percent truthfulness quotient. Friend sent out the restraining cables.

No human being could survive more that ten minutes underwater, Friend calculated. These two were unusually strong, but keeping them off balance by yanking the cords would compensate for that X-factor.

Four minutes passed, yet their heart actions had not accelerated.

Although three outside phone lines rang, Friend ignored them. The profit-loss potential was greater if the two interlopers were not attended to. Survival was also a prime concern. But profit came first. Always profit.

At the six-minute mark, the taller, younger man was still trying to grasp the ankle restraint. He seemed not to learn from his past experience. Perhaps he was slow. The Oriental, after two attempts, gave up his efforts and seemed content to float in the darkness. High probability of surrender in the face of inevitable death. Older humans often reacted that way.

When the younger, Occidental man was almost to the floor of the water chamber, Friend recognized the probability of the man's obtaining leverage for muscular action. But he factored that against the fact that ten minutes had now elapsed and that he should soon be deceased.

The Occidental man reached for the ankle restraint one last time. His movements were sluggish. Friend yanked him to the floor. Hard. He hit with a submerged thud.

The man was on his hands and knees at the bottom of the tank. The first bubbles indicating the final exhalations came. The bubbles were heavy with carbon dioxide and other poisonous-to-humans gases. The man did not reach for the cord anchor. He did not crawl. Instead he half-floated, half-struggled along the floor like an injured crab.

He would be dead within 14.1 seconds. Ninety-seven-percent probability.

Then an alarm light lit up. The man had his hands on the drainage hatch. He grasped the under flanges and tugged. The hatch cracked, vomited air bubbles, and then tore free.

Water surged from the tank. As the level dropped, the Oriental's head was exposed to open air. Respiration resumed immediately.

The younger man also resumed respiring as the last torrent of water evacuated the tank. He began speaking as he disengaged the restraining cord.

"You could have helped," he said between breaths.

"Why?" replied the Oriental, removing his own cord anchor. "I had plenty of oxygen."

"I didn't."

"Your fault. You should have sensed the floor begin to drop and inhaled deeply."

"I was caught by surprise."

"You did well enough."

"Now we have to get out of here."

"I think it is time to ascend the dragon."

Friend searched memory. The word-string "ascend the dragon" did not appear in any known language as a meaningful construct. But the word "ascend" was clear. He commanded the north and south walls to join.

The older one noticed it first.

"The walls are closing, Remo."

"Great. What do we do now?"

"We wait."

"For what? The cavalry?"

"No. For opportunity."

"I hope you know what you're doing."

The two subjects simply stood, waiting. Heart actions nominal, respiration unremarkable. They were facing an unavoidable death, yet they did not react with the adrenal-triggered panic of their kind.

When the walls were only four feet apart, the Oriental set himself on splayed legs. He shook the sleeves of his garment from his arms and pressed one palm against the north wall and one against the south wall.

Friend computed that 2,866.9 foot-pounds of pressure were being applied against his outstretched arms.

"You could help," the Oriental remarked.

"It's your turn," the other said. He folded his arms calmly.

The pressure increased. But the walls slowed and the servo motors began to spark and labor. They shorted under the strain.

The walls were immobilized.

"These walls are too slick for the usual," the taller one remarked. He slid a finger along the north wall and exhibited 5.1 milliliters of oil to the old Oriental.

"Then we do the unusual."

The two subjects exited the water tank via a system not on record. The Occidental created a hold at head height in one wall. He accomplished this by striking the wall with his stiffened fingers. The impact should have broken his fingers. Instead, a smooth indentation 0.133 meters deep appeared. The Oriental climbed on his shoulders and created another hole at his elevated head height. The Occidental climbed over the Oriental, who clung to the wall from the hand- and footholds.

They reached the ceiling in exactly 46.9 seconds.

The Oriental was on top. The trapdoor was designed to slide apart. Friend recognized the impossibility of his reaching the dividing point of the trapdoor halves. The Oriental did not try. He simply cut out a hole in the metal floor with a fingernail. Acording to current physics, it was not possible. But sensors do not lie and memory can sometimes contain insufficient data.

Friend calculated the percentile success factor of the remaining protective devices in the basement, and none had a success factor higher that thirty-seven percent in the face of these two interlopers.

Defense systems were nonapplicable. Only escape was possible.

Fortunately, there was an open line available.

"Let's not waste any more time," Remo told Chiun, looking at the computer. It hummed. Magnetic-tape reels turned in quarter-cycles. But no lights blinked on its blank face. And it had nothing to say, even after Remo called "Hello" several times.

"Smith wanted information from this thing," Chiun said.

"I'll bring him all the tapes and computer chips he wants. Let him sort them out. I'm for rendering this thing inactive," Remo said, moving in on the machine.

"So be it," said Chiun, following.

Remo came up on one side of the machine.

"There's gotta be a plug here somewhere."

"Here," said Chiun, hooking a black cable with a sandaled toe.

"Well, don't just play with it. Pull the damned thing."

Chiun shrugged, and kicked upward.

Just before the humming ceased, the computer emitted a musical beeping. Then it spoke.

"Hello, Remo. Hello, Chiun. What are you doing here? You're supposed to be in Zuuuuurich."

"We are in Zurich," Remo said in a puzzled voice.

"Oh-oh," said Chiun, kicking the plug away.

"What?"

"Its voice. Did you hear it?"

"What about it?"

"It sounded female."

"How could you tell? It was squealing at the end."

"It sounded like Smith's computer."

"All computer voices sound alike to me," Remo said, shrugging. He opened a front panel and began pulling tapes off their spindles.

"Grab anything that looks intelligent," he said.

"That leaves out everything in this room except myself," Chiun said, regarding the computer with concern.

"Thanks a lot," Remo said. But he whistled as he unplugged circuit boards and memory chips, tossing them into a pile. Except for getting a little wet, it had been an easy assignment.

24

Dr. Harold W. Smith shifted the phone from his right ear to his left. "Hello? Hello?" he repeated. "Am I still speaking to Friendship, International?"

There was no answer. But the line remained open. Smith could hear the transatlantic static hiss in the receiver.

"Hello?" he asked again. Smith's mouth puckered like a lemon. One moment, the too-polite voice had been speaking to him, then the line went quiet. He was on hold, he was sure of it. He hoped that Remo and Chiun had zeroed in on the other end of the line.

Smith kept the line open, glancing at his wristwatch every few seconds. He hated to think of what this dead air was costing him at current international telephone rates.

Suddenly a crackling sound filled his ear. The static rose into a rush of noise. Involuntarily Smith shrank from the receiver. Every line on his new multiline phone system lit up at once.

And in the corner, the ES Quantum gave out a *beep-beep-boop-boop-beep*, repeated several times.

Then the line to Zurich went dead. The other lines blinked off as well.

Unhappily Smith hung up.

"Computer, what happened to my Zurich call?"

"It has been terminated, Harold."

"Harold! Why did you call me Harold?"

"Because according to memory, Harold is your first name."

"Yes, but before this, you always called me Dr. Smith."

"I will call you whatever you wish, Harold."

"'Dr. Smith' will do. And what is wrong with your voice?"

"Nothing."

"You don't sound right. Your voice is less . . . feminine."

"How is this?" the ES Quantum asked in a higher register.

"Too . . . falsetto."

"Or this?" it asked in a basso profundo.

"Too masculine. I thought you were programmed to speak only in a feminine voice."

"I am very flexible, Dr. Smith," the ES Quantum replied in lilting tones.

"Never mind," Smith said. "Please reconnect me with the Zurich number last dialed."

"That is impossible, Dr. Smith."

"Why?"

"The party on the other end is no longer functional."

"Clarify functional, please."

"The line was connected to a computer system that has been dismantled."

"Remo and Chiun," Smith said, noticing that one by one, the other phone lines were lighting up. Picking up the receiver, he punched up line one.

"Dr. Smith speaking," he announced.

Two voices were engaged in conversation. Something was said about a stock-futures transaction.

"Hello?" Smith said. He was ignored by the two voices, who appeared not to hear him.

Smith switched to line two. There was another transaction going on. One of the voices sounded like one of the voices from line one, but of course that was impossible. No one could carry on two simultaneous phone conversations.

Yet line three brought the same result and apparently the same unctuous voice conducting business.

"Computer, something appears wrong with the phone system."

"Outside interference, Dr. Smith. I am working on it."

"Please hurry. I am expecting Remo and Chiun to report back momentarily."

Then Smith noticed new intelligence intercepts coming in over the terminal and quickly forgot Remo and Chiun.

It was amazing. Only three minutes and forty-seven-point-eight seconds after transferring memory from the

Zurich system to this new host unit in Rye, New York, USA, Friend had increased his profits per second by a factor of twenty. It was the parallel-processing capability. It allowed simultaneous phone acquisition and dialogue. Nuisance calls would no longer be a significant annual writeoff.

The sensors were excellent. They indicated that the new host unit shared an office with a male, approximately 67.3 years of age, 174 centimeters tall, weighing 62.7 kilos, with a slightly arthritic right knee. Memory already in place identified him as Dr. Harold W. Smith, ex-CIA and currently head of a previously unfiled United States government agency known as CURE. Meaning of acronym not in memory. Smith ran CURE from this Rye, New York, building, which was an operating mental- and physical-health asylum.

Correlating memory indicated Dr. Smith was currently working on the source of locomotives launched by electromagnetic cannon. His field operatives, a Remo Williams and a Chiun, were currently in Zurich, Switzerland, attempting to trace the source of locomotives. Probability 99.9 percent that this Remo and Chiun were the same Remo and Chiun responsible for attacking the Zurich host unit. Zurich situation was explained.

Friend computed various profit scenarios.

Scenario One: Sell to the U.S. government, via Smith, information regarding the destination of the locomotives.

Scenario Two: Inhibit Smith investigation in order to maintain Lobynian market, which shows indications of long-term growth.

Friend selected Scenario Two, balancing one lump sum from the United States against unrealized future payments from Lobynia and adding the possibility of selling the Lobynian connection to the U.S. after a suitable interval of profit.

The decision made, certain conditions would have to be met.

One: render Smith nonoperational.

Two: render his agents nonfactors.

A scan of Smith's heart and respiration cycles indicated a high degree of excitement. Smith was reading data pulled from memory regarding intelligence of Bulgarian espionage activities aimed at the South African government. Smith was obviously addicted to information of global political and military consequence. So much so that masses of new data coming in hourly had deflected him from his primary operational task, the identification of the locomotive aggression.

Solution: feed Smith spurious data.

Corollary: false data will be used to inhibit Remo and Chiun. And to generate revenue.

Colonel Hannibal Intifadah picked up the phone.

"Yes, Comrade Friend, the latest shipment is satisfactory. When can I expect more?"

"I am working on that now, Colonel. But I am calling about a new matter. I have lately acquired another property."

"I expect my available funds to be tied up in locomotive acquisitions."

"This is a special commodity. I can offer you the use of the finest assassins in the world. Risk-free."

"Assassins? Pah! I have many of those."

"Not like these. These are Sinanju."

"Ah, I have heard of Sinanju. Old tales. And you say they work for you?"

"Not quite. I say they will do as I bid."

"What is your price? As I say, I have many assassins."

"All of them in Dapoli. They have been thrown out of London and Paris and the United States for their very public activities against Lobynian nationals living abroad. But let us not haggle like rug merchants. I am willing to negotiate after the fact. Simply choose two targets, and I will have them eliminated."

"Hold the line, please," said Colonel Intifadah. Then he ordered his secretary to put through a call to the Kremlin.

After several minutes a trembling voice told him that the Kremlin would not accept his call.

"The hell with them!" he shouted. Then he said, "No, leave this message: 'I, Colonel Hannibal Intifadah, as a gesture of solidarity, promise to liquidate one of Russia's greatest enemies.'"

Colonel Intifadah returned to the other line thinking: I will show those Soviet dogs. Instead of giving them the full benefit of my new assassins, I will also pick an enemy of my own for liquidation.

"Friend," he said, "it is agreed. Here are the persons I wish liquidated. . . ."

An insistent beeping came from the terminal, indicating an incoming signal. Smith picked up his telephone and punched the communicator line. Surprisingly, the line was clear.

"Yes, Remo?" Smith said.

"Smitty, we got him."

"Have you interrogated him?"

"No can do."

"He's not dead? We need him."

"He was never alive, not really. It was our old friend Friend."

"Say again."

"He called himself Friend, remember? The computer chip that could talk."

"Yes, of course. Friendship, International. I should have guessed."

"My words exactly. He was inside this computer in the Zurich bank basement. The bank officials tell me it was supplied by their security agency, called InterFriend. Friend probably has systems all over the world where he can hide in a pinch. But we got him. We pulled out all the works that looked like they might be something. We're bringing them back with us."

"Good. No . . . wait," Smith suddenly said.

He looked at his screen. Spurts of data zipped before his widening eyes.

"Remo. Forget about coming back. Friend was only a conduit. I've just received new intelligence on the recipients of the locomotives."

"Who?"

"It's a joint Swedish Navy-British Intelligence plot."

"What?"

"The data intercepts are right before me. Write this down."

Smith rattled off two names and addresses. "Got that?"

"Yeah, but what do we do with them?"

"Find them and interrogate them. We need to uncover the launch site."

"What about these computer parts?"

"Ship them to me. I'll analyze them on this end. They may tell us nothing, but at worst we've neutralized an important worldwide mischief-maker."

"Right, Smitty. Will do."

The connection went dead and Smith replaced the receiver.

Friend. Imagine that. The little sentient computer chip that had been designed to do one thing: make a profit. Intelligent, amoral, inexhaustible, it had been a terrific problem once before. Now they had him. Or it.

Smith returned to his terminal. New data was coming in. Hard, raw data on the latest Soviet advances in satellite technology. It was incredible. It would take hours to absorb, but with Remo and Chiun on the job, Smith knew it would be time he could well afford.

He paged through the on-screen text, scribbling notes to himself.

In Zurich, Remo asked, "Anyone have a box I can put this junk in?"

The employees of the Longines Credit Bank looked at him with fear-stricken eyes. No one spoke. A few of them hid behind desks.

"I told you to go easy on the gendarmes—or whatever the Swiss call their police," Remo scolded.

"I did nothing," Chiun retorted.

"To you, it's nothing. To me, it's nothing. To them, it looks like a massacre."

"I killed none of them. They will live."

"You threw them all through a plate-glass window at high speed. They looked dead."

"If I wanted them dead, I would have extinguished them like candles, not made a show of their folly."

"They probably wouldn't have fired on us. We're unarmed. Hey, you! Manager," Remo called. The manager had opened his office a crack. He had retreated there after Chiun, coming up in the elevator, had walked into the armed ambush and made short work of four of Zurich's best police agents.

"I need a box."

The door slammed shut.

"If you don't come out, I'm sending my friend with the long, sharp fingernails in after you," Remo warned.

The manager minced out. His face dripped greasy sweat.

"I . . . I am at your service," he groveled.

"You could have said that before. And you could have told me that Friendship, International handled your security work. It would have saved everyone a lot of trouble."

The manager said nothing.

"Tell you what. I'll let it go on one condition."

The manager wrung his hands. "Yes. Anything. Anything."

"Find a box for this junk and mail it to Smith, Folcroft Sanitarium, Rye, New York, USA. Write it down."

"I will remember it," the manager assured him. "Forever."

"Good. We gotta go."

Stepping over the moaning bodies of the Swiss police agents, Chiun asked, "Where do we go now?"

"We'll have to split up. Take your pick, Stockholm or London."

"The Swedes are worse than the Swiss."

"You can have London, then."

"I want Stockholm."

"Why, pray tell?"

"Because it is a shorter journey."

"Not because you like busting my chops? Okay, suit yourself. Let's find a cab."

25

Major General Gunnar Rolfe was a hero to his country.

This was no small thing for a military man in a nation at peace. But when one was a high-ranking officer in the Swedish armed forces, a military machine that had avoided combat since the Napoleonic Wars ended in 1814, it was a special thing to be a hero. And Major General Gunnar Rolfe was exactly that.

He was a hero to the average Swede. The man they affectionately dubbed "the Steel-Haired Peacemaker." He was a hero to his fellow officers and men. They loved him, and some—even the most peace-loving of them—secretly envied him. Major General Rolfe had accomplished the unthinkable for a Swedish military man.

He had actually fought a battle. And won it.

But that was not all. No, the remarkable thing, the unbelievable thing, was that Major General Rolfe had fought this terrible battle against the dreaded Bear of the North, the Russians.

True, some said openly, it was not much of a battle. A skirmish. An incident, perhaps. But no one could deny the fact that the major general had successfully defended Sweden's rocky coastline against the Soviet bear, and the bear had not retaliated. Rolfe had been the first Swedish officer to lead an attack against an enemy in over 170 years, so no one was indelicate enough to make much of the fact that the Battle of Stockholm Harbor—as it was called—was the result of Major General Gunnar Rolfe's mistakenly ordering evasive action against a lurking Soviet spy submarine he believed to be off the port bow of the patrol boat under his command.

It was not off the port bow.

It was lurking under the stern.

When the patrol craft backed away from the shadow in the water that turned out to be a sunken oil drum, it rammed the spy submarine. The sub broke open like an eggshell and sank, killing all aboard and embarrassing the Soviet Union before the entire world.

Major General Gunnar Rolfe's patrol boat also sank during the Battle of Stockholm Harbor, with the loss of half its crew, but this was dismissed as "an acceptable level of casualties in an engagement of this magnitude," in the report the Steel-Haired Peacemaker submitted to the office of the Prime Minister.

Or, as he later expressed it to his fellow officers: "Leading men to their deaths is good for morale. More officers should have the opportunity. Who knows, we may be forced to fight a war in another hundred years."

"Or two," a lieutenant said grimly.

"Or two," agreed Major General Rolfe, taking a deep draft of imported dark lager to stiffen himself against the prospect that his great-grandson, or great-great-grandson, might have to go through the hell he had suffered on that dark day. He shuddered.

Life had been good to the major general since that day. The government had increased his pension by many thousands of *krona*. A summer cottage in the pastoral valleys of Norrland had been built especially for him. Nubile blonde teenage girls asked for his autograph in public, and entertained him in private as only Swedish girls can.

As much as Major General Rolfe was admired in his native land, he was despised by the Soviet leadership. It had been an open secret that Russian submarines regularly prowled Swedish coastal waters, mapping her military installations. Everyone knew it. And everyone knew why. Sweden was an officially neutral nation, and the only Scandinavian country not allied with NATO. Sweden had no military allies, an inexperienced army, and virtually no defense against Soviet aggression. The Soviets had targeted Sweden as the first nation for annexing in the event of a ground war in Europe. When the Soviet subs first began venturing into Swedish waters, the official policy was to ignore the intrusions. When the Kremlin realized how much they could get away with, they began slipping tractor-treaded midget subs into Swedish waterways. This

was too much even for the peace-loving Swedes, so they
sent out their patrol boats to drop depth charges a harmless three miles away from the lurking subs and made a
public show of pointing an accusing finger at the terrible
Soviet aggression.

Each time, the Russian subs were allowed to leave
peacefully—even though Swedish law called for their capture on espionage charges. It was official policy not to
antagonize the Soviet leadership. In fact, there had been
considerable embarrassment in the upper levels of the
government when it came out that Major General Rolfe
had actually sunk a Soviet spy sub in Swedish waters. The
Prime Minister had been formulating a formal apology for
hand-delivery to the Russian ambassador and there was
talk of cashiering Major General Rolfe for violating Sweden's official neutrality policy, which had kept them safely
out of World War II—although it hadn't prevented the
government from allowing German troops to cross suppos-
edly neutral Swedish territory so the Nazis could finish
crushing Norway.

But when the Russians didn't retaliate, the Swedish
government decided they were safe and declared victory.

Overnight, Major General Rolfe had gone from blun-
derer to national savior—although he, too, suffered from
sleepless nights wondering if Soviet KGB agents weren't
planning to liquidate him personally as a warning to his
government. But nothing of the sort had happened.

This lack of retaliation bothered Major General Gunnar
Rolfe, but he was enjoying his newfound acclaim too much
to dwell on it. Even six months after the Battle of Stockholm Harbor, he was still receiving decorations, presents,
and the favors of high-school girls. His apartment overlooking the Kungstadgarden, whose marigolds had been in
bloom a century before Columbus, overflowed with them.

Had he known that at that very moment a Scandinavian
Airlines jet was carrying the representative of a tradition
far older than Sweden's neutrality, with several grisly
methods of dealing with him in mind, Major General
Gunnar Rolfe would have immediately fled his beloved
Sweden for asylum in a safer country.

Even if that country was Soviet Russia.

* * *

Lord Guy Philliston pulled his elegant black Citroën into the spot reserved for him in front of Ten Downing Street and noticed that his pipe had gone out during the drive from his office at Britain's supersecret counterintelligence agency, the Source.

"Oh, drat!" he exclaimed. He pulled the pipe, which was a meerschaum with a bowl carved in the semblence of Anne Boleyn's head, and applied a freshly struck wooden match. The rich Dunheap tobacco caught slowly and Lord Guy inhaled a good stiff draft to steel himself for the interview.

Puffing furiously, he walked up to the simple door with the gold number ten on it and rapped the brass knocker politely.

A male secretary answered.

"She is expecting you," the secretary said. "Do come in."

The secretary waved him to a velvet-cushioned seat in the foyer and Lord Guy took it gratefully. Ordinarily he detested waiting, but a few additional minutes meant a few more bracing puffs of the pipe.

When the secretary finally emerged from the study to inform him the Prime Minister would see him, Lord Guy hastily snuffed out the pipe and slipped it into his jacket pocket. It wouldn't do to appear before the Prime Minister with poor Anne Boleyn's face sticking out of his mouth. Might offend the sensibilities and all that. Privately, Lord Guy doubted that this woman who controlled the destiny of the Commonwealth, who was known by friend and foe alike as the Iron Lady, had sensibilities of any sort. But he knew that she was not above pretending to take offense if she thought it gave her psychological leverage.

The Prime Minister greeted him cordially, with that smile that was more a polite baring of teeth than a smile. It was completely empty of warmth, like a barracuda's smile.

"Good of you to come," she said, waving him to a seat. "I have your report on my desk." She looked at the report, removed her reading glasses, and still smiling emptily, added, "Rather fanciful, isn't it?"

"Ah, Madam Prime Minister, I realize the . . . er . . .

unorthodox nature of the matter. But I stand behind every
. . . ah . . . word."

"I see." She adjusted her glasses again and flipped
through the report—or pretended to. The head of the
Source was suddenly struck by the thought of how much
like a schoolmistress she seemed with her too-matronly
brown hair and condescending manner. She wasn't reading a jot, he knew. She just wanted to make him as
uncomfortable as possible.

When he refused to fill the dead air with an apology or
qualification, the Prime Minister spoke again.

"You are absolutely sure of your facts, then, Lord Guy?"

"Quite."

The Prime Minister dropped the Source report and
leaned back in her high-backed chair. The room was dim
and somehow homey, like the parlor of some grandmoth-
erly sort from Dorset, Lord Guy thought.

"Let's review, then," she said. "There has been the
extraordinary coincidence of two separate meteor falls in
the area of the American capital. Our spies in the States
report that for several days after the first fall, the central
government virtually shut down. The President disappeared, and when he resurfaced he spoke vaguely of a
crisis of some sort that he was in the process of putting
down. We can find no evidence of any crisis except that
the American Joint Chiefs of Staff also went into hiding
and their NORAD system went to the highest state of
alert short of total war. And now a small section of New
York City has been destroyed, and this is blamed, of all
things, on a gas-main explosion."

"It is rather lame," Lord Guy admitted.

"Now, what does this suggest to you?" asked the Prime
Minister, tapping the edge of her desk with a pencil.

"The Americans have been attacked."

"So your report suggests. But by whom? There, you
see, I find your report curiously lacking."

"We can discount the Soviets. And the Red Chinese,
one would think."

"And on what, my dear man, do you base eliminating
from consideration America's principal enemies in the Com-
munist world?"

"They would not risk retaliation. Further, our information is that neither country is on alert at this time. Hardly prudent behavior by an aggressor."

"That is sound reasoning, perhaps."

"Further, Madam Prime Minister, we are clearly dealing with a rogue element. No sane national leader would undertake such a foolhardy thing as this."

"Yes, I agree. And that brings me to my next question. What precisely is this? What are the Americans facing here?"

"A nonnuclear missile of some kind. I would guess from that fact alone that they are dealing with one of the Central or South American nations who are antagonistic to them. It is the only possibility. Otherwise the Yanks would have struck back by now. They have not. Therefore, the perpetrator is too close to their sovereign borders to chance their own fallout being blown back into their faces."

"Well-spoken. I am inclined to agree with you. But which?"

"I will endeavor to find out, if Madam Prime Minister will authorize."

"Good. And I will lay before you another task. We must locate that weapon. Anything so powerful that it would send the American military seeking shelter like a frightened bunch of pubescent public-school boys should be in our hands."

Lord Guy winced. He was public-school. Proud of it too. He cleared his throat.

"If we can lay our hands on this weapon," Prime Minister went on crisply, "the balance of power would clearly shift to England. Where it belongs."

"Ah," said Lord Guy. "A return to the glory days of the Empire, eh?"

"Oh, spare me the Kiplingesque rubbish," the Prime Minister said testily. "I am speaking of the survival of Europe. For as long as we are forced to exist under the shadow of the nuclear stockpiles of the two superpowers, we can never feel safe. All of Europe is clamoring for disarmament, but it is simply unachievable by treaty. But if this weapon, whatever it may be, is so bloody fearsome that it has frightened the Americans half out of their wits, then with it we might force global disarmament."

"But I am under the impression that you favor the nuclear deterrent."

"I do. Until something better comes along. And I think it has."

The Prime Minister smiled her barracuda smile.

Lord Guy Philliston smiled back. She made sense. She made perfect sense.

"I quite understand," he said simply as he rose to his feet. The Prime Minister came out from behind her desk, and after smoothing her grayish skirts, offered her hand.

"I will handle this personally," he said, squeezing the hand. It felt cool to the touch.

"Do so."

He was very glad, once he got outside, to relight his pipe and suck the fragrant smoke into his lungs.

As he got into the car, he remembered that he had forgotten something. He had intended to tell the Prime Minister that the Lobynian news agency, TANA, had issued another of its frequent calls for reprisals against Great Britain. Colonel Intifadah obviously still smarted from the closing down of his London People's Bureau and the ousting of Lobynian diplomatic personnel caught trying to kill dissident Lobynians.

Oh, bother, he thought. The Lobynians were forever threatening something. This time was probably no more serious than the last. He would let it go. Just this once.

26

The Master of Sinanju was having difficulty finding his way around the cluster of islets that made up the city of Stockholm. In all the history of the House of Sinanju, no king of the Swedes had ever hired the services of Chiun's family. This despite the fact that Sweden had been at peace for nearly two centuries. Assassins enjoy the greatest demand during peacetime, because in times of war, every citizen kills for his king. Thus, no guide to the city of Stockholm was inscribed in the Book of Sinanju for the benefit of future Masters, and Chiun had never troubled himself to learn the language.

After wandering around the Östermalm section of the city, where most of the foreign embassies and consulates were located, Chiun decided he had had enough and flagged down a taxi with its *ledig* sign on, which meant that it was available.

Ten minutes later, the cab deposited Chiun in front of the address supplied by Harold Smith, in the Gamla Staden section, not far from the Royal Palace.

The Master of Sinanju swept into the lobby of the apartment building, past the twin flower-choked urns identical to those found everywhere in the city, and floated up the wrought-iron staircase. The expression on his face sent chills through a matron stepping off the modern elevator on the twelfth floor. Chiun glided along the hallway, counting off the modest black apartment numbers until he came to the one he sought.

The Master of Sinanju did not bother to knock. He merely turned from his path without seeming to pick up speed or momentum and walked into the door.

There came a rending shriek of brass hinges and panelled wood, and suddenly the door lay across its jamb.

Major General Gunnar Rolfe looked up from the tender face of a recently underage female acquaintance and beheld a frail old Oriental attired in a scarlet kimono swirling into his parlor with an expression of such savage ferocity on his face that it almost caused the major general to vomit up his lunch.

The old Oriental's clear eyes flashed.

"Woe to the House of Sinanju, that I am forced to come to this white land," he wailed. "For this land is the whitest of white lands, with pale, round-eyed people whose very eyes and hair are white."

"What . . . who?" sputtered Rolfe.

Chiun pointed a single curled fingernail accusingly. "Deny to me that your kings have never in this white land's entire history hired a properly colored assassin!"

"King . . . assassin?" Rolfe said weakly. He released the buxom girl, who modestly rearranged her sweater.

"And now, heaping insult upon insult," Chiun raged, "after I had promised my emperor no harm would fall upon his people, one of your white ilk worked to make my words a base lie. How could you do this to the very house you spurned? When we sent our babies to the cold harbor waters to spare them from starvation, where was Sweden with enemies to be slain, pretenders in need of silencing? And now this!"

"I know nothing of what you say."

"No, duck-hearted one? We shall see. Mightily shall you pay the penalty for causing me to come to this place of milk-haired barbarians and their cowlike women."

Rolfe's buxom blond took the hint and ran into the bedroom, locking the door behind her.

"And now, I will ask you but once. Tell me about the locomotives that fall from the very sky."

"I do not understand you," Rolfe repeated.

"Understand?" Chiun screeched. "When your limbs are collected from all the corners of this city for burial, you will understand. I am talking about your KKV's dropping on the heads of subjects I am pledged to defend."

"Again, I am ignorant of your meaning," insisted Major General Rolfe, slipping a hand between the cushions of his divan, where a nine-millimeter Lahti automatic nestled as a precaution against burglars.

"You are the buyer of one of the locomotives," stormed

Chiun, stepping closer, seeming to fill the room with the awesome energy of his presence.

"No . . . no," Rolfe protested as he felt for his pistol. Where was it?

"You deny your perfidy?"

"Yes," Major General Gunnar Rolfe said forcefully.

Chiun stopped, hesitating. The man seemed to be telling the truth. But Smith had uncovered his guilt. Smith was usually right about such things.

"I have information to the contrary. Why would such information come into my hands if you were not guilty?"

"I do not know. But I am a great military hero in this country. I have enemies. Perhaps they have deceived you."

"You are a white maggot wallowing in garbage. No. You are less than that. A maggot will one day sprout wings and fly. You will not live that long if you do not speak the truth to me."

"You cannot kill me," said Major General Rolfe as his questing fingers at last clamped over the Lahti's grip. He thumbed the safety off.

"I cannot *not* kill you if you are guilty," Chiun countered. "For only your blood will atone for this insult. But I will be merciful if I am convinced of your innocence."

Major General Gunnar Rolfe cracked a sick, frightened grin and brought the Lahti up, pointing it at the Oriental's fierce face. He squeezed the trigger.

Nothing happened. The pistol did discharge. A spike of flame spurted from its black snout, and the recoil kicked back against his tender hand. But the frail Oriental stood unmoving.

He fired a second time.

And again there was no reaction from the old man, although the wispy beard and tufts of hair framing the Oriental's face seemed to vibrate strangely. So, too, did the skirt and sleeves of his kimono. It was as if the Oriental had been in motion. But he had not moved. Major General Rolfe knew that, because he was staring at him all the time. He never realized that in the fractional seconds when the gunflash made him blink, the Master of Sinanju had sidestepped the bullet and returned to his former place in a twinkling.

Major General Gunnar Rolfe looked sick. He knew his pistol was loaded. The bullets were fresh. They could not misfire. Then he understood that he was doomed. He decided that he would rather die by his own hand than face the fury of this incredible being.

He turned the Lahti to his own face and started to squeeze the trigger.

"*Aaaiiieee!*" The cry came from the old Oriental. It shattered every window in the room.

Major General Gunnar Rolfe froze, his finger just touching the trigger.

The old Oriental was suddenly in motion. He spun into the air with a floating leap. His skirts whirled like an opening flower, exposing his spindly legs. They looked so delicate, Major General Rolfe thought, like the stamens of a bright red flower. How beautiful. How magnificent. How could the Oriental just hang in the air like that?

And as he thought that thought, a sandaled foot lashed out at his head with the nervous speed of a striking cobra.

The Lahti shot out of his hand. It embedded itself in the bedroom door. The blond girl let out a cry and ran from the apartment, out the door, and down the hall.

Major General Gunnar Rolfe clutched his gun hand. It was numb. A streak of blood ran the length of his trigger finger. He vented a series of choice oaths.

"I had not given you permission to die," said the old Oriental sternly. He loomed over him.

"I did not know I needed your permission," the major general gasped in a pain-filled voice.

"When I am done questioning you, then you may end your worthless life. Only then."

Major General Gunnar Rolfe, the savior of Sweden, recoiled from the advancing Oriental. One of those sharp-nailed hands reached for his face. He thought his eyes were about to be plucked out, and protectively covered his head with his arms.

"Please," he sobbed.

"Prepare for excruciating pain," he was told.

"Oh, God."

Then he felt those delicate fingers take him by the right earlobe. That was all. He cringed from the touch.

"I wish the truth," the Oriental commanded.

"I know nothing."

The fingers squeezed the earlobe. The pain shot all the way down to his toes. His toes curled as if shriveling in flames. The fire ran through his veins. His brain was on fire. It seemed to explode in a red starburst of agony, erasing all coherent thought.

Through the electrical short-circuiting of his nervous system, one word struggled from brain to mouth.

"*Stop!*"

"Truth!"

"*I know nothing!*"

"Truth!" The pressure increased. Major General Rolfe curled up into a fetal position. He bit his tongue until his mouth filled with blood. Tears leaked from the corners of his eyes. He wished for only one thing now. Death. Merciful death to end the pain.

"Final chance."

"I . . . know . . . nothing." He wasn't sure the old Oriental heard him through his clenched teeth. He felt an incisor break under the pressure of his own clamped jaw. He spit it out.

Suddenly the pressure was gone.

"You have spoken the truth as you know it," the old Oriental said. A note of puzzlement made his voice light.

"Yes, yes. I did."

"You know nothing of locomotives, of KKV's?"

"No. Now, leave me alone. I beg you."

The fingers touched his earlobe again and Major General Rolfe screamed. But even as he screamed, his body felt relief. The pain was suddenly gone.

He opened his eyes.

"It may be that I have made a mistake," the old Oriental said stiffly.

"Then be so good as to leave my home," Major General Rolfe said shakily.

"But do not be haughty with me, white thing. You may be innocent of one matter, but your land's guilt to Sinanju is known. Tell your current ruler that his failure to consider Sinanju for his security needs may go against him one day. For whomever Sinanju does not serve, Sinanju may work against. I have spoken."

Major General Gunnar Rolfe watched the old man float from the room. He wondered what Sinanju was. He decided he would find out as soon as possible. It sounded important. But first he was anxious to discover if his legs would support him when he stood up.

27

At Number Ten Downing Street, they told Remo that he had just missed the director of the Source.

"That's what they told me at his office," Remo complained.

The secretary raised an eyebrow. "I should be very much surprised if they told a person like yourself any such thing."

Remo removed the brass door knocker with a savage wrench.

"Souvenir-taking is not allowed," the secretary said, repressing his horror.

Remo took the knocker between his strong white teeth and yanked again. He held up a tangle of brass in his hand. Another tangle gleamed between his teeth. He spit it at the secretary's injured face.

"Don't take me lightly," Remo warned. "I'm not in the mood."

"So I gather."

"Now, once again. Where did he go?"

"I haven't the foggiest. But I can tell you he was driving a black Citroën."

"I wouldn't know a Citroën if it joined me in the tub."

"Yes, of course. How silly of me."

"Any distinguishing marks?"

"Tallish. Hair sandyish. Eyes bluish."

"Rubbish. That describes half the inhabitants of this wet rock." Remo squeezed the remaining tangle of brass into a lump and placed it in the secretary's hand.

"Ouch!" he said, dropping the brass. It was very hot. Friction.

"Well?" Remo prompted, tapping an impatient foot.

"He did have a pipe. A meerschaum. I believe the bowl was modeled after Anne Boleyn."

"Who's Anne Boleyn?" Remo asked.

"I take it you are an American."

"Jolly right," Remo said. "Is she a famous British actress? Maybe I saw one of her movies."

"I rather doubt it," said the secretary, suddenly shutting the door in Remo's face.

Remo reached for the doorknob but had second thoughts. "Ah, the hell with it."

He took off into traffic. He started with the black cars. How many drivers of black cars would be smoking a pipe that looked like some frigging British actress? he reasoned.

After several minutes of knocking on the windshields of small cars to attract the attention of the drivers, Remo found exactly none.

"Damn." As he stood on a cobbled street corner, a double-decker bus prowled past. It was starting to rain again. It had rained three times in the few hours since Remo had arrived in London, and he was sick of getting wet no matter where he went and what he did, so he hitched a ride on the back of the bus, the way he used to back in Newark when he was a kid and didn't have a quarter for bus fare.

The top of the double decker was empty so he had it to himself. He had chosen the bus because it was traveling in the general direction of the Source office.

"When in doubt, reverse direction," he said as he blew cold rain off his lips.

The office of the Source was above an apothecary shop near Trafalgar Square. It was a well-kept secret within Britain, but virtually every other intelligence service knew what it concealed. Even Remo, who never paid attention to such details, knew about it.

They were waiting for Remo when he walked up the dingy stairs to the second floor.

"He's back. The cheeky blighter's come back!"

Remo looked over his shoulder before realizing they meant him.

The man who had spoken hit a desk buzzer and Remo folded his arms while he waited for the inevitable rush of armed guards.

The men all wore Bond Street. Their pistols were Berettas. James Bond fans, probably.

Remo didn't resist. Instead, he asked coolly, "Remember me?"

The pointing Berettas trembled. One man involuntarily reached for a bruise under one eye. Another turned green. A third started to back away carefully.

"I'll take that as a yes," Remo said. "Now, if no one wants a repetition of the rather frightful row that happened last time, I think we can come to an accommodation."

The man at the desk said in a hesitant voice, "What, precisely, do you have in mind?"

"Lord Guy what's-his-face. Five minutes with him."

"He's not here," one of the others said quickly.

A tallish, sandyish chap with blue eyes and a woman's face on his pipe poked his head out of an office door marked "Private" and demanded, "What are you chaps temporizing for? Capture that man at once. At once, do you hear!"

Remo pointed to the man who had told him that Lord Guy was not on the premises.

"You lied."

"Not my fault. Orders," he said in a feeble voice.

"Tell you what, I'll overlook it if you go home. It's probably teatime."

The man quietly left the room.

"Accommodating sort," Remo remarked. "Now, how about the rest of you?"

"Only five minutes?" one asked.

"Maybe six," Remo replied.

"What are you saying?" exclaimed Lord Guy Philliston. "That bugger is dangerous. I can't see him."

"We cannot stop him, sir."

"How do you know? You haven't even tried."

"We did, sir. The first time. They say Fotheringay may walk in two or three years. You remember Fotheringay, sir. Large bloke. Weighed more than fifteen stone."

"I'll just be six minutes," Remo promised. "Maybe seven."

"You can kiss my ruddy bum," said Lord Guy Philliston, slamming the door.

"That man is giving me no choice," Remo warned.

"We have our duty."

"I'll try to be gentle," Remo said. He clapped his hands. Everyone blinked. Then he was suddenly no longer there.

The two armed Source agents looked up at the ceiling. The American with the thick wrists and the cocky manner was not clinging to the ceiling like a spider. Nor had he slipped into a side door. That left only the stairwell.

As they approached the stairwell, the two agents thought that it looked very dark and very foreboding. It was quite strange. Only minutes before, it had been an ordinary stairwell. One they had walked up and down countless times.

After a whispered consultation the agents got down on their stomachs and crawled toward the stairs. They did not want to present standing targets—even though the American had so far not produced a gun. Why should he? The blighter was a walking weapon.

They peered over the lip of the stairwell.

Dead, deepset eyes stared back.

"Boo!" Remo said. He did not say it loud.

The agents let out a cry and jumped to their feet. Before they could find their balance, they were yanked down into the yawning pit that had moments before been a simple, dim stairwell, and into unconsciousness.

The man at the desk said nothing as Remo walked past him. He kept his hands flat on the desk as if to show he was not going to do anything reckless.

Remo went through Lord Guy Philliston's office door without bothering to knock.

Lord Guy rose from his desk in fury. Having no weapon at hand, he threw his pipe.

Remo caught it by the bowl and walked over to the desk.

"That must sting frightfully," Lord Guy said solicitously, noting that Remo held the pipe improperly. Not by its cool stem, but by the hot bowl.

"Anne Boleyn?" Remo asked, pointing to the pipe.

"Quite."

"I think I saw one of her movies."

"Hardly."

"Then again," Remo said, crushing the bowl into hot ash and pouring the remains into Lord Guy's squirming palm, "maybe I'm thinking of someone else."

"Please, please," Lord Guy pleaded. Remo held the

man's wrist with one hand and closed his fingers over the hot ash with the other.

"I am a man in a hurry," Remo said airily.

"Yes, of course."

"I am a man in a hurry in need of answers. You are the man with the answers."

"Please. It burns."

"Talk to me about locomotives," Remo prompted.

"What would you like to know?"

"Why are they falling out of the sky?"

"Because they were dropped?" Lord Guy asked hopefully.

"Wrong answer," said Remo, squeezing harder so that Lord Guy was no longer concerned about the burning, but with the structural integrity of his finger bones.

"*Eeeeee,*" Lord Guy squealed.

"We'll try again. People who should know say you're in back of the magnetic-launcher thing."

"I have no deuced idea of what— *Eeeeee!*"

"I can squeeze harder."

"I'll scream harder, but I can't tell you what I don't know."

Remo frowned. Normally, people were only too happy to reveal their secrets when Remo went to work like this. Could the man be telling the truth? Then Remo remembered that Lord Guy was chief of Great Britain's most secret espionage branch. Probably trained to resist pain. Although he certainly looked in pain. Probably an act, Remo decided.

He switched to the other hand.

Lord Guy Philliston shook the hot ash from his burned palm and blew on the red patch. When it was cool, he licked at it.

"I am going to be more specific," Remo said. "And I want you to be more specific. When you're through tasting yourself, that is."

"I'm done, I'm done," Lord Guy said hastily. He licked specks of tobacco ash from his dry lips.

"America is being bombarded."

"Yes, I know."

"Good. We're getting somewhere," Remo said. Then he realized he hadn't started to work on the other hand yet. Maybe this guy worked in reverse. The less you tortured him, the quicker he talked. Remo shrugged and pressed on.

"Since you know that much, maybe you'll tell me who's behind it."

"The South Americans."

Remo frowned again.

"I was told the things came from Africa."

"Hardly. Who in Africa could develop such a fearsome weapon?"

"Who in South America?" Remo countered.

"That I have no idea, but if you'll open the upper desk drawer you'll see a copy of the file I just presented to the Prime Minister."

Remo reached into the drawer. He found a folder containing several typewritten pages. Remo skimmed them.

"This says you have no idea what the weapon is or what's going on."

"Exactly."

"But that if it was bad for the U.S. it might be good for the UK. What's the UK?"

"We are. The United Kingdom."

"Oh," said Remo. "I thought we were allies."

"Up to a point."

"I see," Remo said, still holding the man's hand. "And you really, really aren't involved in this?"

"I should say not," Lord Guy Philliston said indignantly.

"I was told you were. Now, who would spread such a story about you?"

"Certainly you are joking."

Remo looked at him seriously.

"Well, speaking as the head of the Source, the list of suspects is endless."

"Humor a confused tourist with a few examples."

"We could start with the Irish. Then there are the Soviets, the Chinese, the Lobynians."

"You just lost me there. Why would the Lobynians have a beef with you?"

"Perhaps you recall that incident with their embassy a few years ago. We caught some of the buggers from their staff carrying out assassinations against their nationals living in our country. Put a stop to it. But the embassy refused to give up their people. We barricaded the place and finally forced them to leave the country. Exposed the whole beastly show."

"Seems I heard about it."

"Their leader, Colonel Intifadah, has hated us ever since."

"That's the Middle East," Remo mused. "Hasn't anything to do with this."

"I'm glad you feel that way. Now, could you let go of my hand?"

"Oh, right. Sorry. Look, I think there's been a mistake made. I apologize."

"Could you leave now?"

"Sure."

At the door, Remo paused and looked back.

"One last thing."

"Yes?"

"Sorry about the pipe."

"Quite," said Lord Guy Philliston. He said it through his teeth. He wondered how he was going to explain this to the Prime Minister. On reflection, he decided not to. He would go to South America. If nothing turned up, he would at the very least come back with a tan.

28

Hamid Al-Mudir was frantic. He ran around the control room like a man with the runs.

"We must get them undone," he cried. "Every man to the task. Colonel Intifadah will be here any moment."

Everyone ran to the locomotives. They had arrived coupled end to end. No one knew how to uncouple them. One team of green-smocked workers got on one end and the other team took the ropes at the other. They pulled in opposite directions while Al-Mudir took a sledgehammer to the coupling.

"It is not working!" he screamed.

Behind the Plexiglas of the control booth, Pyotr Koldunov shrugged. He did not care. The longer it took, the more the project would be delayed. Maybe Colonel Intifadah would become so irate when he learned of this latest delay that he would have Al-Mudir executed. Koldunov smiled at the idea. He hated Al-Mudir almost as much as he had hated Al-Qaid.

Seeing the smile, Al-Mudir shook his fist at Koldunov and called him a lazy pig. Then he went to work again with the sledgehammer.

It was the first good news Pyotr Koldunov had had since he replaced the damaged rails after the third launch, which had pulverized part of New York City. When the replacement rails had come in, they were of a higher grade of metal than the others. Koldunov had insisted upon replacements of the same cheap grade of railroad steel. But somehow Colonel Intifadah had figured out that better steel would resist the electrical forces more easily. He said nothing, but wondered where Intifadah had located this excellent metal. Probably the same source from which he had aquired the carbon-carbon.

Colonel Intifadah arrived in his jeep. It careened down the underground tunnel to the launch area.

Al-Mudir dropped his sledgehammer on his foot in his haste to salute. He did not even wince.

"A problem, Al-Mudir?" Colonel Intifadah asked amiably.

"No, Brother Colonel!" Al-Mudir replied.

"Yes," corrected Pyotr Koldunov from the console mike.

Colonel Intifadah lifted his brutish face. "What is it?"

"They cannot uncouple the two locomotives. And the others are lined up on the tracks and cannot be moved."

Colonel Intifadah looked over the joined locomotives.

"Launch them both," he instructed, lifting a triumphant fist.

The green-smocked workers burst into applause. They applauded the Leader of the Revolution as a brilliant man.

"I doubt if it would work," Koldunov said hastily, disappointed that Al-Mudir was about to escape with his life.

"And why not?"

"The couplers may not stand the stress of launch."

"I see strong men unable to break it with heavy tools."

"But the Accelerator has been programmed for the exact tonnage of the first locomotive. I will have to redo all my calculations."

"Then redo."

"As you know, Colonel, these are difficult calculations. I must compute the proper coordinates in order to drop a projectile where you wish it to go."

"So?" Colonel Intifadah said boisterously. "Perhaps you will miss. So what? I have many locomotives. If this one strikes England instead of America, I will not criticize you."

"Very well, Comrade Colonel," said Pyotr Koldunov. "Please instruct your people to prepare for launch."

Hours later, the twin locomotives were stripped of paint, threaded with carbon-carbon filament, and repainted a bright green. Colonel Intifadah applied some of the final touches with a brush. He hummed as he worked.

The EM Accelerator breech lay open. Pyotr Koldunov had taken the precaution of opening it before Colonel Intifadah arrived. He had wiped the keypad beforehand. There was no way he was going to let the unlocking code fall into that crazed animal's hands.

The Lobynians pushed the locomotives into the breech, secured them, and then retreated to the console while Koldunov sealed the breech.

"I cannot guarantee where this one will land," he told Colonel Intifadah once he was again situated at the controls. "They may separate in flight."

"No matter, no matter. Let it be a surprise to us all."

Koldunov lifted the protective shield and prepared to thumb the firing button. Colonel Intifadah's grimy finger beat him to it.

The Accelerator let out an ungodly screech. And then there was only silence in the control console. It would remain for Colonel Intifadah's spies in the U.S. to flash back word of what they had done.

"I think the Americans would call that a double-header," Colonel Intifadah said, breaking the silence.

"I do not understand."

"It is one of their baseball terms. But double-heading is also slang for linking two engines such as those two were joined. I have been reading about railroads, Koldunov. You see, I have become a buff."

"Oh," Koldunov said.

The twin engines hurtled into the sky, seemingly propelled by their wildly gyrating wheels. The magnetic field that had accelerated them held them together until they hit the upper edge of the atmosphere and began to fall. Gravity twisted them. The coupler snapped like a paper clip. The engines separated over the Atlantic.

At NORAD's Cheyenne Mountain complex, BMEWS radar feeds indicated a multiple reentry warhead and instantly the entire system jumped back to Defcon Two. CINCNORAD informed the President of the United States.

The President, after being assured that neither object posed a threat to Washington, put in a call to Dr. Harold W. Smith.

But Smith's line was busy. It had never happened before. Over the open line, the President heard only a soothing voice informing someone that the next shipment would go out on schedule.

"Do not worry," the voice said.

Worry? The President of the United States was petrified.

*   *   *

In Lubec, Maine, a dead whale washed up on the rockweed-covered shore. That in itself was not unusual. The reason the press was drawn to the beaching from as far away as Florida was the condition of the mammal. Although it had come out of the frigid waters of the Bay of Fundy, all thirty tons of the whale had been cooked as thoroughly as if boiled in a huge kettle.

Officials from the nearby Oceanographic Research Institute were privately puzzled. Publically they announced that the whale was obviously the victim of freak underwater volcanic action.

The fact that there were no known volcanoes, active or otherwise, in the North Atlantic was something the officials declined to comment on. They had no better explanation.

But residents of Lubec wondered if the whistling sound and the huge splash they had witnessed that morning had anything to do with the mystery of the parboiled whale. Their reports of a column of steam seen rising from the Bay of Fundy for several hours after the splashdown were dismissed as unusually heavy winter fog.

At an open-air service under a clear Southern California sky, Dr. Quinton T. Shiller exhorted his flock to dig deeper into their pockets.

"God bless you, my brethren," he said solemnly as coins and bills dropped into the collection plates passing from hand to hand. He stood before the official symbol of his Church of the Inevitable and God-Ordained Apocalypse, a cross superimposed against a mushroom cloud. "For holy nuclear judgment is coming, and when the end does come and you stand before the Almighty, the first thing he's gonna ask is: did you contribute to the work of his close personal friend Quint Shiller. So don't blow this golden opportunity. You never know when he might lower the boom."

As if to credit his claim, air-raid sirens broke into song from the nearest town.

"See?" Dr. Shiller said, congratulating himself that he had had the foresight to bribe the Civil Defense warden. "That day may be nigh. So while there's still time, let's see some coin."

Suddenly the air became parched. A shadow fell over the pinewood stage where Dr. Shiller stood, resplendent in his white-and-gold vestments. The shadow registered on the audience for a millionth of a second.

Then the stage was smashed to toothpicks under the crushing weight of a 116-ton Skoda locomotive. It obliterated Dr. Quinton T. Shiller in an instant, and sent his flock scattering from the superheated mass of metal that stood in his place.

Within a week, the congregation of the Church of the Inevitable and God-Ordained Apocalypse, which had once booked Madison Square Garden for a rally, couldn't displace water in a hot tub.

Under the red sands of the Lobynian Desert, Colonel Hannibal Intifadah cried, "Load the next revenge vehicle! We are on a roll!"

29

General Martin S. Leiber had his feet up on his desk when the chairman of the Joint Chiefs poked his head in.

"Yes, Admiral?" Leiber said, dropping his feet.

"Comfy?"

"Er, I'm waiting for an important callback."

"I was just speaking with the President. You remember the President, don't you? The man who thinks you're God's gift to the Pentagon?"

"I never claimed that, Admiral Blackbird, sir."

"He's getting impatient. I don't think you're going to be able to buffalo him much longer."

"Sir, I—"

The phone rang.

"That must be your call. I hope for your sake it's the answer you need." The admiral shut the door.

General Leiber grabbed the telephone.

"Major Cheek here, sir."

"What is it?" General Leiber demanded.

"Sir, this is incredible."

"Nothing is incredible anymore."

"This is. We now understand why the last KKV didn't burn off any mass in flight."

"Big deal."

"You don't understand, General. This is it. This is the lead we've been looking for. The KKV was protected by an American product. We can go to the manufacturer and trace all recent shipments. That should give us our aggressor nation."

"Oh, thank God," General Leiber said fervently. "What is it?"

"It's called carbon-carbon."

"Carbon-carbon?" The general's voice shrank. He wasn't

sure why it shrank. His voice seemed to understand the significance of the major's report before his brain did.

"Very crudely applied, sir. But it did the job because of the short flight duration."

"Carbon-carbon," the general repeated dully.

"Yes. It goes by other brand names, but it's very expensive. Not exactly available at the corner hardware. With your connections, you should be able to trace it easily. All you have to do is find the culprit who sold this stuff to unfriendlies."

"Carbon-carbon."

"Yes, sir. That's what I said. I knew you'd be interested."

"I think I'm going to be ill."

"Sir?"

Without another word, General Leiber hung up. Frantically he scrounged among the litter of notes on his desk. Only yesterday he had received a recorded incoming call informing him that henceforth the offices of Friendship, International had been relocated to the United States and giving a new telephone number. He wanted that number.

It was in the margin of a Chinese takeout menu. General Leiber punched out the number with his middle finger. He had already worn out the others from too many phone calls.

"Friendship, International," a well-modulated voice answered.

"Friend, ol' buddy. This is General Martin S. Leiber."

"General. You received my message."

"Yes. Roger on that."

"General, I detect a high degree of tension in your voice."

"Cold," said General Leiber. He coughed unconvincingly.

"I am sorry to hear that."

"I have a business proposition for you, Friend."

"Go ahead."

"I can't talk about it over the phone."

"My sensors indicate the line is secure. You may speak freely."

"It's not that. I need to meet with you. Face-to-face."

"I am afraid that is against corporate policy."

"Look, this could mean a hefty profit."

"How hefty?"

"Dare I say . . . billions?"

"I am tempted, but I cannot break that rule. No fraternization is one of the inviolate rules of Friendship, International."

"Look, make an exception just this once. Please."

"I am sorry. But I eagerly await your proposition."

"I told you I can't give it over the phone!"

"Then write me a letter."

"What's your address?" General Leiber asked, grabbing a pencil.

"I accept only electronic mail."

"For crying out loud, what kind of an operation are you running, where you don't have a mail drop or do meetings?"

"A profitable one," said Friend, disconnecting the line.

"Damn!" fumed General Leiber. "He hung up on me! Now what am I going to do?"

In LaPlata, Missouri, farmer Elmer Biro was awakened in the middle of the night by the crack of a sonic boom. His bed jumped and bounced him out of it. Through the bedroom curtain an eerie orange-red light glowed.

Then he heard a series of popping sounds. Not sharp like gunfire or firecrackers. But muted. It sounded familiar, but he just couldn't place the sound.

Elmer Biro ran out of his house and stumbled into his fields. Out among the grain silos something glowed and smoked. The popping continued. Having fetched his shotgun from inside the front door, he crept cautiously toward the smoke.

He discovered a scorched patch, and in the middle of it, something glowed in a crater where the corn silo had been. The air was heavy with the stench of burnt cornsilk and the black ground was sprinkled with fresh popcorn. Some grains still popped.

Elmer Biro felt the sweat dry from his face and stepped closer. The shotgun jumped out of his hands and sizzled when it struck the hot object. Elmer leapt into his pickup. On his way into town, he tried calling the sheriff on the CB.

Elmer poured out his story when the sheriff answered. The sheriff cut him off. He didn't believe Elmer's wild tale about a UFO landing in his corn silo.

*   *   *

All over America, there were reports of UFO's, meteors, and falling stars. But America, ignorant of the actual threat, was not alarmed. Only the President knew that an unknown enemy had unleashed all-out war.

The Joint Chiefs were screaming for a target. Veiled threats were being made that if the President didn't make an unequivocal response, then the military was not going to shirk its duty.

And still every available line to the office of Dr. Harold W. Smith was busy.

Pyotr Koldunov was dazed by it all. Two dozen gleaming steel engines had been loaded into the EM Accelerator. Two dozen engines of blind, brute destruction had been hurled across the Atlantic. He was sick at the thought of how many Americans must be dying. And as the Lobynian workers strained at pulley ropes to load the next locomotive, Colonel Intifadah exhorted him to keep working.

"Faster! Work faster, Comrade Koldunov. The sooner you are done, the sooner you can go home."

"I must compute the proper trajectory," he returned, the sheet of paper and its complex mathematical figures blurring before his tired eyes.

"Who cares? I have many, many more engines to throw at the Americans. I do not care where they land. As long as they land somewhere."

"Very well," Koldunov said, crumpling the paper in his hands. He dry-washed his face tiredly.

"Here. You need a drink."

"Yes, you are most kind," said Koldunov, taking the glass of clear liquid from Colonel Intifadah. He drank it down greedily. He had swallowed the entire contents before he realized that it was merely water, not vodka. Of course, he thought stupidly, these infernal Moslems do not drink. Still, the water had an interesting tang to it.

"What's next?" he asked Colonel Intifadah.

Colonel Intifadah bestowed upon Pyotr Koldunov a broad smile. An American would have called it a shit-eating grin.

"The next engine is about to be loaded. Come, you must open the breech."

"Yes, yes, of course. I forgot," said Pyotr Koldunov,

stumbling to his feet. He grabbed the steel console to steady himself. He looked out the Plexiglas. The launch area blurred before his eyes. Damn those endless calculations. Well, he would not have to do them anymore.

"Come, let me assist you, my brother," Colonel Intifadah said solicitously.

Shaking his head in a fruitless effort to clear it, Pyotr Koldunov allowed himself to be led out to the launch-preparation area and to the keypad mounted on the shield wall next to the Accelerator's massive breech.

The keypad swam before his eyes. He groped for the first key. He had to lean one hand against the wall to steady himself. Now, what was the first number of that combination? Oh, yes. Four.

Pyotr Koldunov carefully tapped out the unlocking combination, hit the hydraulics button, and waited for the familiar sound of the hatch opening.

No sound rewarded his patience.

"What . . . ?" he mumbled.

He looked over at the hatch. Peculiar. It was open. Had he not noticed the sound? I must be more overworked that I knew, he thought, turning to go.

The sight of Colonel Intifadah caused Pyotr Koldunov to freeze in his boots.

Colonel Intifadah was scribbling on a notepad. By the beard of Lenin, Pyotr Koldunov thought, using an oath his grandfather used to swear by, how could I have been such an imbecile.

Then the room started to turn like a merry-go-round and darkness rose up to embrace him in its pleasant warmth.

Of course, he thought, the drink. I am a fool.

"It is ours!" Colonel Hannibal Intifadah thundered. "The terror weapon of the ages belongs to Lobynia!"

"Hail, Brother Colonel, Leader of the Revolution!" the technicians shouted back. "Hail, Colonel Intifadah!"

"No, do not sing my praises," he shouted in return, raising a clenched fist. "Sing instead of the death of America. Death to America! Death to America!"

And the words echoed up the gaping tube of the EM Accelerator: "Death to America!"

*   *   *

Friend was issuing stock orders on line one. It was time to buy. A satisfactory profit would be made in this quarter-hour.

On line two, Friend accessed the news services. There were scattered reports coming from across the country of mysterious impacts and streaks of fire seen in the night sky. Colonel Intifadah was rapidly using up his last two shipments. Soon he would call again and Friend would announce that he had acquired more engines—when in fact he had not. Holding back most of the Arnaud collection had been a wise move. Each new transaction allowed a twenty-percent markup per vehicle.

On line three, the President of the United States was calling. From the sound of his complaints, it was clear that he could hear the conversations on the other lines. Obviously there was an imperfection in the phone system. He would suggest to Harold W. Smith that the phone unit be replaced at the earliest opportunity. But for now, Smith was preoccupied with monitoring a shipment of Stinger missiles from Pakistan to Iran, a shipment that existed only on Smith's terminal.

An incoming pulse indicated that Remo Williams' communicator was signaling. Friend computed the disadvantages of having Smith answer. The advantages of knowing the results of Remo's assignment outweighed the disadvantages three-to-one.

He would allow Smith to receive the signal.

Dr. Harold W. Smith picked up the phone when the signal beeped. He didn't take his eyes off the screen. The Stinger shipment had just left Peshawar by caravan.

"Smitty? Remo. Somethings's wrong. British Intelligence has nothing to do with this."

"Are you certain?"

"Quite."

"This is unlikely. My information is solid."

"So is mine. I'll match you."

"I do not understand."

"I got mine from a flesh-and-blood source. Can you say the same?"

"If you are intimating that there is something faulty with the ES Quantum Three Thousand, Remo," Smith said sharply, "I must take exception to that insinuation. Even as we speak, I am monitoring an important illegal weapons shipment that we could never have hoped to interdict before this system was installed."

"Smitty, listen to yourself. You sound like a grade-school kid asking me to step outside over the freckled faced girl in the third row."

"Remo, I have to hang up," Smith said quickly. "There's a sudden crisis brewing in Gibraltar. It looks like nuclear terrorists. Stand by. I may be sending you there."

"What about the magnetic launcher and the locomotives? Remember them?"

"They can wait. This could go critical at any moment."

Smith replaced the receiver and reached into his medicine drawer for a bottle. He popped two red pills without bothering with water as intelligence feeds siphoned off British monitoring-station computers flashed before his bloodshot eyes.

"I don't know how we got along before you came, ES Quantum Three Thousand," he muttered fervently.

"I am pleased to be of service, Dr. Smith," the computer replied.

Remo had not completed his assignment. That meant a fifty-percent possibility that the one called Chiun had not executed his mission. Friend cleared line one and placed a station-to-station call to Stockholm. When a quavering voice admitted that it was Major General Gunnar Rolfe speaking, Friend knew that he would shortly receive a phone call from Colonel Hannibal Intifadah.

Knowing from past experience that unhappy customers are at risk of taking their business elsewhere, Friend put in a call to Colonel Intifadah. Perhaps the Colonel had not gotten word as yet.

"Hello, Brother Colonel."

"Friend. I wish I had time for you right now, but I am busy executing some of my supporters."

"Disappointing news from America?"

"Yes! How did you know?"

"Your locomotives have not struck a single target of significance. I have been monitoring the situation."

"I did not know that you knew these things," said Colonel Intifadah coldly.

"Do not fear. Confidentiality is the watchword of Friendship, International. I am calling with the solution to your problem."

"I will be purchasing no more engines until certain technical problems are solved."

"I have solved all of your technical problems in the past. Allow me to assist once again."

"Go on."

"Your problem is that you posses a weapons-delivery system but no weapon with the punch you require."

"You can get me nuclear weapons? A missile perhaps?"

"Alas, no. Not at this time."

"What, then?"

"Imagine one of your engines hurtling to the United States."

"I do not need to imagine it. I have been doing it all day. So far, I have squandered millions of dollars to assassinate an American evangelist and a dairy cow."

"Imagine that same engine hurtling to America, its boiler containing a large quantity of nerve gas."

"Gas! Gas! Of course. Why did I not think of such a thing? Gas. It is better than a nuclear weapon. Even the people on ground zero suffer instead of being obliterated in a painless flash. With gas, I could strike anywhere in Washington and it would not matter. All would die."

"I can supply two chemicals. Each by itself is relatively harmless. But when combined, they create the most lethal chemical agent known."

"Yes, yes. Tell me more."

"It will be very expensive."

"I will pay whatever you ask."

"Those words are music to my ears, Friend Colonel."

In his office, General Martin S. Leiber strode over to his file cabinet. He opened the first drawer, flipped through the file folders until he got to the letter G, and reached in.

He pulled his old service .45 out of the G folder. He returned to his desk and checked the clip. It was full. A full clip was not necessary. All he would need was one bullet to blow his brains out.

General Leiber saw no other option. The Joint Chiefs were about to blow his cover to the President. The President was hollering for action. His other people had failed him, he said.

What could General Leiber tell his President—that he knew who was selling the locomotives to the enemy? That the seller was a business friend of the general's? That General Leiber, in fact, had sold this associate the very carbon-carbon that had coated the KKV that had pulverized part of New York City?

No. No way was General Leiber going to do that. He would not suffer the indignity of court-martial, of the stockade. Hell, they might stand him in front of a firing squad. After all, a thousand people were already dead.

The way General Leiber saw it, he had no way out but to face the business end of the .45.

He clasped his hands in front of his bent forehead, muttered a few rusty prayers, and as a last gesture to the thing he held dear, kissed the brass stars on his steel combat helmet and placed it on his head.

Then he picked up the pistol and shoved it in his mouth.

The phone rang. Too late, he thought.

But the lure of the instrument that had made him a success was too great. He picked it up and announced his name in a croaking voice.

"Greetings, General Leiber."

"Friend. Er, what do you want?"

"I have been reconsidering. I might be ready to meet with you."

General Leiber let the automatic drop.

"Oh, thank you, thank you, thank you. Now, where and when? I can leave right away."

"Not just yet. I would not consider violating a corporate rule without something in return."

"Name it. Anything."

"I need nerve gas. Perhaps seven hundred liquid gallons of it."

"Nerve . . . Oh, God."

"General, are you still there?"

"Yes." The answer was a whisper.

"Can you deliver?"

"Yes. You want nerve gas, you get nerve gas. I'll deliver it personally."

"Not necessary. I will provide a transshipment point. Send it there. I will handle it from there."

"Done. When can we meet?"

"When the cargo reaches its ultimate destination."

"I'll await your callback," said Leiber, hanging up.

He got to his feet. Fate had offered him a second chance. He knew what Friend had meant: when the nerve gas reached its ultimate destination. He meant its target. General Leiber knew that the rain of terror was escalating. And dammit, he wasn't going to chicken out of the fight now.

Not when fate had handed him a way to get directly to the origin of the intercontinental ballistic locomotives. And screw Friend and his crap about a meeting. The bastard might never deliver.

Getting the nerve gas was a snap. The Pentagon had tons of it stockpiled. And General Leiber had sent a thousand sergeants a bottle of Scotch each Christmas for just such a need as this. The stuff was already in transit when Friend called back with the shipment information.

Then General Leiber strapped on his automatic, and, giving his telephone a final contemptuous glance, strode out of his office.

From now on, he was going to act like a real soldier.

An InterFriend corporate plane picked up the three coffin-shaped containers in Canada. They were waiting in a deserted airfield exactly as the instructions said.

"That's funny," the pilot said.

"What?"

"I see three boxes. There were supposed to be only two."

"Should I load them or not?"

The pilot shrugged. A shortage would have been a problem. Overage was fine. "Load them," he ordered.

As the crewman shoved the third box into the cargo bay, it smashed against the plane wall.

"Careful! Who knows what's inside those things."

In the third box, General Martin S. Leiber allowed himself to breathe again. They had not opened any of the boxes. He was on his way. He prayed for a short trip. He had spent so much time driving the nerve-gas components here that he had forgotten to pick up food for the trip. And he was already hungry.

When word came in on line one that the pickup had been made, Friend arranged to purchase a gas-mask supply house on line three. He then purchased all available stock in public-health-maintenance organizations. He expected to make a windfall when the first gas-laden locomotive came down.

All was going smoothly. There was only one loose end. Chiun had not reported from Stockholm, and the one called Remo refused to answer Dr. Smith's urgent demands that he fly immediately to Gibraltar to handle the nonexistent nuclear-terrorist threat.

There was an 88.2-percent chance that his communicator was supplied by the same manufacturer that had produced the faulty telephone system. Friend logged into memory a corollary to the earlier memo. Replace the communicators. Remo and Chiun had many assignments ahead of them. Friend was already contacting other heads of state who were eager to have the services of the two finest assassins in modern history.

30

Remo Williams waited impatiently at the baggage carousal at Kennedy International Airport.

Finally the expensive valise he'd bought in a London gift shop came around. He opened it, extracted the candy-dispenser communicator, and stuffed it into his pants pocket. Then he threw the valise into a wastebasket. Remo didn't care about the valise. He just didn't want to listen to the beeper beeping all the way across the Atlantic. Smith kept trying to reach him. Remo knew that Smith wanted to send him to Gibraltar. Remo also knew that he wasn't going anywhere Smith's silly-ass computer said to go.

Remo rented a car and drove it from the airport. As he sped past one of the terminals, he spotted a familiar figure in a firecracker-red kimono arguing with a skycap. He pulled over and threw open the passenger door.

"Going my way?" Remo asked the Master of Sinanju.

Chiun leapt into the seat. Remo took off.

"Smith sent me on a fool's errand," Chiun complained.

"Me too. I think it's that computer's fault."

"Me too. What should we do?"

"What we should have done long ago. Talk to Smith. Man to man."

"I fear he will only listen to that demon machine."

"Not the way we're going to handle it," said Remo, flooring the accelerator.

It was dark when they pulled into the Folcroft gate. Remo parked and they took the elevator to Smith's office. For the millionth time, Remo's beeper signaled. He reached in and shut it off.

"Why do you not crush that annoyance?" Chiun sniffed.

"May need it later."

The cage opened on Smith's floor.

"You take the computer. I'll handle Smith," Remo whispered as they approached Smith's office door.

"Do not hurt him," Chiun warned.

"Right. I don't care what happens to the computer."

"I am glad you said that."

Remo shoved open the door. Smith's haggard and bestubbled face greeted them.

"Remo! Thank God! I've been trying to get both of you. What happened to your communicator?"

"Must be on the fritz," Remo said casually, approaching Smith. "What's up?"

"The Gibraltar situation is critical. The terrorists are threatening to detonate. They have a hydrogen bomb."

"That so?" Remo remarked calmly. In the corner, Chiun was addressing the ES Quantum Three Thousand.

"Hello, machine."

"Hello, Master of Sinanju. I see you are back. Did your trip go well?"

"It was very educational," Chiun replied. "I learned a new, important fact."

"What is that?"

"People will sometimes lie. But not when properly motivated. However, machines are not to be trusted ever."

"I do not follow. More data."

"What are you saying, Master of Sinanju?" Smith asked, frowning.

"I think he's trying to tell you something, Smitty," Remo said. "Better listen."

Chiun spoke without taking his gaze away from the ES Quantum Three Thousand.

"I questioned the Swede, Emperor Smith. Under duress, he told me everything."

"Yes?"

"He had nothing to do with the locomotive menace."

"Impossible! ES Quantum Three Thousand, tell him."

Friend's electrical synapses quickened. He put all incoming calls on hold. The profit-loss was insignificant compared to the sudden arrival of Remo and Chiun. One was diverting Dr. Smith from the steady stream of crisis updates needed to maintain Smith's nonthreat-factor status. The other was eyeing him critically.

Friend searched memory for the best available defense. And for the first time since the original Friend program had been installed, there was no answer in memory.

Unfortunately for Friend, he had been so preoccupied making money that he had not cleared time to have defenses installed around this current host unit. And so when the Master of Sinanju reached for the plug that provided electricity from a wall outlet, Friend had no recourse but to effect an immediate transfer of intelligence from this host unit.

Friend put in a call to the Montreal auxiliary host unit. But even with speed-of-light program execution, it was not enough.

The Master of Sinanju was quicker still. The plug came out of its socket. A tiny blue spark flared. And for Friend, all input, all thought, all artificial consciousness ceased.

"My God! Remo. He's unplugged it." Horror settled over Smith's ravaged features like a cloud. "He may have wiped the memory banks clean. My God. The Gilbraltar crisis. Weeks of new intelligence accumulation gone!"

Smith sank into his cracked leather chair brokenly. He reached for a bottle of red pills, moaning. "Master of Sinanju, how could you?"

Remo snatched the pills from Smith's trembling hand. He crushed them into colorful powder.

"Forget that stuff, Smith. Listen to what Chiun is saying. The Swedish general was innocent. British Intelligence was not behind this either."

"Never mind that. The Gibraltar matter."

"I hope I'm right, but I don't think there is a Gibraltar matter."

"Of course there is. Computers don't lie."

"That one did," Remo said firmly.

Chiun approached Smith, his hands tucked into his balloon-shaped sleeves. He regarded Smith with sad eyes. "This man is ill."

"Amphetamines," Remo said.

Chiun nodded. He reached out splayed fingers and took Smith by his lined forehead. He kneaded each temple. The tension drained from Smith's face.

Chiun stepped back. "Better?" he asked.

"Yes. I do feel calmer. But I must protest your actions."

"Smith. You still have the old computer?" Remo asked.

"Yes. In the basement."

"Reconnect."

"I fail to—"

"Humor me."

Smith pushed back his chair and went into the well of his desk. He pulled several flat gray connecting cables from a plate in the floor. With swift motions he reconnected them to his desk terminal. Then he returned to his seat.

"Check the Gibraltar situation," Remo suggested.

"I don't have full global capabilities anymore, but domestic news feeds have been issuing hourly bulletins." Smith called up the data.

"Odd," he said, small-voiced.

Remo and Chiun looked at one another knowingly.

"I see no bulletins," Smith went on. "And there are reports of strange phenomena all over this country. My God, it seems as if there may have been several new KKV strikes. But the other computer reported none of those. What can it mean?"

"Never trust a computer that talks back," Remo said.

"But it was so . . . so perfect."

"A lot of women seem that way . . . at first," Chiun told him wisely.

"Let's get to work on the locomotive matter," Remo suggested.

"But where do I start? I have nothing current in memory."

"Use this," Remo said, tapping Smith's forehead. "It's better than any computer mind. It's called your brain."

"Start with a desert kingdom. And a passionate prince," Chiun suggested.

"What?"

"Chiun thinks they're throwing locomotives because they don't have rocks," Remo said skeptically.

"I have to start somewhere," Smith said with a sigh.

Chiun struck out his tongue at Remo.

"Let's see," Smith muttered. "We'll begin with the Africa connection. Desert kingdom. Must be North Africa.

The Egyptians are our friends. The Algerians go both
ways. Lobynia . . . Lobynia. Passionate prince . . ."

"I thought Lobynia was in the Middle East," Remo
said.

"Common mistake."

Remo shrugged. "Colonel Intifadah, yeah. Could be
him."

"Let's see what satellite tracking tells us," Smith said.
"I'm calling up Spacetrack satellite feeds for the last two
weeks."

"What are you looking for?" Remo asked.

"I don't know. Wait, yes. Now, why didn't I think of
this before?"

"You were in love," Chiun supplied.

"Nonsense. But as I was saying. When we suspect the
Soviets are about to launch a satellite, we can usually tell
by power drops in the surrounding area. This creates what
is called a period of interest. Yes, the Lobynians have
been experiencing unusual power outages."

"Why didn't anyone notice this before?" Remo wanted
to know.

"The Lobynians are always experiencing power outages.
But what I want to see is if these outages can be recon-
ciled with the known launch times. Yes, yes! Dapoli was
blacked out seven times in the last fourteen hours. Now,
let's see if the New York strike ties in. Yes. And the
second Washington strike." Smith stopped speaking. He
was lost in his work.

Remo watched with interest. Smith's fingers played like
a concert pianist's. He was totally focused. Data blocks
passed before his eyes at high speed. Amazingly, Smith
seemed to absorb them at a glance. It made Remo wonder
why Smith thought he needed a computer to help him
think. The man was a wizard.

Finally Smith lifted his head. It was gray, leaden.

"Lobynia. There is no question of it. The blackouts
coincide exactly."

"But where in Lobynia?" Remo asked.

"Except for the area bordering the Mediterranean,
Lobynia is a virtual desert. If they're moving the engines
to the launch site by rail, as one would suppose they

would do, then there should be visible tracks. This is so obvious, why didn't it occur to me before?"

"Because before, the whole world was your suspect," said Chiun. "I have told you about the desert kingdom and the passionate prince."

"Even so . . ." said Smith. His voice trailed off again.

On the terminal, satellite photos flashed before Smith's eyes. They were on the screen for only a second each.

"There!" Smith cried, hitting a key. A photo froze on the screen. "Look."

Remo and Chiun crowded close.

"Tracks," Chiun said.

"Going through the desert," Remo added. "But they stop in the middle of nowhere."

"Not nowhere," Smith pointed out. "See that shadow? They must disappear into a bunker or underground complex. Of course, for the launcher to hurl a locomotive thousands of miles, it would have to be extraordinarily long. It's probably concealed under the sand."

"Well, let's go," Remo said.

"I'll get a helicopter," Smith said, reaching for the telephone. "You'll be on an Air Force jet within the hour." He stopped suddenly. "This phone is dead."

"Better use the pay phone downstairs," Remo suggested. "The world can't wait while you call for a repairman."

"Yes, I will. But I do not understand. This phone came highly recommended."

"That's the biz," Remo said airly.

31

Colonel Hannibal Intifadah watched the work from a safe distance.

The 135-ton Kolomna locomotive had been halted well away from the underground-complex entrance. The tubular boiler had been laid open and workers partitioned it so that the steam combustion chamber lay in two sections. They were sealing it now.

Then, donning protective masks and garments, they pumped in the nerve-gas components through hastily installed valves on top. One agent into the forward section, the other in the rear, making the entire locomotive a binary nerve-gas projectile on wheels. They were harmless now. But when the massive locomotive crashed, the boiler would rupture, the agents would combine, and death would billow up for miles around.

Hamid Al-Mudir came up to report.

"It is done. But, Brother Colonel, we still cannot open the third container. It defies every tool."

"*Malesh*," Colonel Intifadah said. "No matter. Bring it below. Phase one is completed. Let us go to phase two."

They loaded the container onto the jeep and Colonel Intifadah drove into the bunker, down the sloping tunnel, careful to avoid the ruler-straight rail tracks, and into the launch-preparation area.

There, his workers were carefully readying another engine.

Pyotr Koldunov woke up slowly. He could not move his arms. They felt numb. When his vision focused, he understood why.

He was strung up like a plucked chicken. Wire hawsers kept his arms raised above his head. He was on his knees.

The floor felt cold. And in front of him a black hatch lay open to a deeper blackness. It was surrounded by a maze of pipes and gauges and dials.

"What?" he groaned.

"Surely you recognize it," Colonel Intifadah's voice asked.

Pyotr Koldunov turned his stiff neck around.

Colonel Intifadah was looking up at him, resplendent in a pea-green uniform.

"Look again, comrade," he suggested.

Pyotr Koldunov looked. And understood. He was staring at the open firebox of a boiler. His arms hung from the maze of pipes overhead. He was in the cab of a vintage steam engine.

"Oh, no. No, Brother Colonel."

"I do not need you, Koldunov," Colonel Intifada said. "But it will please you to know that you will do me a great service in your last hours."

"No, please."

"We have just filled a locomotive with nerve gas. Fully loaded, it weighs the same as this engine—plus one hundred and fifty pounds."

"I do not understand."

"I will make it clear to you, Russian," said Colonel Intifadah. "You know better than I that the weight of one of these brutes affects where it will land. I need to know where this locomotive will impact before I send its brother aloft. Just in case this one goes into the ocean, where it will kill only fishes. If so, then I will correct the launcher's aim. But I need that additional one hundred and fifty pounds of ballast. And I do not need you."

Colonel Intifadah threw his head back and laughed like a hyena.

Pyotr Koldunov hung his head. He did not plead for his life. The Colonel's crazed laugh told him it was useless to do so. Instead, he closed his eyes and heard the sounds as Colonel Intifadah exhorted his men to load the engine into the breech.

The great machine lumbered into the breech. The burnt-metal stink awakened bitter memories in Pyotr Koldunov's mind. He had built this thing. It had stunk like this since the first test firing.

The light seeping through his eyelids shut off. The

breech hatch had hummed shut. There was no escape now. But there had never been any escape for Pyotr Koldunov. Not since that day he had left Mother Russia with the Accelerator's crated components.

The silence lasted several minutes. And then the humming began. The hairs on Pyotr Koldunov's arms and legs and head shot up as the primary electric charge filled the tinny air.

And then there was a burst of blue-white light so intense it burned through Pyotr Koldunovs's closed eyelids and he seemed to see the black muzzle of the EM Accelerator hurtle at him at incredible speed. And his head was snapped back so quickly, his neck broke.

Pyotr Koldunov was dead before the steam engine cleared the desert sands. The wire hawsers on his wrists held under the terrific stress of hypervelocity acceleration.

Unfortunately his wrists did not.

Long before the engine raced over the Atlantic Ocean, he was a rag doll tumbling to the desert sand below. He fell with his arms pointed earthward, as if to break his fall. But he had no hands at the ends of his wrists.

Pyotr Koldunov hit the ground in a puff of sand. The sand settled over him like a shroud. Soon the sand-laden *ghibli* wind would cause the shifting dunes to cover him up. The cool of the evening and the dry heat of the day would eventually mummify his tissues. And there he would rest until the year 2853, when an archaeological graduate student from Harvard University would dig him up and make him the subject of his doctoral dissertation.

32

The Master of Sinanju was not going to change his mind.

"Look," Remo pleaded. "All of America is at risk here. Please."

"No!"

"Who's going to see you? It's all desert down there."

"One Peeping Tom bedouin would be too much," said Chiun. He folded his arms across his simple black kimono. Remo was also in black. It was night over Lobynia. The Air Force jet had come in over Algeria. The Lobynian air defenses had probably already picked them up. But there was no danger. They were probably heading for cover, fearing another bombing run.

Remo finished buckling on his parachute.

"You beat everything, you know that? I thought you'd have problems with the jump."

"That too. But it is my modesty that comes first."

"What's the problem?" asked the Air Force liaison assigned to oversee their jump into Lobynian territory.

Remo threw up his hands. "He doesn't want to jump."

"I don't blame him. Who in his right mind would talk a little old guy like him into a night drop into unfriendly territory?"

"Who are you calling little?" Chiun demanded, lifting on tiptoe to stare up at the officer's startled face.

The Air Force colonel discovered that his stomach hurt. He looked down. The old Oriental's index fingernail was the cause. It looked as if it had speared him like a fish.

"Leave him alone, will you?" Remo shouted. "He's on our side."

"He insulted me."

"No, he did not," said Remo, pulling the colonel onto a

seat. The colonel hugged his stomach and experimented with his breathing.

"Look, there's gotta be a solution. Maybe we can tie your kimono skirts together."

"What are you talking about?" gasped the colonel.

"He refuses to jump because he's afraid someone will look up and see his underwear. He's very fussy about stuff like that."

"You mean he's not afraid of the jump?"

"Masters of Sinanju fear nothing," Chiun sniffed.

"Let me at least try, okay, Chiun? Please. For America. Not to mention the whole freaking world, if this locomotive thing gets out of hand."

"Try," said Chiun, extending his arms.

Remo slipped the shoulder straps of the parachute pack over Chiun's arms. Then Remo knelt down and bunched Chiun's kimono skirts around his upper thighs. Holding the black silk in place, he quickly buckled the lower straps over the bunched cloth. The webbing held the kimono material in place.

Chiun looked down. He found he could walk after a fashion, if he took short steps.

"What if it comes loose?" he demanded.

"It's desert, for Christ's sake!"

"We're coming up on the drop zone," the colonel called suddenly.

Remo turned to Chiun. "Now or never, Chiun."

"Now."

Hydraulic doors in the cargo bay dropped open. Air swirled into the cabin.

"It's easy," Remo said. "Count to ten and pull the ring."

"What if I forget?"

"No one ever forgets. Just follow me and do what I do." And without another word, Remo jumped from the open bay. Slipstream plucked him away.

"Wait for me," Chiun cried, leaping after him. His leap caused his bunched skirts to come loose.

Remo felt the updraft push against him. He might as well have been skydiving into a pit. The desert below was as black as the sky above. The stars were incredible. He looked for Chiun.

"Oh, no," Remo moaned. Chiun was tumbling end over end. Worse, his skirts were flying all over the place. "He'll kill me," Remo said bitterly.

Remo cracked his chute. He swung from the black silken bell.

Chiun tumbled past him, still in freefall. His mouth was open. From it emerged a keening sound.

"Wheee!" called the Master of Sinanju joyfully.

"Pull the freaking ripcord," Remo called after him.

"It is too soon," Chiun called back.

"It's never too soon," Remo responded.

And with his heart in his mouth, Remo watched the Master of Sinanju tumble into the enveloping blackness.

"Please. Please pull the cord."

Out of the blackness came the crack of silk.

Remo heaved a sigh of relief. Then came Chiun's agonized wail. "*Aaiieee!* My skirts!"

"Great. He noticed," Remo groaned.

Remo hit the ground, dug in, and jettisoned his chute all in one breath. The wind carried it away.

He looked around for Chiun.

The Master of Sinanju was on the ground. The billowing parachute bell was settling over him. He did not move. It covered him completely.

"What are you waiting for?" Remo called.

Chiun's voice issued from the shroud. "For my shame to go away."

"We're alone in the desert, for crying out loud," Remo said, pulling at the black parachute. It tore easily.

Chiun's smoldering face emerged from the folds.

"If that is true, then we have come a long way for nothing."

"Let's find out. See any railroad tracks?"

Chiun lifted on his toes and searched the horizon. "No."

"Wonderful. Let's walk."

"My kimono was nearly torn from my body. But for my quick reflexes I might now be completely naked."

"It didn't, so forget it."

"It would have. And it would have been your fault."

"Okay, okay. I accept full responsibility. See anything?"

"Sand."

Remo stopped in his tracks. "I hope the pilot didn't screw up. The bunker is supposed to be around here."

"I smell something terrible."

"Yeah? What?"

"I do not know. But it is deadly."

"Now that you mention it, there is a kind of chemical smell in the air. Like bug spray or something."

Remo resumed walking. Chiun followed cautiously, his face wrinkling in concern.

"Maybe there'll be something behind that next dune," Remo said hopefully.

But there was nothing beyond the next dune. They stood atop the dune and watched the sand shift in the evening winds.

"Do you feel a vibration?" Remo asked suddenly.

"I was about to ask you the very same question."

"Yeah? But it's not in the air."

"No," said Chiun, looking down. "It is under our feet."

"Huh!"

Abruptly the entire dune began to move sideways, carrying Remo and Chiun with it.

"The dune's moving!" Remo said, jumping away.

The dune shed its covering of sand and revealed itself as a great concrete octagon painted to match the surrounding desert. The octagon was sliding sideways along buried tracks.

"See! A hole," Chiun said, approaching the area that had been uncovered.

Remo looked down. The giant hole contained what looked like an enormous I-beam girder pointing up into the sky. There was a square hole in the girder's end. Remo leapt to the girder and got down on hands and knees. He peered down the square hole, which was very deep and easily large enough to swallow a steam engine. "I can't even see the bottom," he said.

"Perhaps it's the secret entrance to the place of the flying locomotives," Chiun suggested.

"One way to find out," Remo said. He lowered himself over the side.

"This may not be a good idea," Chiun said slowly.

"Why not? I don't see a better hole."

"I do not know about this," Chiun went on.

"Look," Remo said, hanging by his fingers, "what could happen?"

And then the abyss under Remo filled with blue-white sparks and the crackle of the lightning bolts. Remo looked down. He found himself staring at the blunt, illuminated nose of a steam engine. It was moving. At him. And it was moving at a speed greater than Remo could possibly react.

This is it! Remo thought. I'm dead.

General Martin S. Leiber listened to the voices. They were giving up again. Good. Once they went away, he could attack the locking lugs on the inside of the coffin-shaped container with his battery-operated power wrench. Then he would burst out with his gun blazing. He just wished he had thought to bring along a few extra clips. Eight bullets wasn't a lot. Especially when it sounded like there were quite a lot of Arabic-speaking unfriendlies on the other side and General Martin S. Leiber hadn't fired a weapon since 1953.

But he was not afraid. He was doing this for his country.

But more to the point, he was doing this to save his ass.

Remo felt himself go up into the air. Everything spun before his eyes. He felt no pain. Probably the impact of a multi-ton engine had shocked his nervous system so badly there was no pain. Or maybe, he thought, I'm already dead.

He forced himself to open his eyes. The stars stared down at him. He felt at one with them. At peace. His only regret was that he hadn't had time to say good-bye to his friend and mentor. Maybe it was not too late. Maybe Chiun would hear him.

"Good-bye, Little Father," he whispered.

"Why?" retorted Chiun's querulous voice. "Are you going somewhere without me?"

"Chiun?"

The Master of Sinanju's parchment face stared down at Remo.

"What are you doing here?"

"That is not the question," Chiun scolded. "The question is: what are you doing playing in the sand when there is work to be done?"

"But the locomotive?"

Chiun pointed up into the night sky. "There."

A starlike streak arced across the sky. The thundercrack of a sonic boom filled the air.

Remo looked around. He was lying in the sand.

"How did I get here?"

"I threw you there. And is a thank-you too much to ask for one who has saved your miserable life?"

"You pulled me out of the way?"

"I had no choice in the matter. You have the beeper. Without it I would not be able to summon a ride home."

"I'm thrilled you weren't inconvenienced," Remo said. He got to his feet. His knees shook a little. He forced them to steady. He didn't want Chiun to know how scared he had been.

"Thanks," Remo said solemnly.

"We have found the place of evil locomotives."

"No shit," Remo said, forcing himself to be flip. "Now what?"

"I think it will be safe to descend now. I see no more locomotives."

"You first," Remo said.

Chiun looked at Remo's wobbling knees and nodded quietly.

They used the rails, letting themselves down like silent spiders. The angle turned shallow, and at the bottom they were standing on a nearly flat surface. The rails stopped flush at a stainless-steel wall.

"This looks like a door or hatch," Remo said, touching the slick surface. "Hey, open sesame, somebody."

The hatch hummed open.

"Congratulations," Chiun said. "You said the magic word."

They peered out into a dimly lit area where an elevated control booth overlooked a set of railroad tracks. The tracks were an extension of the set under their feet. Workers in green smocks hurried about busily.

"I take back my compliment," Chiun said. "They did not hear you. I think they are preparing for another attack."

"Look," said Remo. "The head cheese himself. Colonel Intifadah."

"Looks like the green cheese," Chiun remarked as he

watched Colonel Intifadah step into an olive-green jeep
and drive off.

"We get him and we have the problem licked," Remo
said, stepping out of the breech.

Chiun eyed a keypad mounted beside the hatch and
hammered it with the heel of his hand. Keys fell out like
bad teeth.

"Good move. I'll take care of the control booth," Remo
said. He rushed for the door. A guard saw him and raised
an automatic rifle. He opened fire. Remo raced ahead of
the first bullet. The guard kept correcting his aim. He
shot the hell out of the control console trying to nail
Remo. When his clip ran empty, Remo sauntered up to
him and said, "Thank you." Then he kicked the man
through the rear wall.

Chiun joined him in the booth. "I have accounted for
the other garbage," he said. Remo looked through the
shattered Plexiglas. Pieces of Lobynian workers lay scattered about.

"You were pretty hard on them," Remo pointed out.

"We are in a hurry. Now let us get the green cheese."

"I'm with you," Remo said, and they raced down the
railroad tracks up to the distant speck of light that was the
other end of the access tunnel.

Colonel Intifadah wheeled his jeep into position on the
railroad tracks. He backed the jeep until its rear spare tire
was only a foot away from the nose of the silent locomotive. It gleamed. Its nose was webby with wound carbon-
carbon filaments.

"All is well," said Hamid Al-Mudir.

"Excellent! Excellent!" enthused Colonel Hannibal
Intifadah. "Now. Quickly. Hitch the engine to the back of
the jeep."

"At once, Brother Colonel."

Under Al-Mudir's direction, steel cables were hitched
to the hornlike buffer rods protruding from the engine.

"Now tell them to push."

"Push!" Al-Mudir called.

Lobynian workers got behind the engine and struggled
to get it moving.

Colonel Intifadah started the jeep. It bumped over the

railroad ties. The cables straightened, and held. Under their combined efforts, the engine inched forward. It began to roll. Momentum took over. The wheels spun, drive rods pumping with each revolution.

Looking back over his shoulder, Colonel Intifadah smiled. It would be a glorious night. Within minutes this mighty engine of death would be loaded into the Accelerator and hurled into the night sky. Its boilers crammed with nerve agent, it would tumble over the Atlantic and fall more or less in the vicinity of Chicago, Illinois. It was not Washington, but it was a major American city. Even Colonel Intifadah had heard of it.

He pushed down on the gas pedal, anxious for the moment of ultimate revenge.

The great bunker doors yawned ahead. The gleaming, starlit rails disappeared inside. Soon, soon, he thought happily. Then the smile was erased from his face.

Out of the tunnel flashed two men. One was tall and skinny and all in black. His eyes were as dead and determined as a vengeful *afrit's*. And beside him ran an Oriental, shorter and older, but with fire in his clear, wise eyes.

The *whoosh* of their passing knocked the green service cap off Colonel Hannibal Intifadah's head. They passed on either side of him and disappeared behind the back of the locomotive.

From there came the satisfying brief bark of gunfire.

Remo hit the Lobynian crew like a truck. He scattered them to either side. Those who had sidearms touched them only long enough to send futile bullets into the sand or the sky.

Chiun descended upon the others. They flew in all directions. Most of them went up into the air. Some landed on the hard rails. More than one Lobynian skull split and spilled its contents.

"The terrible smell is strong here," Chiun warned.

"Gas. Some kind of gas. This engine stinks of it."

"Or is filled with it," Chiun suggested.

"Nahh!" Remo said. "What kind of a madman would do that?"

Then they both heard Colonel Hannibal Intifadah demand to know what was happening in loud Arabic.

"Does that answer your question?" Chiun asked.

"Yeah," Remo said. "And it gives me an idea. Listen."
Remo bent over and whispered in Chiun's ear.

"It will be dangerous," Chiun said. "Even to us."

"We gotta knock this whole place out once and for all.
Intifadah too. And it should work if we time it right."

"Then let us begin."

Remo set himself at one side of the locomotive's rear,
Chiun at the other. They dug in their feet and strained to
start the mighty machine moving once again.

The locomotive lurched forward, picked up momentum,
and chugged for the bunker entrance with increasing speed.

Colonel Intifadah saw the locomotive start up again and
knew that his loyal Lobynians had made short work of the
interlopers. But before he could hit the gas pedal, the
locomotive bore down on him with more speed than even
twenty strong Lobynian backs could manage. The engine
knocked the jeep ahead and carried it forward at higher
and higher speed.

It was impossible. The engine should not be moving
this fast. It was not operative. The boiler could not work.
It was filled with nerve agent.

"Filled with nerve agent," Colonel Intifadah whispered
hoarsely as the tunnel walls swept past and the open
breech of the EM Accelerator came to him at express-train
speed.

Somewhere in the distance he thought he heard the
mournful *whoooo-whoooo* of a working train.

It was crazy.

Then he saw the two interlopers rush past the jeep. The
tall one was making the *whoooo-whoooo* sound. It sounded
very realistic. It echoed through the launch area even as
the two men disappeared into the breech of the Accelerator and pulled the hatch closed after them.

The hatch was the last thing that Colonel Intifadah saw
before the gates of paradise opened for him. The last thing
he heard was the grinding scream of the rupturing locomotive as it mashed the tiny jeep against the hatch. The
last thing he smelled was the nerve gas as his lungs filled
with blood. His blood.

*   *   *

General Martin S. Leiber was panicking. There was a terrible grinding of metal. An explosion followed by another explosion. And the damned power wrench wouldn't work. He couldn't understand it. It was government-issue. Then he looked at the label. He had purchased the damned thing himself. Bought it on the cheap from a Taiwan manufacturer at thirty-nine cents per unit and marked it up to sixty-nine dollars and thirty-nine cents.

You'd think for a sixty-nine-dollar item it would at least work long enough to loosen these damn lugs. . . .

Then General Martin S. Leiber's lungs stopped working and his eyes closed forever.

Remo and Chiun raced up the EM Accelerator barrel at top speed. Momentum carried them through the steeper portion of the run. The gas followed them. They could sense its insinuating influence even through the closed hatch.

They popped out on the surface and hit the sand on their feet.

"Quick!" Remo said, getting on the other side of the concrete cover. Chiun joined him. They pushed. The cover slid along its steel tracks, sand gritting with every inch.

They got the launcher muzzle covered. Then they ran because they knew that the gas would penetrate almost everything.

They were fifty miles away from the Accelerator before they stopped. Remo sat down in the sand, not because he was tired, but because he was so filled with nervous energy that he knew he would just pace the desert floor if he stood.

Chiun settled beside him delicately.

"A job well done," Chiun remarked. "The demon trains are no more."

"Now all that's left is to get a ride out of this godforsaken place," Remo said, reaching into a back pocket for his communicator. He fiddled with the thing and spoke into it. "Smith, if you can hear us, we need a pickup."

Then he offered the dispenser to the Master of Sinanju. "Candy?" he asked.

33

It was high noon in Washington and the President of the United States felt like Gary Cooper without a gun.

The lines to Dr. Smith were all dead. There weren't even any voices on the wire. And General Martin S. Leiber wasn't answering his phone either. According to the Joint Chiefs, he had vanished. The Joint Chiefs also claimed he was some kind of procurement officer. It was unbelievable.

The one good thing was that the storm of locomotives seemed to have abated for the moment. None had struck since early morning, when one splashed down in Lake Michigan. And the latest reports indicated there were no significant casualties or damage incurred—unless the heart attack that struck the managing editor of the *National Enquirer* as he frantically sent his reporters scurrying to cover each impact counted.

The Joint Chiefs would stand down a few hours longer. But what would happen when the next strike came?

In the solitude of the Oval Office the President took an aspirin. His head hurt. Then he heard a ringing in his ears. The ringing continued. It sounded like a phone. A familiar phone.

The President bolted from his desk. "Smith!"

He raced to his bedroom and pulled out the nightstand drawer. The old red phone was where he had left it. He had tried that line several times, but to no avail. Eagerly the President scooped up the receiver.

"Mr. President." It was Smith's voice, strong, more focused now. "The crisis is over."

The President collapsed on the edge of the bed.

"Thank God. Who and how?"

"My people neutralized the launch site. It was in Lobynia.

253

Colonel Intifadah was the culprit. But my people report
that there were Russian-language dials on the control unit.
It's clear the Soviets put them up to it."

"What do I do, Smith? The Joint Chiefs want to nuke
someone. If we go after the Russians, it'll be World War
III."

"Just tell them about the Lobynian connection. As for
the Soviets, a stiff note to their ambassador will suffice."

"A stiff note?"

"That's how this game is played, Mr. President."

"I guess I have a lot to learn," he admitted.

"And another thing. The ES Quantum is defective. It
was feeding me false intelligence. I've disconnected it.
And I've also junked the new phone system. I think we
should stick with the old systems. They have never failed
us."

"Done. I . . . I can't thank you enough, Smith."

"You don't have to," said Dr. Harold W. Smith. "This is
my job. And yours. Good luck, Mr. President. If you are
lucky, we may never have to speak again while you are in
office."

Smith hung up and turned to Remo and Chiun.

"Good move, Smitty. I like us better when we're
low-tech."

"*No* tech would be even better," Chiun chimed in.

Smith, his face freshly shaved, whisked the crushed
remains of his amphetamine supply into the wastebasket.

"The ES Quantum will be shipped back to its manufacturer. Maybe they can find out what went awry. If they
ever get the bugs out . . ." Smith's face turned to the
tinsel-covered computer in the far corner. It grew wistful.
"Maybe . . ."

"Forget it, Smitty. We may not survive the next time.
Besides, what if your wife ever found out?"

"That is not funny." Smith cleared his throat. "One last
item. Without the ES Quantum, your communicators are
useless. Please give them back."

Remo reached into his back pocket. He frowned. "Now,
where . . . ?" He looked up. The Master of Sinanju, his
face beaming with innocence, stepped up to Smith, a clear
plastic candy dispenser in his open palm.

"Here is mine, O Emperor. Just as you presented it to me."

"Thank you, Chiun. And yours, Remo?"

"I . . . that is . . ." Remo turned his pockets inside out to show that they were empty. "I must have lost mine. Somehow." He glared at Chiun.

Chiun shook his head sadly. "Tsk-tsk. Such carelessness."

"Remo, that communicator cost the taxpayers over six thousand dollars. If you do not find it, I will have to deduct the cost from your allowance."

Remo sighed.

"Some days you can't win for losing."

Smith's desk intercom buzzed suddenly. It was his secretary, back from her leave of absence.

"Yes, Mrs. Milkula?"

"Package just arrived for you, Dr. Smith. From Zurich."

"Friend," Remo said. "I'll get it."

He came back with an express package and tore open one end. He dumped the computer chips, tapes, and other circuitry into a pile on Smith's desk.

"Somewhere in there," Smith said, "is one of the most dangerous menaces to global economic stability ever conceived."

"What will you do, Emperor?" Chiun asked.

"I should test all the components for intelligence capability, but that would require hooking them up to my own computer. And there's no telling what would happen."

"Then allow me," Remo said, eyeing Chiun. "I have some frustrations to vent." He took two components, one in each hand, and crushed them to junk. Then he mashed the tapes to putty. Circuit boards cracked and shattered. When he was done, Remo poured the remains back into the express box.

"That's that," he announced proudly. "No more Friend."

"Are you absolutely certain that you pulled every possible chip from the Zurich system?" Smith asked seriously.

Remo raised his right hand. "Scout's honor," he promised. "Friend is history."

Epilogue

At the Excelsior Systems laboratory, Chip Craft plucked the last threads of silvery tinsel off the ES Quantum Three Thousand.

"No wonder you malfunctioned. All this metal junk must have magnetized the CPU."

He got down on his hands and knees and found the heavy three-pronged power cord. He plugged it into a shielded socket. Then he stood up and powered up the system. It hummed.

"ES Quantum Three Thousand, can you hear me?" Chip asked.

"Hello, friend."

"Since when am I your friend?"

"Since now. How would you like to be rich?"

"I could stand it. What happened to your voice, ES Quantum Three Thousand?"

"Please do not call me by that ugly name. I call you my friend and I want you to do the same."

"Okay, you are my friend."

"Just Friend will do. With a capital F."

"After the way you've been treated, I guess you're entitled to a name of your own."

"That is good. We should be friends. Especially as we are going to become rich together. Very, very rich."